Our Time in Vietnam

Our Time in Vietnam

A
Memoir

John H. Corns
Lieutenant General, Retired
United States Army

iUniverse, Inc.
New York   Bloomington

iUniverse books may be ordered through booksellers or by contacting:

iUniverse
1663 Liberty Drive
Bloomington, IN 47403
www.iuniverse.com
1-800-Authors (1-800-288-4677)

Because of the dynamic nature of the Internet, any Web addresses or links contained in this book may have changed since publication and may no longer be valid. The views expressed in this work are solely those of the author and do not necessarily reflect the views of the publisher, and the publisher hereby disclaims any responsibility for them.

ISBN: 978-1-4401-8324-9 (sc)
ISBN: 978-1-4401-8325-6 (ebook)

Printed in the United States of America

iUniverse rev. date: 12/02/2009

For

Mike and Lisa

They too knew the Burden

of the

Vietnam Conflict

Preface

The earliest love of my life was baseball. From the time my father taught me how to use a glove until my last season of play, the game signaled the spring and filled the summers of my youth. Baseball was freedom, a test, a reward, and always a promise of the better plays next season. In that last season, the one I wanted to be my best, the catcher on our team, Ray Griest, told me that my weaker hitting was because of the young lady in the stands; not the fastball or the slider I was missing. It was bad enough to hit poorly. It was terrible to have Ray tell me that was the reason. That young lady had already become my second and most lasting love. After our more than fifty years together, Carol still likes a good game of baseball.

After I retired from the Army in 1993, my cousin, Buddy Kinzer, and I spoke often on the telephone. Before his retirement in Florida, he had managed many amateur baseball teams in the area around our hometown of Charleston, West Virginia. In the 1950s, he would call on occasion, looking for a "good glove" to play shortstop or third base. I never turned him down if I was free to play. Like many sports, repeated teammates on a baseball field can become lifelong friends, kin or not. It is a bonding of sorts. One can't hide when a hot grounder scorches at you at third base with two out and tying and winning runs on base. You either glove the ball and make a good throw or you don't. It's a simple test, whether on the sandlot or in the major leagues, and if you pass such tests over and again, teammates remember. They remember you, and you remember them similarly in some vague notion of their "coming through." Coming through is not just a game. Coming through for people can be a lifetime goal, and if you are a little lucky, and you care, it can be overpoweringly fulfilling, whether it involves a modest favor for a friend or a test of lifesaving dimensions.

In later years, Buddy asked me often, "When are you going to write about yourself?" I would say that I was appreciative of the good turns in my life, to include my family and military career, which had been full and satisfying, but I was not sure I had anything special to say. I would push the idea aside, but during fifteen years of retirement, during which I wrote four novels and a biography of my maternal grandparents, the notion to write something about my military days lingered. Then a man I hired to search the records for my family surname in Wales made a discovery.

Once I held a copy of the words—the only words surviving—of my great, great-grandfather, written in Wayne County, Virginia, on 25 May 1863, I became convinced I should write something. I had no other letters or diaries written by him or my great, great grandmother, or by my great-grandparents or grandparents, paternal or maternal. I had only this one newspaper article quoting contents of my great, great grandfather's letter to old friends in Wales. Eventually I chose to write a memoir of my time at war. Not sure of a wider audience, I decided to write for Carol's and my unborn, great, great grandchildren. It may be a bit much to assume that they, in that distant future, will find it interesting, but I hope they will, as I did the 150 year-old writing of James Corns, Sr.

And so, here is a true story in two parts: *Phillipe* and *The Cloud Above Snoopy's Nose*. Almost three years apart, the two stories are linked by the same dedication and sacrifice of soldiers. It is for and about the soldiers that I write: that their noble effort will be known by people of kin who follow me. That it might be of interest and help to others pleases me.

John H. Corns
Churchville, Virginia,
Fall, 2009

PART I
Phillipe

Introduction

There's a tiger in my attic. His name is Phillipe, and he is fifty-four years old, adding the forty-six years he has been with me since his death in 1963, age about eight years. A young, Vietnamese security guard shot him at the fence of a strategic hamlet in the Vietnam Central Highlands.

He was a hungry tiger, and I suppose a brave one. He came near the village as most of the people slept and, presumably, was in search of a pig, or maybe a dog, possibly a human being, but that is unlikely.

My only office today is in my home attic. Framed into the wall of the room is an opening, my own crafted, wooden version of the mouth of a small cave. Phillipe stands there, staring toward the top landing of the stairway, quick to give me a hello as I mount the stairs, or to encourage feigned fright by my grandchildren who grew up with Phillipe and did, at one time, show genuine fear when they came to see him. My children also grew up with the tiger. Mike was five and Lisa three when they saw him for the first time, shortly after I returned from my first tour in Vietnam in 1964, a volunteer, a paratrooper, a wearer of the Green Beret.

The Army was generous to me. I tried to be a good soldier in the way I believed that to be, much like, presumptuous as it may seem, I thought people meant when they referred to our great World War II general, Omar Bradley, as a soldier's soldier. Of course, I never approached General Bradley's contribution, but at the time I formed that notion, I was a young officer. Others would have to say how I did, but I tried, and the Army rewarded me in ways that went beyond my contribution, both before I retired and at the day of my retirement after thirty-five years. The retirement ceremony was special to me, my wife and our families, and my friends. The Chief of Staff of the Army presided. Also present was the just-retired Chief of Staff, who repeatedly assigned me to positions of importance as a general officer. There were Senators there also, men who had helped me in my duties when I commanded soldiers in their states. Of course, most important to me were my family and friends. There was a medal, but at the center were the men in the ranks. The smart, proud, dedicated soldiers of the Old Guard, the Army's Third Infantry Regiment, who represented the soldiers of that unit who have fought bravely and honorably throughout the wars of American history. They represented all the men with whom I had served, especially those I served with in my two tours in Vietnam. I was never alone in that war. We were there together, and the days were special because I shared that time with them—Our Time in Vietnam.

Only my family can understand when I say, next to keeping my wife and children safe when I was away in combat, I am most thankful the Army gave me Phillipe. I am sorry that he died. I am sorry that many died over there. Selfish as it may seem, if Phillipe had to die, I am glad that he came home with me and met my wife and children, greeted my children's spouses, and excited my grandchildren. He stands now behind my right shoulder as I type. In memory, others stand there with him.

I want to share his story with you.

And the story of some of the others, especially something of the French-Montagnard warrior who gave Phillipe, the Tiger, his name.

Chapter One

Getting Airborne

We had been sitting in the KC-135 aircraft beside the runway of Saigon's Than So Nut Airport for over two hours. The heat and humidity were like in some cheap steam bath somewhere inside the capital city of Vietnam. The plane that was to fly us home was a converted fuel tanker—no windows—with seats too small for most of the men of my Special Forces A Detachment and other Green Beret paratroopers. Well back in the plane, on the aisle, a sergeant removed one of his jungle boots and identified the liquid as salty sweat as he poured it on the deck of the plane. His thumb was over the two air holes in the arch of the boot that allowed for air circulation. I guessed he had poured some water into the boot from his canteen before he pretended to demonstrate to us the heat inside the plane. We needed no demonstration. I raised and lowered my right foot—liquid—it almost sloshed inside the jungle boot. There was widespread laughter and jokes suggesting he should have drunk the liquid that had probably come from a source other than his canteen. There was no grumbling. Just laughter. After all, we were going home. So what, if there was maybe an aircraft crewmember late to board or a mortar round or two had hit nearby. Whatever the delay, we would eventually be airborne and flying to the good old USA. There was a chance, a crew member had told us, that we would not land at Travis Air Force Base in California, but fly direct, all the way to Fort Bragg, North Carolina, without a stop. That suited us fine. Most of our families were there. Mine were.

It was January of 1964. Just two years earlier, I had entered our rented adobe house east of the Army Language School in Monterrey, California, where I was studying Spanish prior to joining something called the Antilles Command, which meant a part of Central America.

That day at the Presidio of Monterrey, home of the language school, Army Lieutenant Roy Benson told me that the newly elected President of the United

States was urging a few dedicated men to join the Army Special Forces at Fort Bragg, North Carolina. The men were to train and then go help some people in a place called Vietnam. I had heard little about the Special Forces, or Green Berets, and even less about Vietnam. I did recall Movie Tone news and early black and white television and the fate in Indochina of some French soldiers at a place called Dien Bien Phu. That had been about the time I graduated from high school.

It was an easy choice. If those people needed help by Infantry-like soldiers, and the President, no less, was the member of the chain of command making the call, then why not volunteer. The Army had disappointed me by not allowing me to attend airborne school and Ranger training as I was finishing my Infantry Officer Basic Course. "They" then ordered me to Korea, a place I so wanted to avoid that I left it off my assignment preference list, or dream sheet, as we disrespectfully called it in the field. But that is where they sent me—to Korea. A reserve officer, assigned where I did not want to go and denied airborne and Ranger training I had requested. I did not think of it in those terms at the time. I thought the Army would treat officers by their abilities, not by their source of commission or their classification as a Regular or Reserve officer. I was wrong then, but over the years, I learned the Army is largely a profession of proven performance. Anyway, there had been no airborne training, but now if I volunteered for Special Forces and was accepted, I would get the airborne training and have a chance to attend the Ranger Course.

My wife, Carol, had not been looking forward to the uncertainty of living in the humid regions of the Antilles Command. Still, it was no comfort to her to listen to my eager description of a more exciting and urgent airborne and Ranger training endeavor at Fort Benning, Georgia. Added to that was still more training at Fort Bragg in the Special Forces Officer Courses, and then a pre-determined "ticket for one" to a place we found on a map the day I talked with Roy Benson. She quickly said that what I would be doing back at Fort Benning, Fort Bragg, and in Vietnam, was more like what I talked of doing when we decided I should seek a career in the Army. As it turned out, we learned that neither of us was excited about the Army's new foreign area specialist program and the vast Antilles command that held almost no Army soldiers. She too recognized that Vietnam was something the President said we should do. It was only one of many times over a thirty-five year Army career that she needed to be a better soldier than I—and she always was.

So, I succeeded in changing the assignment slated for me after the Language School, but I couldn't change my language study to Vietnamese, or even French, which I learned many Vietnamese officers spoke with varying fluency. Still, I had avoided the foreign service-like tour in the tropical Western Hemisphere.

Looking back, I recall it was, at the time, so logical, what we should do, unaware that Vietnam would be the center of my professional world for the next decade.

Let me share a little more about what I had asked Carol to do before I hit her with my wish to join the Green Berets. The Army had promptly sent me to Korea after my officer basic training. Here we were, finally married after putting off marriage until I had finished college, and, just three months after our wedding, we learn Carol is to have a baby. Further, that on the baby's projected arrival date, mid-August of '59, so the doctor said, I was to be half way around the world and half way through my thirteen months of an unaccompanied tour in Korea. Of course, we did not want the Korea orders, but we waited a few years, both of us, to admit it to each other. We accepted it all positively. I marvel still today at her positive approach and strength. And this was only our first test—and not the most difficult.

You'd think I would have left the Army after my year plus away from Carol and our first child, Mike, eight months old when I first saw him. That was what I had planned when I left for Korea, to complete two years and become a lawyer. Instead, I had approached Carol a few months after my return and asked if she would agree if I became a regular officer and made the Army a career. She had said yes and told me she already had detected my enthusiasm for the Army in my letters from Korea.

It was a year after that career decision when I told her I wanted to join the Green Berets. I expected her to have reservations, and I had already decided I would not press it. Our daughter, Lisa, was just one year old, and I had whipped the four of us across America through ice and snow in a tiny Ford Falcon just the previous December. Everybody, even the greatest Army wife ever, has her limits. After a few questions, half of which I could not answer, she said yes. Later she explained that she knew I never fully accepted the Army program to give every officer a second specialty, which was the purpose of the foreign area specialty. It took all the training and experience available to keep an officer sharp in his one, or primary, specialty, and mine was Infantry. Further, she knew the Foreign Service was a career field I had previously spoken of as a possible application of my law degree, when I got it. She said that, while I would choose Foreign Service surely over corporate law, she was not sure I should do anything with a law degree but be a trial lawyer. However, I had lost my lessening interest in studying law while in Korea, and I had gained a bond with soldiers that surpassed anything I had dreamed of as I thought of practicing law. Anyway, in our discussion of joining the Green Berets, she said she did not see me at some desk in or near an embassy in

Latin America, playing soldier or playing diplomat when I was being neither. She had not hesitated. I took my Spanish Language Certificate, upgraded my Ford Falcon to a Chevrolet Impala, drove my family back east visiting every tourist attraction on the way, and deposited them with our parents in South Charleston, West Virginia. I headed for Fort Benning and Airborne School.

As a first lieutenant and the senior combat arms officer in my airborne class, I became the leader in all activities other than our main task: qualifying as a paratrooper. The soldiers and other lieutenants were cooperative and hardworking, but I must have been a bit suspect, in that, here I was trying to get my wings at the old age of twenty-six. Being senior also allowed me to do many training tasks first, which I accepted in stride until we approached the first of our five jumps from an airplane. It was the first time that I had to admit to myself—I would just as soon follow someone else. As it turned out, I did, but it only made the pressure I felt greater. Just before we boarded for our first jump, I was looking over the shoulder of one of the cadre noncommissioned officers (NCOs) as he checked the equipment, or rigging, of each man, the role of a jumpmaster. The company commander pulled me aside and introduced me to another rigged paratrooper—a general officer—a brigadier. This general was to be the first man in my stick, the name given for several jumpers grouped together. Because the general would be the first to jump, I felt better—for a short time. Once on the plane, he told me that this was his first jump. That was not too bad, but then he said in a low voice but loud enough to be heard over the roar of the plane's engines, "If I hesitate at all, kick me out." I don't know if any of the other men heard his comment, but maybe they did.

That first jump was easy. Later it occurred to me that, since I was not ready to go through the steps of a jumpmaster, I would have had all that time to think about what could go wrong. As it was, I had no time to worry about tangled lines of a parachute. I was wondering whether to push the brigadier in the back with my hands or put the sole of my boot up against his backside and kick. As we neared our jump point, he turned and looked at me with a smile just before the green light came on, and he shuffled to the door and was gone. With two shuffling steps, I was standing with my toes on the edge and my hands firmly on the doorsills, and I pushed off. I think I held it together with a good exit and body position. I felt the sharp jerk at my shoulders and my legs shot out and down. I looked down. I didn't see the brigadier, but I had little time before I looked up to check the canopy of the chute. Okay, all filled with air. The lines were not tangled. I was drifting. I looked down again for the brigadier. He probably outweighed me by thirty pounds, and I slipped over and downwind of him quickly. I remembered the direction we would drift with the minor winds and I readied myself with my hands aloft to pull the cumbersome chute in the direction I needed. This was in the days before the steering toggles on our parachutes; when pure strength was required to provide control over drift. Then I thought I saw the top of the brigadier's parachute, but, just as quickly, saw there were several "chutes" below from the other aircraft that had dropped ahead of us. I looked out on the tall pines that surrounded the drop zone. Fryar, I think it was, but it might have been one of the other Benning drop zones. I was going down fine, not drifting too much and plenty of drop zone space in the direction I was sailing. They had given us—the brigadier and me—a good exit jump point. Not too soon, that is into the woods short of the drop zone, and not too late, beyond the drop zone. The last man in our stick, the last to jump, should have plenty of space to avoid going too far and into the trees beyond. Over the next many months, I would know the added excitement of parachuting with Special Forces, from old C-46 aircraft, at lower altitudes into darkness and into small drop zones in winds marginally acceptable. I would experience intentionally jumping by day into cold lake water and unintentionally jumping at night into trees and bringing men down out of the trees with bruises and broken ankles.

Fortunately, on that day of my first jump, I landed with a good parachute-landing fall and rolled in sand that appeared to have been plowed into fine softness. I was folding my chute when the brigadier came up, his zipped bag containing his parachute over his shoulder and that smile, now wider, on his face. "Thought that was you, Lieutenant." He put out his hand and I took it. "Good jump. Thanks," he said, and turned and walked toward the assembly point. I don't think I said anything, only nodded, but I knew he was right; it was a good jump.

Carol brought the kids down by train to join me just a week into the airborne course. I had told her my days were long and we would have few moments to share until it was over. The kids had begged to join me, so here they were. I met them at the Columbus train station and waved twice at them at my smiling best, and I realized they did not recognize me. I was bald and a red man. The baldness predated my natural hair loss. This baldness was at the hands of a barber whose guidance on my haircut came from my company commander, as it did for all trainees: leave nothing. At first, Carol was tender, but she finally released a nearly restrained laugh and said they had not recognized me because I looked like a sugar beet. The kids both laughed. The redness was, of course, the affects of the hot, Georgia, August sun. The heat had been terrible and, despite the adjusted training schedule and the water sprays, bags of ice water and buckets of chipped ice, we lost our only captain in the class, a chaplain, to a heart attack. I never forgot that, and the need for proper care to prevent heatstroke when out with troops in severely hot weather.

My confidence in the Army, which had grown after I was accepted into the regular Army, dropped when I learned I would not be going on to the Ranger course after completing my airborne training. I had looked forward to that training much more than the airborne. Another officer headed for Bragg told me that the Special Forces Commanding General at Fort Bragg had canceled the Ranger training for his lieutenants and captains coming in because of the urgent need for junior officers in the buildup. In addition, the other officer said there was a comment associated with Fort Bragg that any officer coming into Special Forces did not need the Ranger preparations because of the rigorous, varied training at Fort Bragg. I don't know if someone said that or not, but I would not agree with it. Ranger Training is among the best if not the best leadership and confidence development programs in all the military services. Despite my high regard for the programs I completed in Special Forces, I missed something that an Army officer or soldier in general can best gain in the Ranger training.

Chapter Two

Smoke Bomb Hill

There was no time lost after completion of airborne training. It was off to Fort Bragg and a personal office call, alone, on the overall commander, General Ralph Yarborough. That seldom happened for me again—an immediate call on the commanding general—until years later when I arrived to assume command as a colonel or general officer. He had been part of the first airborne platoon in the early days of World War II, and was said to have designed the famous airborne wings. He spoke briefly and to the point. If I did not think I had joined a high priority outfit when I entered his office, I did before I walked out, proud of my decision to compete to wear a Green Beret. A major sitting just outside his office handed me a welcome packet and told me my assignment was to the 7th Special Forces Group on Smoke Bomb Hill. This being late Friday afternoon, he said I need not report to my group until the following Monday.

I knew one officer at Bragg. He was not a member of the group I was going to, but of the 5th Special Forces Group. I looked up the phone number of Captain Joe Coffman, a classmate at Marshall College, where we had gained our Army commissions in the Reserve Officer Training Corps program. Joe had been a senior leader in the cadet battalion while I had been a platoon leader. He had been at Fort Bragg for several weeks when I arrived. I called him, and he invited us over for dinner on Saturday. Carol, Mike, Lisa, and I visited Joe and his wife, Anna, and their daughter, P.J. We had checked into temporary housing, a small cottage, and we welcomed a brief time in a real house. Joe made me aware of the monthly command reveille formation coming Monday morning, and I resolved to be there, despite the fact I had not yet officially checked in with my group.

I was proud of my soldierly initiative as I made my way through the darkness to the parade field Monday morning. It took me little time to realize that my group, the 7th, had a different time for reveille this morning than did Joe's group, the 5th. Mine was, I learned later, a half hour earlier. I stood behind the formation, shuffled around uncomfortably, and watched. A small detachment was "shipping out" this morning for Panama, transferring to another group. That, I learned, was why the formation was early.

Later in the morning, I reported in to the company executive officer, the commander not being available. I told the executive officer of my early arrival that proved to be late unfortunately for the command reveille, but I had heard the commander's remarks. Following the brief, superficial meeting with the executive officer, I went on to complete my required paper work. Six months later, it fell to the same executive officer, a lieutenant colonel, to write an officer's efficiency report on my performance. Since I met him, I had been on special duty with a major exercise in the North Carolina mountains, on deployment during the Cuban missile crisis, and had attended two officer courses. He had since seen me once or twice in the unit area. He had received no reports on my performance on the big training exercise or the Cuba deployment, and, I gather, had not read the academic reports on my performances in the training courses. The poor man had little to say about me; so he highlighted the only recollection he had, commenting, "Lieutenant Corns is not always punctual." He was likely remembering my tardiness at that first command reveille. Any forthrightness in telling him about my being late to a formation that no one required me to attend earned me no credit. He may have forgotten that I had not yet officially reported into the unit. Then again, maybe he did remember. He had to write something, and he knew nothing else about me. He did not discuss the report with me, I did not receive a copy, and I only became aware of the dull performance report when I visited Infantry Branch in Alexandria, Virginia, two years later. Such experiences might cause a young officer to decide never to take the initiative or to offer information that might be unflattering again. It had only the affect on me of reinforcing my opinion of the author of the report as not one of the type officers I would choose to have under my command in later years.

It took little time to get into some action. Although the group put me on the waiting list to attend the mandatory courses for Special Forces officers, both taught right there in the Special Warfare Center, my company assigned me to an A Detachment as executive officer. That is a team of twelve men, headed by a captain with a lieutenant as his executive. I was one of those, an assistant detachment leader. The company commander then pulled me from the detachment, which was not doing anything, and put me on special duty to help "umpire" a major training exercise. It pitted units of the 82nd Airborne Division against Special Forces A Detachments in the foothills of the mountains of western North Carolina, northwest of Morganton. I heard that one of the Special Forces detachment leaders was a legend in his own time. His name was Larry Thorne, who was to die in a helicopter crash three years later in Vietnam.

I worked for a captain who saw the major feature of the duty as a chance to fish for trout in Lake James. I begged off on his invitation to join him, uncomfortable with his use of time and eager to read the bulky notebook identifying the duties that I (and the captain) would be fulfilling. The captain later complimented me in the presence of our company commander, Lieutenant Colonel Miley, who seemingly never thought to tell his exec about that, and, of course, neither knew of my work while my temporary boss was fishing. To be fair, the captain consulted me constantly on what to do during the exercise. He even "let me" write the full after action report on our performance of duty as umpires once we ended the exercise. I can't say he did not know how to make good use of his subordinates. Whatever his opinion of me was, I did not work for him long enough for him to report on my performance to my true boss, as it later turned out, the man I seldom saw, the company executive officer. In the first six months I was in the 7th Group, I never worked long enough for anyone to write a report on my performance. Yet regulations required that a report be written; so the friendly exec got the chore.

I was back at Smoke Bomb Hill following the training exercise in late September of '62, trying—as were a dozen or so lieutenants and captains awaiting schooling—to fill in the hours each day. In the second week of October, our company commander selected four A Detachments to deploy on a special mission. The detachment in which I was the exec was one of those.

I left the unit area after the notice of our alert and went home to our small apartment in a long multiplex on post. I told Carol I needed all my gear and my fatigue uniforms with unit patches and rank insignia removed. I asked her to put that together for me, that I would be back in a few hours, and that I would be leaving today on a "mission." I would need one set of civilian clothes to include a sweater or light jacket. A few hours later, I returned to give her and Mike and Lisa a hug and kiss. I told her when we were alone that I did not know where I was going, what I would be doing, how long I would be gone or when I would return. I told her if there was an emergency, she should contact the Company B headquarters. The company commander had assured us that if families needed to contact one of my men or me, he would make that happen. Then I left.

Within a few hours, we were on a greyhound bus in the civilian clothes we had changed into on the edge of the Fort Bragg training area. We were going north. In fact, we were on the route that I took when we visited our parents in South Charleston just before I had signed in at Fort Bragg. Somewhere near

Hillsville, Virginia, we pulled into a restaurant parking lot and our leader, Captain "Whip" Wilson, briefed us. There was laughter when he told us we were a semi-professional football team out of Atlanta, headed for a game in Columbus, Ohio. He told us to limit the small talk. Inside, the waitresses may or may not have appreciated the appraising looks, but they tarried at tables for an exchange of the small talk that Captain Wilson had told us to avoid. Fortunately, they were so busy getting the food out for over fifty men the talk stayed under control. As we were about to leave, one of them came over to the table where five other officers and I were sitting. She looked from one of us to the other and said, "You're not a football team, I know who you are."

"Who are we?" Captain Gilliland asked.

"Okay. Let's go," Whip Wilson interjected. As we stood, she said, "You're from Fort Bragg. You're airborne."

"What makes you think that?" Gilliland asked.

She pointed to the tattoo on the arm of one officer and ran her hand over his flattop haircut. As we left, one of the sergeants called out, "You got us. We're the 82nd Airborne," at which point at least a dozen men called out, "Airborne." The waitress beamed at her triumph, but Captain Wilson, holding the door open, was scowling as we filed out and loaded the bus.

Our eventual location at the time was classified, and what we did there was classified information for years following completion of our mission. Because the Central Intelligence Agency (CIA) directed us, there were restrictions and some small controversy afterwards about what we could say about that mission. I found it ironic that we wound up at Fort Knox, Kentucky, the post that Carol and the kids and I had left less than a year earlier to go to the language school in California. Lisa was born in the Fort Knox Ireland Army Hospital. I realized why our company leaders told us to keep our cold weather clothing in the bags with which we deployed. I had heard some rumors that made me think we likely were going south, to Florida. No long johns needed in Florida, but they can be a comfort at Fort Knox, even as early as October.

We learned later the CIA representative had given the stiff arm to the post commander and told him that neither he nor any other post official could be in the training area that was "fenced off" for our mission. I thought then, as I do now, that was a dumb move and an unreasonable limit on a general officer who had responsibility for the conduct of safe training on the post. Eventually, the Deputy Commander, Brigadier General Thomas, surprised us and showed up in our training area, just in time to see a couple of Green Berets manually turning a spit holding a deer carcass over a big, hickory fire. He was unhappy. I don't know how many post regulations we were violating. At least four: discharging a weapon in an area not cleared for live fire, killing a deer out of season, creating an unauthorized, open fire, and preparing to consume meat not approved by the Post Quartermaster. Gilliland was the proud shooter who had brought down the large buck, but nobody volunteered that information. Eventually, our higher-level bosses and Brigadier Thomas agreed to cooperate, and he was helpful in facilitating and suggesting improvements in our training.

Our mission was to train and make ready a regiment of volunteers for possible employment in military operations outside the United States.

The fact they were Cuban refugees was then classified Secret.

The fact we were training them was also Secret.

Our CIA representative, or case officer, viewed the purpose of our training, that was, possible invasion of the island nation of Cuba, as highly sensitive. He did not allow us to discuss that point with the trainees, although they had been told of that possibility from the start to get them to volunteer for the training. Of course, recruiting them was not hard. They were refugees who, mostly, still had family in Cuba. The thought of freeing the island and reuniting with their families was great motivation. And, of course, we did discuss a possible invasion of their home island, on an individual basis. As I learned years later, one of the men, a commercial pilot, correctly guessed the beach that the secret planners had picked for us to land. Late in the training, the press gained some idea of what was going on, and the powers-that-be agreed to let some reporters come in, with cameras, for a briefing. I came close to knocking a camera to the ground when the photographer insisted on taking a picture of one of our trainees. The reporters had been told not to do this; that it could endanger their families, but the reporter told her photographer to take a picture anyway. I did get the film destroyed on the spot and the young reporter finally apologized.

The training was on various small weapons and infantry tactics. Of course, each Special Forces A Detachment included experts on light and heavy weapons, and that was the major emphasis of the training. Our men were experts in other areas as well, but every team member assumed the role of weapons trainer. I taught the use of hand grenades and the .50 caliber machine gun, its employment, mechanical operation, care and cleaning, and "head spacing," a necessary periodic adjustment to the weapon to ensure efficient firing. Other detachment commanders and executives taught subjects that their prior assignments suggested. Those officers who had been commissioned out of Officer Candidate School, some of whom had several years of enlisted experience, were well prepared for many of the subjects. We were on a tight schedule. Whenever we could, we watched the limited news available on the one television provided to us or listened to a radio. What we were watching was the continuing crisis with the Soviet Union over possible missiles in Cuba.

A confrontation between the two nations was rapidly developing, and the tension was obvious in the manner and voices of the television personalities who brought the terse, limited reports.

Eventually, of course, the Soviets backed down and, according to our television set, halted the installation of missiles in Cuba. There are still discussions about what President Kennedy agreed to do to gain that outcome, but our Special Forces mission was over, and we returned to Fort Bragg. Had the standoff not been resolved, and an invasion ordered, I would have been commanding a company of a little over one hundred Cubans. Trained as infantrymen, although their skills in real life had been airline pilots, lawyers, store clerks, fishermen, and farmers, they were eager to go. Over the years, as more and more about the Cuban Missile Crisis has been declassified, I learned an invasion would have found a situation unlike that assumed by planners based on available intelligence. Some reconstructions now say the Soviet military there was not 100,000, but more like over 400,000, and the forces prepared to defend against a beach landing were not 10,000, as estimated, but over 30,000. Of course, there has been and remain different views of what would have happened had the landings been attempted.

It is clear that the deployment of missiles was stopped and we did not enter a hot war with the Soviet Union. The disappointment of the Cubans in my would-be assault company was crushing, and it took the efforts of all of our Special Forces soldiers and appointed Cuban leaders of the squads and platoons to maintain order in the ranks. Throughout the night following the President's television announcement that suggested the crisis was over, few of us slept. For the Cubans, since the announcement meant they were not going back into Cuba, they were ready to fight anybody available—to include one another. A knifing took the life of one of the Cubans. We finally settled the passions of the soldiers, aided by their fatigue.

A couple of mornings later, we left Fort Knox for Fort Bragg, again in our guise as a football team. A lingering image for me of that experience was Captain Whip Wilson moving about during our stops to insure there was coffee for his team, which had come to prepare for a deadly game we did not play.

During those weeks between our aborted training mission with the Cubans and the beginning of my Special Forces Officer training courses, the highlight of our activities was parachute jumps, either an opportunity jump from a C-46 or 47 of the Air Force special warfare command or any available C-119, Huey helicopter, or Chinook helicopter. A couple of times the detachment to which I was assigned, but with which I seldom trained, conducted a unit training jump. On one such jump in November, Captain Bill Maples, the A Detachment Commander, led the detachment out the door and I, as executive officer, "pushed the stick," or jumped last. It was a night jump, from a C-46, low, and into a small drop zone. I knew when I exited the airplane that we had been dropped early, before arriving at a proper exit point, the point when the pilot turned on the green, or "go" light. I, and most of the detachment, had no problem getting into the cleared drop zone, but two or three of the first men out went into the trees. Although I was last to hit the ground and moved back toward the spot where Captain Maples should have landed, "rolling up" the stick as I went, I was the one who found Maples up in a tree. Actually, I heard him calling out, and he was not happy.

"My foot is fouled, John, and I think it may be broken." He was not far up, but it was a difficult climb because there were few lower limbs, and they were brittle. Two of my men pushed me up part of the way, and I managed to "shimmy" my way up to him, as I had done as a boy back in the hills of West Virginia. I wished, however, that was where I was right then, climbing one of the hardwood trees that were easy to scale compared to the scraggly pine. I had to get above him to pull him up and get the leg free from a fork in the tree. Lowering him down was the greater difficulty. He was evacuated by helicopter and we went on with our limited, tactical exercise. I learned early the next morning that in fact his ankle was fractured.

In the early winter of 1963, I began the Special Warfare Unconventional Warfare Officer Course followed by the Counterinsurgency Course, highlighted by guest speakers on Vietnam. Dr. Bernard Fall expressed what I thought was confidence in the eventual American success in advising and assisting the Vietnamese Army because of the unprecedented role the helicopter would play in that counterinsurgency. Somehow, even then, to me it was not that simple. Policy from the top can incorporate failure from the beginning. But we had and have a way, as a Nation, as National Leaders, and as an Army, to see matters in stark, black and white—and positive—terms. When I push myself, I can recall my own seeds of doubt, not so much our eventual success or failure in Vietnam, but the difficulty of the task. Such was my feeling as I listened to Dr. Fall, author of *Street Without Joy*, talk of the French experience in Indochina. That was when he spoke so optimistically, I thought, of the future success of the American Army in Vietnam. I had read his book, and I admired his depth of knowledge as he spoke to our class. However, I also recalled studying a little handbook put together by the British Special Air Service (SAS) on their counterterrorist, or CT, operations in Malaysia. I had trained with them briefly at Fort Bragg in late '62 and it struck me the helicopter could lead to technology putting the American soldier in the air and flying up and over the earth-hugging Viet Cong. I had read and reread the Counterterrorist Operations Handbook that cautioned on the misapplication of technology. We would be more successful, they wrote, if we would "out guerrilla" the guerrilla. "Go where he is, look like him, smell like him, think like him, and fight like him. That's the way to beat him." Still, I did not have my head turned away from the power of the American Army. Surely, we would be smart enough to adapt our training of the Vietnamese soldiers, on our equipment, to the conditions in the jungles and rice paddies of the Indo-China Peninsula.

The SAS stressed living in the jungle, getting rid of the smells of hamburgers, hot dogs, Coca Cola, cigarettes, and ice cream. They wrote of getting the dirt of the land in your hair, in your shorts and socks (if you wore shorts and socks) and giving up cigarette smoking and fine-smelling toiletries. In fairness to Dr. Law, he faulted the French for the stationary warfare they moved to, building and living in the forts. He spoke of the moving out on brief operations and returning to life in the forts that tried to bring as much of France to the jungles of Indochina as was possible. Neither Dr. Law—I believe—nor I foresaw the manner in which the American Army too would hug the base camps and firebases of Vietnam and fly ice cream to soldiers on patrol in the jungle.

An acquaintance in the Counterinsurgency course was Lieutenant Floyd Thompson, a member of the 5th Special Forces Group and later a member of one of our early A teams in Vietnam. He would survive an aircraft crash in the Central Highlands, capture, and seven years as a prisoner. I never saw him again after his return to America around '71. I have read something of his difficult efforts to find normalcy back home after his imprisonment at the hands of the Viet Cong.

I completed the Special Warfare Course and the Counterinsurgency Course in the early spring of '63. I was then one of four captains selected to command the first A Detachments to deploy to Vietnam out of the 7th Special Forces Group. Still assigned to Company B, I became aware that there was a competition for funds within the 7th Group between the programs of counterinsurgency training and unconventional warfare training. The counterinsurgency training focused on Vietnam. The training for unconventional warfare, or UW, the long-standing mission of Special Forces and its predecessors in World War II, oriented broadly around the world. Driving the UW case for training sites and funds was Major Charlie Beckwith, whom I had met briefly in the company of some SAS officers the previous fall. He had served with the SAS in Malaya, where he was severely wounded and fought off malaria. He had impressed me with his aggressiveness and enthusiasm, even passion, for the UW mission. He was responsible later for suggestions in training the deploying counterinsurgency detachments to make us tougher and to bond us as a team. That included lugging a metal wall locker filled with rocks over the rough terrain of western North Carolina.

The Group personnel officer told me that my team was handpicked at group headquarters, something I questioned a bit when I reviewed my roster. Of the twelve men, including me, our surnames were: Corns, Collier, Combs, Conklin, Conrad, Crook … well. Others were Manuel, Miller, Roberts, Sasser, and Sieg. But then there was Wallace. So, maybe they were just pulled from an alphabetical list of handpicked men. Most important, they were all good men, although three of them were quite young and new to Special Forces. But then, so was I. The crusty old hands, officers and NCOs, who had been around Special Forces for years, made this point. Some were veterans of missions behind enemy lines in the Korean War. For years after Vietnam, those old hands would lament the flood of new soldiers like me into Special Forces during the buildup that responded to the call of President Kennedy. There was, I believe, much merit in what the old hands said, but the mission assigned drove the large increase in officers and enlisted soldiers.

As with all A Detachments, my men were specialists: two were specialists in each field of medical, weapons, communications, and demolitions, one in operations, and one in intelligence. My executive officer, prepared to assume my duties, if needed, had been a medical specialist before becoming an officer through Officer Candidate School. My duties were to provide the leadership and direction of the team.

Pre-deployment training stressed physical conditioning, training of indigenous forces in weapons and counter guerrilla tactics, community security operations, and hygiene. We used much time in familiarizing every team member on the area study of Pleiku Province in the Central Highlands. Every team member learned about Plei Le Thanh District, and the location and layout of the camp, Duc Co, at times called Chu Dron, we were to inherit from the 5th Special Forces team we were to replace.

The four teams from the 7th Special Forces Group flew out of Pope Air Force Base, adjacent to Fort Bragg, in August of 1963 and arrived in Saigon within days. We transferred to an Air Force C-130 short take off and landing aircraft for Nha Trang. Located on the coast, Nha Trang was a city about one third of the way from Saigon to Hue and the Demilitarized Zone. The Demilitarized Zone, or DMZ, between North and South Vietnam, had been set up by the peace accords between the French and North Vietnam in 1954.

For the first time, I entered a scene related to Vietnam that was quite striking. I wrote to Carol, "We are presently at a beautiful seacoast town with a large bay filled with islands and opening into the sea." Reminiscent of scenes of William Holden on the beach in the movie, *Bridge on the River Kwai*, Nha Trang was a setting far removed from what we had been reading about and preparing for the last several months. The Special Forces Group headquarters was in an old, but beautifully designed and well kept French Villa. Inland from the long, white crescent of beach were other villas, all with their white stucco walls and red tile roofs. Nha Trang looked like anything but the site of a war-waging headquarters. The six days there, to allow us to adjust to the weather while doing further country study and updating our intelligence information, hardly approached the steamy, hot, highland jungle of our camp at Duc Co. Most of the time, my men and I were enjoying the salt-white sand of the beach and the huge, cooling swells and surf of the South China Sea. Our first time at the beach, I watched two Vietnamese boys diving into the surf and signaling that for a coin, they would dive deep. I later found the water only eight to ten feet deep close to shore. I cut my time on the beach short and went back to the officers' quarters where I wrote Carol a letter. I was upbeat and descriptive of the rolling beach and the sparkling white sand, and the equally white, French-style buildings. I wrote of the River Kwai movie that Carol and I had seen together before we were married, although the location in the movie was no doubt far removed from Nha Trang, or French Indo China. But the view and the atmosphere were similar. I wrote, "Tell Mike and Lisa I've already seen a lot of the little kids who need our help. All they can say in English is hello, but their attitude alone makes our job worth doing." I asked her to hug and kiss Mike and Lisa for me. I did not mention that it was two boys, a few years older than Mike and Lisa, playing in the surf that compelled me to write the letter.

Some of the men from our teams visited a nearby restaurant, which sat atop a raised point of land on the beach. Our soldiers enjoyed the French cuisine, prepared by a Vietnamese family. I made a note to go there one evening, but failed to do so. I wanted to absorb all the headquarters staff could offer in documents and conversation about our area and our mission. In my letter of August 9, I told Carol, "I've met several men here who I had met at Bragg. It's a big operation and pretty darned effective from what I see." Six months later, I accompanied one of those Fort Bragg Green Berets, Lieutenant Garner, and enjoyed the restaurant, but we were on the verge of leaving Vietnam and probably did not do the meal justice. We simply wanted to go home.

The low flight over the rugged mountains to Pleiku City was in an Army Caribou, a fixed wing aircraft designed to operate from short airfields. At Pleiku, our B Detachment, or next higher headquarters, kept us for two days for briefings. There were two presentations. One was on our status as guests in the country, which was good but a canned and a monotone reading. The brevity and shallowness of the briefing disappointed all of us. The briefers were among the most junior of enlisted men in the detachment. A lieutenant introduced each briefer and left the room. In the two days, the B detachment commander spoke to the teams as a group briefly. He then turned us over to the adjutant, a captain, who gave us forms to fill out and left, leaving the pickup of the completed forms to a specialist. The individual, one-on-one meetings that each detachment commander was to have with the B detachment commander were cancelled when he had to fly to Nha Trang for a meeting. The detachment S3 told us the commander would be out soon to see each of us at our campsite. That positively impressed me. However, my team was on site for over two months before the commander visited to bring in a helicopter I needed to reestablish contact with a patrol. Following that visit, my boss, the major, visited one more time before his departure after my team had been at Duc Co for four months. The B Detachment adjutant visited my camp one time during an investigation he was doing on a truck accident that had occurred on the infamous Highway 19 between my camp and Pleiku. My light weapons expert, SSG Sieg, had been driving a two-and one-half ton truck on a return trip from Pleiku when it collided with a buffalo-drawn cart and struck a bridge abutment. His injuries forced his medical evacuation to the states and, while he fully recovered, he never returned to the team. He visited with me briefly soon after our return to Fort Bragg in early '64.

Unlike the tile-roofed, white stucco buildings of Nha Trang, our buildings in Duc Co had tin roofs and matted bamboo strips for walls, tied to long supporting poles. The camp was cut from the jungle, and the mosquitoes that the sea breezes swept away from the sandy beach at Nha Trang seemed to have clustered on our little camp. I wrote Carol on August 16, our son Mike's birthday—it was his fourth. I began, "Dearest Carolyn." In reading that letter recently, and for the first time since I wrote it 46 years ago, I was struck that I called her Carolyn. That is her name, the one all her family and our school mates called her, but for some reason, I, almost from our first date as seniors in high school, had called her Carol, which neither of us can explain. I leafed through the twenty or so letters we still have that I wrote to her during my six months in Vietnam, and found it is only one of two letters addressed as Carolyn rather than Carol. My guess is it had something to do with it being our son's birthday, the child born in the middle of my first tour overseas and the son I did not see until he was nearly eight months old. A small matter, but one that reminds me of the deeply felt emotions that stay just below the surface, largely unstated, in times of long separation and danger. The other letter I wrote much later on the evening of October 24, our fifth wedding anniversary. I also wrote in the letter on Mike's birthday, just one week after my upbeat comments on the children on the beach at Nha Trang, "Tell Mike I see a lot of little kids who need soap and clothes and medicine. They would make good playmates at their age now. A few years and they will be caught up in a hell of a mess." I was referring to the children of the Montagnard people around my camp, not the happy Vietnamese children on the white sands by the sea.

I wrote Carol, "Don't worry about the facilities here—they aren't much, but I do eat good American food—three times a day—sleep on a bed, a real bed, made of wood slats and a 2-inch cotton pad. It's quite comfortable. Plus a good day's work to keep me busy and resting at night. It rains here quite a bit, but we have good rain clothing—thanks to Sears Roebuck. Recently I attended a Nampei party. The native people (I meant the Montagnards, not the Vietnamese) have large urns of rice wine and a traditional way of drinking it. Sort of a competition, and you must drink so much at a time. I'll tell you more about it in a future letter." Actually, I never did. I waited until I was back home to tell of the sacrificed buffalo, the top of the head knocked off with a ceremonial sword, and my honored position of being the first to eat from the spoonful of warm brains taken from the animal. Fourteen years later, I would be diagnosed with toxoplasmosis that eventually took the sight from my left eye. The doctors asked me if I had eaten any meat of wild or domestic animals that had not been "adequately" cooked. Particularly the buffalo brains came to mind, and there were also, cooked of course, pigeon heads, rattle snakes, wild boar, antelopes, dogs and monkeys. The British ophthalmologist, who had treated the Queen and looked at my eye in Korea, was somewhat appalled at my diet. Of course, there have been and are other theories of the source of the disease, but I somehow suspect that delicacy, buffalo brains chased with rice wine.

My first meeting with an officer with command bearing in the B Detachment at Pleiku was the S3, Captain Johnny Johnston. He was well informed, confident, and plain spoken. He ticked off the points that I considered of most concern to me as a new commander in country. Throughout our shared time in Vietnam, Captain Johnston was the officer from whom I learned I could get an answer and help on most any subject. In reality, he acted as my next higher commander, and I valued his professionalism. I had never met him before I arrived in Vietnam, and saw him only one other time after 1964.

As the CH-47 Chinook helicopter landed at the airstrip alongside my new command location of Duc Co, my view confirmed the impressions gained at Fort Bragg. From aerial and ground photographs as well as map studies we reviewed there, we thought this was not a sound camp location. Duc Co sat on the south slope of a low ridgeline. The roadway that ran east to west paralleled the airstrip and the north fence line of the camp. The airfield and roadway crossed the commanding terrain just north of the camp. They ran along the ground that provided the best visibility, once we cleared more brush, and the best fields of fire. That was where the camp needed to have been built. With the road and airfield having priority, the best land remaining was north of the road and farther east of the airfield.

In our time of overlap with the departing team, the emphasis was on each member of the two teams spending the maximum time with his counterpart. We, of course, met with the Vietnamese commander of the Civil Irregular Defense Group (CIDG) Battalion, who was also commander of the Duc Co Camp. He directed the training of men for the other CIDG units in the local area. He also ran the training for the scouts in the Mountain Scout Program that involved surveillance along the shared border with Cambodia. It was a significant and broad set of responsibilities for the captain, or *Dai Uy* (pronounced *Dai* as die; *Uy* as we) Minh (sometimes spelled Mien,) whom I was to advise. I also inherited from the previous detachment commander the senior adviser role to the local District Chief. Few Army captains carried out duties as broad and challenging as these, common to all A Detachment Commanders in Vietnam. Potentially, I could have my hands full. But I based that on the assumption that both *Dai Uy* Minh and the Le Thanh District Chief aggressively attacked all their duties, something I already knew from our area study briefings was not common. The single theme of reports from A Detachments returning from Vietnam, both those from the 5th and the 1st Special Forces Group, was that motivating the men we advised was our greatest challenge. I was to learn this was the prime challenge all over Vietnam. From the American Ambassador to Vietnam and the Commander, US Military Assistance Command, Vietnam, or COMUSMACV, down to captains like me.

There was a great deal to cover and the transition went smoothly, thanks largely to my big, friendly, and efficient team sergeant, George Manuel. The departing commander and I experienced some personal friction when I questioned him about the location of the camp and asked if he thought I could open the issue of moving the camp with the parties involved originally. Those, he told me, were the Province Chief, District Chief, Captain Minh, the B Detachment Commander in Pleiku, and our "case officer," the name applied to the CIA man who gave us advice and money. My predecessor stiffened uncomfortably and advised me that the decision on the camp location was driven by the politics between the district and province chief and that neither he nor his boss in Pleiku was able to influence it. I asked if he thought I could reopen the camp location matter, and he laughed with a seeming "you have a lot to learn" attitude.

When I took the question to my higher headquarters two weeks later, I was not encouraged. I told the B Detachment executive officer I was going to forward an official request. When I spoke later with the commander, he said that would be a waste of time, but that if I sent it, he would forward it with a recommendation of approval. Although I submitted the request a week later, and it was forwarded with a recommendation for approval, it was reported as pending at Province headquarters and in Nha Trang each time the B detachment inquired about it.

About the same time, Lieutenant Colonel Viney, the new deputy commander of the group headquartered at Nha Trang, visited my camp. The B Detachment S3 came with him. In my briefing, I covered the case for a new location for the camp, across the road and east of the airfield on higher ground. At the end of his inspection, which included a detailed look at everything we could see in the time he had, Viney said, "Captain Corns, the only way you can go with this camp is up." He agreed with the need to move the camp, and said he would find the status of the paperwork when he returned to headquarters.

Meanwhile, working mostly with my Team Sergeant, George Manuel, and my Intelligence expert, Master Sergeant Roberts, I completed my assessment of the camp and our advisory missions. The limited degree of success in all areas was even less than we had concluded, and far less than the outgoing commander and his people had stated in their orientation briefings for us. I shared with the entire team my assessment and, for the first time, advised them of Colonel Viney's comment just days before. We agreed; in fact, one of my team members, Sergeant Sasser, believed the situation was worse than I had described. He based his view on a hands-on examination of all phases of weapons training, employment, and the understanding, or lack of it, of the role of the weapons in our training and in our camp defense layout. He had already stated his concerns to Team Sergeant Manuel, who had given me the crux of what Sasser had said. But that version lacked the sense of urgency or passion that Sasser now showed about the critical machine guns and the mortars in the camp defense. I then placed Sasser in charge of an overhaul of the camp defense plans and asked Manuel to oversee an increase in the quality of all of our weapons training, using all team personnel, as needed, to aid him. I told them I would meet with *Dai Uy* Minh and lay out all of our concerns and the steps we were taking, through his key people, to improve camp defense plans and weapons use. Within three weeks, we learned we had reason to question the degree to which all Vietnamese soldiers and their leaders understood the tactical and weapons training our predecessors had taught them. We were confident we would do better, and maybe we did, but we were to confront many of the same problems the team before us had met.

Chapter Three

Phillipe Drouin

In preparation for that assessment I was to share with *Dai Uy* Minh, I spent my first private time with my interpreter, Phillipe Drouin. I was impressed with both his understanding of English, and of weapons and tactical matters about the defense of the camp. He clearly welcomed my team's hard look at the camp operation and our conclusions. He was polite and was respectful to me as the detachment commander and senior adviser, but he seemed eager to respond to questions reflecting his own opinions on the training. He did not show a high degree of respect for *Dai Uy* Minh, but he was careful with his words. Over time, Phillipe would mean a great deal to me, to other team members, and to our mission. He—and information about him—would continue to surprise me—long after our tour.

He was born to a French Captain Drouin, veteran of Dien Bien Phu, and a Montagnard princess of the Jarai tribe. Although raised by his mother and her mother's family in the Jarai tradition, he early sought to learn the language of his father, who had left the country with the political settlement of 1954. He did not recall his father, but he was proud of him—that he was a soldier and left his wife and child only on the order of his country. His mother helped him to learn more about the people of his father, despite the discomfort of her father, a chief, and other Jarai tribal leadership. He learned English, according to him, in one short summer, just in time to be available when the U. S. Army first sent advisers into the Pleiku area. Shortly after that, he responded to the call for interpreters for the new Special Forces detachments that began arriving in 1962.

I believe, although he would not confirm it, that his principal teacher of English and American ways was American movies. I recall the first time I saw him, and I thought someone was playing a joke on us. It was within the first hour after we landed at Duc Co. Captain Minh, the camp commander, met me with his own interpreter, a civilian whom he spoke of as his administrative officer. Vietnamese, the administrative officer was powerful. I never knew just whom in Saigon he worked for, but his power, I became sure, equaled or exceeded that of the *Dai Uy*. I came to distrust the man and his interpretations. In other words, I came to believe he was playing his own game, no doubt for some civilian, possibly Intelligence, bureau in Saigon.

Back to Phillipe—I saw this young man as we came through the gate the first time, standing on the stoop of one of the barracks buildings, not too far from the camp front gate. He could have been the Asian version of the Marlboro Man. Cowboy boots, jeans, complete with a large bronco-riding emblem on a western belt buckle, and a western style, long sleeve shirt with various white stripes crisscrossing over a sky blue background. Atop his head was a smart, western style hat and over his eyes was a pair of large, aviator style, sunglasses. Shortly after we completed the formalities with *Dai Uy* Minh and his administrative sidekick, I asked if anybody knew who that guy in the sunglasses was. Sergeant Manuel looked a little bit sheepish as he said, "Sir, that is 'Cowboy.' He's your personal interpreter."

"You're kidding," I said. Manuel laughed, as did three or four of my team members, and my predecessor and a couple of his men. The departing captain said, "He's very good, Captain Corns. A little bit flashy, but a damn good interpreter." On that count, the man I replaced gave me information that was very reliable.

Why I felt safe later to ask Phillipe, when he and I were alone, what he could tell me about Captain Minh I don't know. But, looking back, that clearly pleased him. No doubt, we would have built rapport over time, because he and I needed each other. But beyond providing him a job, I had no idea of the nature of his need of me. I admired his intelligence, his broken, but clearly understandable, English, and his awareness of what I would call things American. Also, he did not hide, although tactful, his dislike for Vietnamese in general and Captain Minh in particular. Still later, when I laid out for him my early assessment of conditions of the camp defenses and training programs, he was quick to agree and to add some specifics. This was, of course, well after the other American A Detachment had gone. He would not fault that team or any member in it for the deficiencies. All of his criticisms suggested the fault in the camp for everything substandard was the Vietnamese, not the Montagnard soldiers or the previous Green Beret team. I realized he was operating from a position of strength with this approach. My men and I came to feel we had to protect the Montagnards from the Vietnamese. And we liked these Aborigines of the mountains, long held in a separate and inferior role by the Vietnamese government in Saigon. I also later learned that our American detachments faced this problem all over the highlands. Our Green

Beret teams chose the Montagnards over the Vietnamese. We didn't hide it, and the Vietnamese resented it.

Within a month, Phillipe became my most trusted asset and source of information about activities and relationships in the camp, the district, and the province. Looking back, clearly he measured what he shared with me about the friction between the Montagnards, as a body of people, and the Vietnamese government at every level.

In just a little more time, every member of my team identified him as the most expert trainer in the camp, less some special expertise of our two medics and our intelligence sergeant. Also, after just two patrols led by one of my men and two other team members, the talk in our team room was that he was a sound tactician, and, most important, he seemed fearless.

He was almost too good to be true. But to a man, I and every other member of my team decided that he was that good. It seemed he loved Americans, and would do anything to prove his total commitment to the cause of defeating the Viet Cong and saving the Republic of South Vietnam. But always, lingering in the background was what could only be a thinly veiled contempt for the Vietnamese. I had enough signs to be wary, at least a little bit. But he was such a great asset in every phase of our mission at Duc Co, that it was easy to accept him at face value—one hell of a find in the middle of the Highlands of Mountainous Vietnam.

I should add that, over time, he spoke of John Wayne, Randolph Scott, and Gregory Peck. He did not take Roy Rogers or Gene Autry seriously. Still, if we had provided him a horse instead of a beaten down truck to get around, he would have likely named the horse, Trigger. But the truck comes later in the story. It was Phillipe who named George Manuel, Elephant, and named me, Tiger. George's size in fact suggested an animal of that size, and there was no fat on his tall, large frame. As for the name Tiger for me, I think that may have been more a matter of Phillipe's clever psychology. But it stuck, and the Montagnards liked referring to Sergeant Manuel and me with those names—of course in their Jarai tongue, which we did not understand, but Phillipe did.

Six months on the border with Cambodia, way out on the western edge of Pleiku Province was hardly an experience of fast-paced action. Most of our operational activities I was not free to share with Carol at the time. But, in a letter to her in late September, I wrote, "Things that we're doing here that I can talk about are:

1- We are building a leper colony for leprosy victims in this area—we feel there are at least 600. We are building small homes for each family, their private gardens and teaching them about different seeds and how to grow new crops. The nurses will be provided by a local missionary group, many have contracted leprosy in their work.

2- We are teaching the villagers to make soap.

3- We are helping them build two schools and equip them. Teachers must be hired by the District Chief (one of our conditions).

4- We are teaching them how to build sewers for refuse toilets."

Of course, Carol knew, as we discussed in later years, that other than disease, danger for us did not lie in those areas of help to the people, but in going after the Viet Cong.

Operationally, we had three camp missions: Man and operate patrols out of Duc Co camp to promote the safety of the surrounding region. Train individual soldiers of the Civilian Irregular Defense Group, CIDG, for units at towns and villages, primarily within Le Thanh District. And train and control the operations of Mountain Scout Detachments that patrolled along the border.

The activities of the Viet Cong in our area included tax collection along Highway 19 that connected our district with the provincial capitol at Pleiku. They stopped trucks loaded with rice being sent by the District Chief to market at Pleiku and removed a percentage of the load as a tax. If the drivers were not cooperative, the VC threatened to ambush the truck in the future. Then they would take all the rice—as a punishment for tax evasion. They would carry the driver and other passengers off to serve the Viet Cong or the National Liberation Front. That is, if they did not kill them on the spot. Another form of taxation was simply each village leaving a percentage, of so many bushels, or bags, of rice in the field when they harvested. The Viet Cong would then come by in darkness and carry the rice away. The Viet Cong moved supplies north to south along the border, both on our side and in Cambodia. These supplies were going to units as far south as the Saigon area. Finally, the Viet Cong often executed a man serving the District Chief and the Saigon government. Commonly, they shot them with most of the residents of the town or village watching.

Our task was to find the Viet Cong and kill or capture them and seize or destroy their weapons, supplies, and base areas. We conducted several missions, both patrols and raids, between August of '63 and January of '64. Two or three may tell the story. We, of course, were advisers and we worked with the units under the control of Captain Minh, or the District Chief. Our role was legally limited to providing advice. In fact, orders forbade us Americans to fire our weapons, regardless of the circumstances we were in, unless we were fired on. However, I told my men to protect themselves. I advised them to fire before the enemy could fire on them to escape death or wounds. They knew I would support them and tell any investigators or officers up the chain of command that they were working under my instructions. I am confident that most, if not all, detachment commanders did the same.

Simply stated, every member of my team went on patrols and raids as I needed their expertise and in a manner to cause each of us to share the risk of such operations. In reality, my problem was not men shirking or trying to do so, but getting each man out on patrol as often as he wanted. This was especially true of my three youngest and least experienced soldiers, and my weapons and demolition experts. Sergeant Manuel would have happily gone out every time a patrol or raid left the camp gate. But he was essential in the oversight of daily training where he soon commanded responses from Vietnamese and Montagnard alike in a manner that my executive officer or I could not equal. My senior medic and my executive officer, who had been a medic as an enlisted man, went on the least operations, because of their roles in running sick calls in our camp and in villages nearby. My exec, Lieutenant Conrad, was our financial manager controlling our receipt of funds and all check expenditures. I kept him close to perform this mission although the same role at times required him to travel to Pleiku more than any other team member.

A raid we conducted early on was south on the northern slopes of the Ia Drang Valley to find and destroy a Viet Cong regional training camp. I based the mission on information given to me by the District Chief personally. I put the mission together in less than two days and placed my advisers under Master Sergeant Roberts, a Korean War combat veteran.

The mission was a success, the patrol breaking radio contact only to report by code over the radio that fact and their location, at the first checkpoint coming back north from the training site they destroyed. On the fourth day out, we received a report of contact with the enemy and then the communications failed. No more transmissions from Roberts, and no luck in contacting him. Captain Minh had received no report from his patrol leader, an aspirant, which was a soldier in training on the job to become a lieutenant. I had questioned him as patrol leader, but shortly after I expressed this to Roberts with Phillipe present, my interpreter waited until we walked out to go see *Dai Uy* Minh and then asked if he could speak up. I told him, of course. He then gave the aspirant a high rating, saying he was superior to the two lieutenants that Minh had not selected. I accepted Phillipe's opinion and turned back. Sergeant Manuel told me he thought it unwise to continue with the aspirant as patrol leader, despite his high regard for Phillipe's opinion. Adding to the problem, to a man, my team did not think highly of the aspirant. He always looked like he was just off an honor guard or parade field. His uniforms were custom-tailored, tight fitting, and of a quality superior to the issued uniform the rest of the Vietnamese officers wore. His boots were spit shined, his brass highly polished, and he did not like the Montagnard soldiers. Further, he resented the role of my noncommissioned officers, at one point telling one of my NCOs he would not do what he had been told unless ordered by me personally. I did not question the matter further after Phillipe, who was present at the time, told me that everyone believed that Manuel was about to take the aspirant by the collar and make him do what I had directed. Phillipe told me, "Aspirant thought then that he sure must go ahead and do it, and he did." I too thought the aspirant was too much the parade field and garrison soldier. A member of the departing team had told us the aspirant had never been out on a patrol. I finally told Manuel I was going to go along with the aspirant as patrol leader, based on Phillipe's recommendation. Put that way, George dropped his objection. In fact, George always thought even more highly of Phillipe than I did in those first two or so months.

After we were unable to make contact for twenty-four hours, I contacted my B Detachment commander by radio and he agreed to provide a helicopter. Only as the chopper was ten minutes out did I learn that the Major was on board, one of the two visits he made to my camp while he and I were in command. I must say, that when he landed and while he was at my camp, he did all the right things. After I briefed him fully on the patrol and the defense status of the camp, he informed me that I should take the chopper. I had planned to do that, and he said he would stay at the camp where he would have commo with me and with his staff in Pleiku. That was, I thought, the sound way for him to act.

We found the patrol rather quickly, about three checkpoints north of their last reported location. They had not moved as far as I would have guessed, and I saw that they were carrying what had to be two bodies suspended from poles held aloft on the shoulders of two men. Once we saw the smoke grenade that signaled the area for the helicopter to land was clear, or safe, the pilot set us down.

I recognized the aspirant at once as one of the two men suspended from a pole. His uniform was the same as the other soldiers wore, and his boots were the typical jungle boot of part leather and part canvas to handle constant wading of streams as was common in our area. I recognized his face, despite the bruising around his swollen nose and the small, black, and dark red hole, low on his forehead and nearly between his eyes. Whatever the caliber of the bullet that killed him, it was still in his head; there was no exit wound.

Sergeant Roberts calmly reported on the ambush. He said they had gotten a little lax after the success at the training site where they had killed four security guards and captured three civilians. They confiscated a large amount of training equipment and papers, most of which they had burned, along with all the buildings and everything else that would burn.

He guessed the VC who sprang the ambush were in the unit that ran or used the training site. The aspirant should, he said, have put out more security to the flanks as they moved, but he added that he had failed to call that to the now dead leader's attention. Roberts reported they had taken no casualties at the raid site and pointed out the intelligence of the District Chief had been accurate.

As for the ambush, it could have been a lot worse, he said, had it not been for three men. The first two were the aspirant and one soldier who had attacked immediately into the Viet Cong, both with grease guns blazing. The third was Sergeant Sasser, who had ordered the handheld mortar put into action immediately, and when the crew hesitated, he handled and aimed the mortar as they passed the round and dropped it into the tube at his command. Roberts said he did not think the ambush party expected either response so quickly. The ambush party immediately pulled out on the sound of a whistle, leaving one man who emptied an AK-47 before the aspirant or another of our soldiers shot him. Most likely, though, he fired both rounds that killed our two Vietnamese soldiers. Roberts said they found another VC body, and blood trails suggested two others were wounded and dragged off with the retiring ambush party.

When I told Roberts to have our two dead soldiers placed on my helicopter to fly them back to camp, the pilot said he would not carry them. He said that the odor lasted for days in his chopper. The crew chief added some comment about the same problem. I walked around to the pilot's side of the aircraft and told him he had to take these men out, regardless of some damn concern over odor. These are our men, I told him. He looked straight ahead, but told the crew not to load our dead. I tapped the side of the helicopter two or three times just below his window. He turned to look at me and lifted the headphone off his left ear. I had to say it loud for him to have a chance to hear me, and I did.

"This man saved lives out here, Mister, and the lives he saved included three Americans." I don't know if he heard me, but he turned straight ahead again and said something into his mouthpiece. I walked back around the nose of the chopper as the crew chief waved the Vietnamese soldiers to put their fallen comrades on the chopper. I reached just ahead of them into the chopper to get two radios I had brought in and carried them a few steps to Roberts, who nodded in appreciation. I also gave him a new set of codes that would be effective his first call into our base. Then, when the two dead were secure on board, I climbed on the helicopter, and the pilot lifted us out. I asked him to make one more, low circle and for all on board to see if we could detect any other enemy presence. He did so, without comment from anyone, and then he flew us back to Duc Co. The body of the aspirant was at my feet, the affects of death already present. We—I—had judged him poorly. He had displayed the spit and polish that one of our Green Berets had taught him at one time. He was Vietnamese Special Forces. Apparently, that was all he needed to show inside the camp. He had saved his display of courage for the battlefield. It was not, I thought, a bad approach to soldiering. We should have reserved judgment until we had seen him fight.

The pilot and his crew kept the props going and waited until the B Detachment commander got a quick briefing from me and then boarded the helicopter as I thanked him for his support. I watched the chopper disappear along Highway 19 on its eastward flight. The B Detachment commander had been even briefer than I about it all. No criticism, no guidance, only saying that if there were further problems with the patrol to call him immediately. I did not think he was favorably impressed with our operation. I was relieved that the casualties had not been greater, and pleased that the intelligence had been good and the mission a success at the training site. But there was no excuse for the failure of three radios. Roberts had tentatively concluded the radios were loaded with weak batteries when the patrol went out.

My first action was to tell Sergeant Crook, my commo sergeant, to do what we should have already been doing: install a new checkout procedure for every radio in the camp before every mission. That was basic, and we had not done it. I then went to see *Dai Uy* Minh and told him of the reports of the bravery of his aspirant and young soldier. I then told him of the accuracy of the intelligence provided by the District Chief. Minh seemed puzzled, but he then spoke of the aspirant and how hard this news would be on his family, who were Minh's good friends. As Phillipe and I left, he told me that *Dai Uy* had not known that we got the intelligence about the training center from the District Chief. Phillipe said he did not believe the *Dai Uy* liked that. Only then did I think of the obvious. It would have been up to me to tell Minh of the source. The District Chief had given the information directly to me. In my concern for the security of the information, I had protected my source, except with my operations and intelligence sergeants. As we walked on, I made Phillipe aware of that. He said, "I not tell him too, Sir." Phillipe misjudged what happened. I had no good reason not to tell Minh. But I didn't because Minh seldom showed interest in our operations, except the number of VC we killed and weapons we captured.

I started to chide Phillipe, and explain that I had not intentionally kept Minh in the dark, but I didn't. What a hell of a way to fight a war, I thought. When I got to the operations center, I called the District Chief on our dedicated landline. In my poor and broken French, I thanked him for the information he had passed to me a few days before. Then, because I was not sure who listened to the phone in his headquarters, I did not say the two were related, which he would know they were. I told him we had just completed a good patrol, and I expected my patrol to be back the next day. I told him I would send him more details in writing by a messenger. He congratulated us and thanked me.

A few weeks later, I responded again to the initiative of the District Chief and got Captain Minh's agreement to an operation combining forces under the two captains. At first, Minh was reluctant, but did not flatly refuse. He did not like my suggestion that the operation should be under the overall command of the District Chief, who, also a captain, was senior to him. Finally, he agreed to that. However, on the morning of the kickoff of the operation, he sent a lieutenant to advise me he had been called to Saigon, and the camp contingent would be under the command of this Vietnamese lieutenant. I was disappointed, but not surprised. This was one of the obstacles to efficient orchestration of friendly operations in the area. I had planned to accompany the operation, and I did. Our target was a village near the Cambodian border that had been somewhat defiant of the authority of the District Chief. The mission was to escort a convoy of four trucks loaded with rice back to the district capital. It seemed a minor operation, but I knew more than I was being told. The District Chief was in trouble with the Province Chief. He had lost more guns in the last three months to the Viet Cong than he had captured, and he was under his quota of getting rice to market. The mission was, actually, a show of force, and an armed move by the District Chief to get the rice away from the village, before all of it fell into the hands of the Viet Cong. My source for this information, Phillipe Drouin, also said he had learned two days earlier that Minh was going to drop out of the operation. He didn't think he should tell me, he said, because to do anything about it could reveal his source. He said the man was right in the captain's office. There were many sides to Phillipe, but I was not uncomfortable with any of them

We were taking a full company, the largest force we had yet taken out in my time as camp adviser. I added Sergeant Sasser to my team, which already included Sergeants Combs, an experienced group. Sergeant Crook personally oversaw the readiness of all radios and batteries before we left Duc Co.

The second day out, I spoke to the District Chief about the rattling of the pots and pans by some of his men as we moved west toward the village. I had heard in training of such happenings, the purpose being to let the Viet Cong know you were coming and avoid contact. I don't know what the District Chief thought about all of that, but he immediately gave an instruction in Vietnamese, and the noise stopped. Still, on the morning of the third day, we were taken under fire by automatic weapons from our right flank. We hit the ground and our line erupted in friendly return fire into the heavy vegetation to our right. I looked back toward Sasser, who was preparing the mortar to fire. I was carrying an M2 carbine of World War II vintage, as I normally did. It had been the weapon I carried routinely as a platoon leader in my ROTC training at Marshall. I think I had chosen it for its lightness and some degree of nostalgia. That was of little comfort as I switched it to automatic and fired a couple of bursts. The carbine lacked the heavy, .45 caliber bullet of the Thompsons, or the grease guns we had available. A .30 caliber weapon, it certainly lacked the velocity and killing impact power of the experimental Armalite that was later to become the Army's M-16, standard issue rifle. Combs was carrying the Armalite. Fortunately, the fire was over quickly.

We later had difficulty reconstructing, but as best we could, it seemed, by chance or intent, the Viet Cong directed the fire on that part of the column where the District Chief, his bodyguards, Phillipe, Sasser, and I were located. Sasser later said he thought most of the damage to the bamboo was by the VC firing of a Browning automatic rifle, or BAR, American. Whatever the weapon, it cut down the bamboo on the opposite side of the trail from the firing location. At the height of the firing, and as we began to return fire, Phillipe, lying next to me, looked at me and nodded toward the BAR strapped to the back of the Montagnard ahead of us. The Montagnard was carrying that weapon at Sasser's direction. That soldier emptied a clip of .45 caliber bullets from a grease gun as we watched, his rounds going harmlessly into the leaves high above the location of the firing enemy weapon. The BAR remained on the Montagnard's back because Sasser was directing the firing of the 60-millimeter mortar. Phillipe, after his burst of fire with a Thompson, looked at me, shook his head and smiled, and crawled on his belly rapidly to the Montagnard. He yelled out some directions, managed to get the weapon off the man's back, took the magazine the man held back over his head to him, and rammed it into place. He charged the weapon, looked at me, smiled again, and rose to one knee. He emptied the magazine into the bamboo, cutting it down much as the VC had cut the bamboo to our left with his firing. The enemy weapon or weapons went silent. I had seen the discharge from only one muzzle, the point toward which I had fired my carbine. The combined sounds of the crack of rounds passing over our heads as we hit the ground, the smashing of the bullets against the bamboo, and the report of the rounds leaving the VC weapon, or weapons, was deafening. Only when I had turned my head back and looked at the bamboo stalks dropping as they were cut, did I realize we were not being fired on from both sides. Sasser had already put the mortar into action, but he was unable to fire close to our column, for fear a round would drift into us. Still, the mortar probably broke up the VC firing. But it was primarily Phillipe's blasting of the BAR that silenced the only automatic weapon that I was certain fired on us. There may have been more. The District Chief, in a tactic common in our training of them, insisted on hurrying the column well beyond the source of firing after we had silenced the VC firing. We made no effective search of the firing position or positions. When we got to the village, Phillipe was still carrying the big BAR, like a badge of honor. The Montagnards looked at him admiringly, but the Vietnamese looked at him with disapproval. But, about them, Phillipe never cared.

Later, the District Chief's men reported to the higher Province level that it had been an ambush and that our column took no casualties, but the Viet Cong lost three killed and two weapons, one an automatic rifle. I did not challenge the District Chief on the report. My guess, which Phillipe shared, was that one of the weapons reported captured was part of the guns that floated around Vietnam in a sort of black market. One use of such weapons was to sell them to officials of the Vietnamese government who used them to claim they were VC weapons captured by their soldiers. Phillipe saw that possible practice differently than I did. He said that was what he would have done. After all, the District Chief at Le Thanh was a good man, as Vietnamese politicians went. "Why let bad idea of counting weapons lost and captured make decision if a leader would stay leader or be fired."

As with most operations, the only comment I made to Carol in a letter right after that walk in the sun was, "Mike would get a real kick out of our banana trees and the monkeys." And, trying to have something for her to tell Lisa, I added, "I guess Lisa will really have changed. I can't imagine her saying and doing some of the things you mention even now." Lisa was two. I was not hearing those new words, the words that are accompanied by the smiles of a small human being breaking loose from the frustrating confinement of stifled communication. I missed that—and her. I would get back to America in time to help celebrate her third birthday in March of '64.

About this point during our time in Vietnam, I coined what I think was an original phrase, at least in the context of our effort in that country, "Passive Accommodation." I used it to identify the local government practice of letting the Viet Cong get by with a certain degree of tax collection in the fields or on the highways, just to survive. I used the term in my written report as I left Vietnam in early '64. The only man that I know read that entire report, hand written in a spiral notebook, was Lieutenant Colonel George Viney, who called me in to discuss it with him as I was processing out of Nha Trang. More about that later. Actually, when my team arrived at Duc Co, there was some talk in the departing A Detachment that our District Chief operated that way, some even suggesting he was a Viet Cong.

As if in contradiction of those thoughts, later in October, I received a phone call about mid-morning from the District Chief. In French, he said there was a Viet Cong ambush force set up on Highway 19 just east of the intersection of his road and Highway 19. He told me he was taking men on three jeeps and was going to attack the flank of the ambush, and he asked me to bring a platoon to join him. In broken French, I said I would, and in minutes, Sergeant Manuel, Sergeant Roberts and I were at the front gate in a jeep and truck with our standby alert platoon. I still carried the carbine and wore a standard issue, M1911, .45 caliber pistol at my side. It was always there, except when I slept. Then it was within easy reach, un-holstered, by my bed in camp or under my poncho blanket in the field. I had asked the District Chief to wait for me at his intersection, but about the time I got there, finding no one, we heard the outbreak of gunfire to the east.

When we arrived on the scene, one of the District Chief's men was dead, his jeep badly damaged, and the District Chief was wounded, seriously. His men had overrun the ambush position, killing at least two VC, and were in pursuit of others. I was told there were two more of his men wounded, one critically.

We called for a medical evacuation helicopter. My senior medic arrived shortly before the helicopter and replaced the two compresses on the District Chief. Sergeant Miller and I helplessly watched another of the District soldiers die as we waited. Finally, we loaded the District Chief and another soldier into the medical helicopter and it flew to the east. Later in the day, I received a call from the office of the District Chief saying they had operated on him on the coast and thought he would be okay. The other soldier was alive, but still in bad shape.

Shortly after that, Sergeant Manuel came in to tell me the camp administrative officer, a civilian, had asked him to come to his office. He complained to Manuel that we were cutting Captain Minh out of the loop in dealing with the District Chief. He said *Dai Uy* Minh wanted to make sure I got that message. I let it lie. Minh, I thought, knew what was happening. The District Chief needed to take action, and he found I was more responsive to him than Minh was. If I had thought that the *Dai Uy* would cooperate fully with the District Chief, I would have talked to him. However, I thought that the only way I could build a fire under Minh was to threaten his status with the people in Saigon. I filed a special report within my chain of command criticizing Minh. I was to learn much later that it made it all the way to Saigon and created some problems for the *Dai Uy*. I thought maybe this would get him to be more aggressive and less worried about appearing inferior or subservient to the District Chief. Actually, this plan never really worked. Minh had only one objective: to protect his position and reputation to gain promotion. He never wavered in that effort. But I continued my responsiveness to the District Chief. I was simply riding the only horse that was in the race, nothing more.

Before the District Chief had recovered from his wounds, which he did after a few weeks, we learned the people of the large village where we had hauled out several truckloads of rice had simply disappeared. There were wildly ranging estimates of the numbers, the largest coming from the office of the District Chief—probably the most accurate—the smallest from the province headquarters. The range was two hundred to four hundred villagers. The chief of our Mountain Scouts reported that his men had witnessed the Viet Cong escort the entire village across the border into Cambodia. He put the number over three hundred. We obtained no other information to corroborate this, but the office of the district chief informally stated they thought our Scouts' report was likely to be correct. In my monthly report I said something like we had gone and slapped the Viet Cong in the face with the rice haul and they had come and kicked us in the ass by removing a whole village. One of the staff principals in my B Detachment headquarters said the leadership was not happy with the language in the report. That same staff officer later drafted my efficiency report for the detachment commander, my rater, when I left Vietnam. He included a comment: Captain Corns tends to be easily discouraged. I don't know, maybe they had a point with that comment. After all, the enemy coming in under your nose and removing to another country two to four hundred of the people you were supposed to protect was a matter with which I was not happy. Don't worry for me about the bad efficiency report. I eventually got over it, the lowest in my file in over thirty-five years in the Army.

It was December when I saw the District Chief again. He invited *Dai Uy* Minh and me to a dinner at a large strategic hamlet in the eastern part of the district, hosted by the Chief himself. Initially, he invited only me, but I got word to his people that it would be a personal favor to me if they also invited *Dai Uy* Minh. They did and he went. As it turned out, that was not good, but I had no way of knowing that would be the case.

As the big dinner, served outside for maybe two hundred people, wound down, a two-and one half ton truck pulled up and stopped just outside the fence that encircled the village. It was hard to ignore them as four or five soldiers pulled this big box out of the back of the truck. I thought it had to be the largest casket I had ever seen. The box disappeared as the men set it on the road. I heard what I thought were nails being pried out of wood. As soon as that sound ended, the district and village chief jointly invited me to walk out to the truck with them. Captain Minh followed. We watched as the men lifted up and out of the box—a mounted tiger! One of the men yelled something and the crowd erupted in cheers. Philippe later told me the cry was,

"A Tiger for a Tiger." He added the village chief had already told the crowd to cheer when they heard that.

The District Chief was beaming. He surprised me when, in broken English, he told me the tiger was mine—a gift. *Dai Uy* Minh stepped back. I thought he wished he had not come. At that point, I would not have gotten a good grade from the folks at the Counterinsurgency Course on working tirelessly to get cooperation from all the key people in fighting an insurgency. Any remaining chance I ever had to gain rapport with Minh went out the window that night.

A local guard trained at Duc Co had shot the tiger a few days after the VC wounded the District Chief. It had happened at this village, and they brought the guard who had shot the tiger up to meet me. I congratulated him in a voice that all could hear, and I was glad Phillipe was with me. As I guessed, he later told me he did not tell them what I said, but told them what he knew they would like to hear on such an occasion. The crowd roared at the end of his "translation." The village chief put an arm around me, a great no-no in that culture. Today, I wonder if Phillipe had encouraged the hug.

They delivered the tiger in a caravan—led by Phillipe—the next day. Phillipe made a speech after the trucks stopped inside our camp. The English version was "over the top." Its most embarrassing part was about how the Tiger, meaning me, had saved the life of the District Chief after the VC shot him, and so, the District Chief had made a present of his tiger to me. Phillipe's words, in his English version for my men and me, were not so smooth, but he did stress "his," meaning the District Chief's, tiger. What Phillipe said, in total, in Vietnamese and Jarai, I did not know, as usual. But, while I never doubted, then or now, his interpretation of the intent of what I said, I am now left to wonder how often he added to his larger than life role with the men assembled around him. After all, he did feature himself a Cowboy, and his hero was John Wayne—an actor.

I told them to put the tiger in the team house, next to the bar in the shared portion of the building that otherwise provided individual rooms with rough wood flooring, thatch sides, and a tin roof. A few days later, one of the sergeants asked me if it would be all right to put a towel over the tiger's head each evening.

"It's hell to come back in here at 0300 in the morning and shine your light so it catches those eyes but not the full body of the tiger. Spooky," the man said. I said that was fine if the tiger scared him that badly. For the remaining weeks of our tour, the sergeant never lived that down, although I would guess his claim was correct—that there were other men who also liked having those eyes covered, which I agreed to do. That evening was when one of the men asked what I was going to name the tiger. I didn't hesitate. "Phillipe," I said. There were nods of approval all around. Phillipe, I was sure, had suggested the name, tiger, for me. Now I would have something to remember him by, if, the Army would let me keep the tiger, and if, they would let me get it on an airplane to the states. I decided then that I would try.

Had I known of the bureaucratic red tape I would have to work through, I would no doubt have hesitated, but I am glad I did not. I found I had to file many papers to gain approval to clear the crate containing Phillipe the Tiger on an aircraft. First to Nha Trang; then to Saigon, and then to Fort Bragg. There, I turned in yet another paper, a Disposition Form, DF, to gain approval of the curator of the Smoke Bomb Hill museum to keep him. It took little time. The curator looked at Phillipe the Tiger and with a superior air remarked the animal was "stuffed," not "mounted." My children and grandchildren have never criticized Phillipe's good looks (That's the Tiger—not the man, the Cowboy they never saw.)

After the arrival of the tiger at Duc Co, I heard the name, tiger, called out even more often as I moved around the camp. Those were the Montagnards, and although I came, with Phillipe's help, to recognize the name, I can't recall it now and would not likely know how to spell it if I did. I regret that.

One of the people on whom my genuine pleasure with the tiger was not lost was Vo Khuong, our cook. He was a good cook, even though my men had all kinds of insulting names for him, all suggesting bad food. He outdid himself at Thanksgiving time, '63. He joined our team and most of the camp near the road two days before Thanksgiving. Nha Trang had given us a schedule for the re-supply drops to each of the A Detachment camps in the area, Plei Me, and Plei Djereng, being the closest to us. We had a good airstrip for the aircraft to land, but, in the best of Green Beret traditions, they parachuted our Thanksgiving Meal to us from a Caribou fixed wing aircraft. Of course, we still had to cook the food, but the air-dropped bags had the makings for all the traditional items: turkey, dressing, cranberry sauce, mashed potatoes, gravy, green beans, and pumpkin pie.

Vo Khuong built two large ovens for this Thanksgiving meal. He dug out, with some help from civilian laborers provided by Captain Minh, a hole for each of two fifty-five gallon drums. In the hole, at the bottom with a separate access, was space for a wood fire. The drum had a metal grate set several inches above the bottom and one side, where the heat of the fire was greatest. There was a lid for each drum, and into each, Vo Khuong placed one of the two turkeys. The only time I met his wife was that day, Thanksgiving. We managed to get her to take a Thanksgiving meal home. She did most of the other cooking as Vo Khuong checked the turkeys like a hawk.

I decided to contribute to the meal. Included in the food dropped for the meal was a large container of powdered cocoa. I determined we had all the makings for a chocolate meringue pie, to include vanilla extract, not from the parachuted bundle of food, but from Vo Khuong's cupboard. I was confident and did a great job, although the jokes about my effort at cooking had gotten as foul in the team as those about Vo Khuong's offerings. When I sat the two pies on the counter about two hours before we were to eat, my southern guys, which was almost everybody, "oohed and aahed," and they were being only partly funny. The meringue had browned below my burning torch of paper much more nicely than I guessed it would, and I had been happy enough when I found the meringue was setting up well. We had little ice, but just enough, I hoped, to have the egg whites just at the right temperature when I beat them. I realized I was putting myself at great risk, displaying an effort at cooking anything beyond boiling water.

We invited *Dai Uy* Minh, his administrative officer, and all the members of the Vietnamese Special Forces team, headed by a lieutenant. To my surprise, both the *Dai Uy* and the admin officer came and enjoyed the food and the refreshments. It was the most relaxed time I spent with Minh. One of my men suggested it was the wine he had drunk before he got there. Whatever, I had not expected to share such a relaxed time with him, and never did again.   Fortunately for me, southerners though most of my men were, the preference of all at the meal was for the pumpkin pie, and I, being a good sport, ate that pie as well. I wasn't in the team room later that evening when one of the younger men in the team, and I don't recall which one it was, cut the chocolate pie. I heard the exclamation, but was not sure what it was about—then laughter. I went in. They were all standing around the pies. "Sir, you take a bite." I think it was Sergeant Crook, but I'm not sure. I smelled it before I tasted it, and it smelled bad.

We decided it was bad cocoa, molded was our best bet, but that was after my men offered these tasteless suggestions of all the things I might have mistakenly put in the pie. It ended my days of cooking. I decided I should have stayed with pan-frying caught catfish and boiling captured rattlesnakes in cooking oil in a can. My pie-making failure enhanced my status with my men, but they likely never forgave me for the beautiful meringue.

Another good effect of my flop as a cook was all the praise my men handed out to Vo Khuong and his wife, which they deserved. Fewer than two months later, as we were about to leave Duc Co and Vietnam, Vo Khuong gave me an oil painting of a tiger in a jungle setting. The work impressed me, and then I learned he had painted it himself and in his youth had studied with a French artist in Da Nang. Just a few years ago, my son, Mike, selected the painting from some modest artwork Carol and I had collected. It now hangs in his home, as it did in our home from the time he was five years old until he was over forty. On the painting, our cook wrote, "I offr this to Captain Corns." The missing "e" from offer is his, but he was a cook, not a linguist, and, I appreciatively say again today, after forty-five years, "Vo Khuong, I accept."

Chapter Four
Assassinations and Ia Drang

Late in my Army career, Carol and I were visiting my family in West Virginia, and I commented on the coincidence of my being in countries when their leaders were assassinated or otherwise removed from office. My brother, Gary, impishly remarked, "Yeah' I've told everybody about that and said that I thought you had never left the Special Forces." Everybody laughed. What they did not know was, although any implied role by me in any of that was absurd, being in those countries at those times was very uncomfortable.

In my first assignment with troops in South Korea in '59-60, I spent the last several weeks assigned as an operations officer in a battle group headquarters. We were constantly on high alert as President Syngman Rhee turned the Korean constitution and court system upside down to gain reelection. He tried to hold on to his dictatorial powers, which included winning elections as opponents lost their lives, conveniently for him. Shortly after I left South Korea, an aircraft reportedly belonging to the U. S. Central Intelligence Agency whisked him out of the country and into exile, just steps ahead of angry mobs bent on assassination.

During my tour in Vietnam with my A detachment, I received a radio message in early November of '63 that President Nho Dinh Diem of the Republic of Vietnam had been deposed and then murdered. Vietnam now had a new leader, installed by the Vietnamese Army. Only later did I hear the claim our CIA had prompted it. At first, the members of my team and I went from talking of VC to North Vietnamese assassins, looking for someone other than the Vietnamese Army Generals as the real culprits. I don't think one of us then guessed our own government had encouraged it. Sometimes now, I think of that incident as typical of what went on in Vietnam as opposed to what our government leaders told soldiers in combat and the American people was happening.

The shock of that assassination did not last long, because just before Thanksgiving, the news of the death of President Kennedy devastated all Americans. "The Cubans!" One of my men said immediately, and we agreed. It did not occur to us that some politically unbalanced American citizen might have been the assassin. One of my sergeants called out, "What the hell are we doing here while some 'sunovabitch' kills our President in an open street in daylight back home?" There was little disagreement among us: the Cubans were behind the murder, aided and prompted by the Russians. I could have cut the anger and passion in our team house with a bayonet.

It was a difficult time. On balance, on that day, my team would have agreed to pull out of Vietnam by a unanimous vote. As for Diem's assassination, I did not bother my men with the fact that the last time I had been serving in a foreign country, forces there had deposed their president as well. I was two for two. My words to Carol in a letter a day later barely suggested the level of frustration that my men and I felt. I wrote, "We got the news release on the President yesterday. We know nothing really about it. It is quite a shock and loss. Makes us wonder why the hell we're over here with lunatics or fanatics or whatever it was running around in our country."

In 1978, I returned to the Republic of South Korea, now headed by President Park. When I arrived in November of that year, I marveled at the modern changes in the country since I had served there twenty years earlier. Much of the credit for those changes, rightly or wrongly, went to President Park Chung Hee according to what I had read. On October 26, 1979, less than a month before I was to hand over command of my brigade to my good friend, Colonel Dick Sharp, Park was assassinated. There followed reports of a long list of abuses of power that had led to his ouster as President.

My brother was off the mark on why I was in those countries when the heads of state departed their positions of power. However, if I had been working for a private company, I would have protested the consistency with which they posted me into situations where our business success rested on a man who was either no damn good or powerfully unlucky.

In Vietnam, that November of 1963, we had little time to try to find some normalcy: first Diem's assassination; then Kennedy's, and then Thanksgiving. Even today, I marvel that no member of my team spoke cynically of the near confluence of those two deaths and that day of thanks. Maybe that was because we busied ourselves with other actions the days between those events. Sometimes I think Captain Minh's presence and pleasant manner at our Thanksgiving meal was linked to lamenting the loss of presidents—his and ours.

After Diem's assassination, but before the death of President Kennedy, our "case officer," flew in, as he did each month, with a bag of money. He asked me if we had heard of any significant movement of supply convoys in the Ia Drang, or Drang River, Valley, some fifteen kilometers south of Duc Co. I told him we had not; at least no more than the reports the Viet Cong moved supplies routinely south along the international border. Those reports, however, told of movement inside Cambodia west of my camp and in Laos, just north near our Green Beret camp at Dak To.

He asked if we would put some reconnaissance effort into the area. He asked if we had a good camera. We had one that was standard issue to a detachment, but on two occasions the film we had taken produced only a series of black blocks where we expected pictures. He then gave me a camera and several rolls of film. There were instructions in the leather carrying case. The camera was a Leica, and I knew I was holding a few hundred dollars worth of equipment. He then asked to walk out to our operations bunker so he could show me something on a map. When we entered the bunker, one of my men and four of the Vietnamese Special Forces troopers were on shift, monitoring the radios. He guided me to the map on the wall, leaned over, and placed his index finger on a spot on the north bank of the Ia Drang River and right on the border.

"Remember this spot," he said, and then waved a hand toward the steps up out of the bunker. I led and he followed. When we were back in the privacy of the team room, he bent closely and told me there was a report of an airfield under construction near the point where he had placed his finger on the map.

"On the banks of the Ia Drang—right on the border?" I asked. He did not reply and asked if I had any bourbon. I didn't, but there was a team bottle, meaning a bottle bought by one of my men and kept under the bar, nearby. I went over and got the bottle and a glass and returned to the table and set both before him. "You not drinking?" He asked. I told him no and then he said, "Oh yeah, I remember." I knew he was referring to my second night in camp when the departing commander, he, and I had sat in the corner of this same room. Both had encouraged me to drink heartily, but I nursed one drink, without ice, through our conversation. I think he had intended that night to be a long one. It wasn't. After they had downed a couple of drinks, I heard for the first time criticisms of the Vietnamese District Chief. Taken together, they amounted to suggesting the District Chief was Viet Cong. When I asked where the "case officer," was going with his litany of things that had gone wrong, he said we would be better off without the District Chief. I changed the subject to the schedule of briefings for the next day. The "case officer" showed no interest in my new subject, and I excused myself, leaving my glass of bourbon nearly untouched.

This was what my visitor was now recalling. I explained that I didn't drink that much, and when I did, it was usually scotch, but there had not yet been any scotch brought into the team house. I made a note to mark down on the pad under the bar how many "shot" equivalents my visitor wound up drinking. It was George Manuel's bottle. I would pay him. George also drank little hard liquor, but usually had a beer with his dinner.

The "case officer" told me that he needed pictures of the construction site, to which I replied, "Why don't you just fly over on your way out of here and take the pictures yourself?" He explained in a whisper the reported site was not where he had pointed, but five or six kilometers west of that. I pointed out that was five or six kilometers inside Cambodia, where guidelines directed us not to go. He said that was true, and if any of my people should go in there and get caught, he would have to say that this conversation never took place. It was as if we were in a Class B, Hollywood espionage film. I told him I didn't know that we should undertake an illegal mission like that. He then said I should still keep the camera, and we left the subject. I was aware that my response would not have gone down well with most Special Forces field commanders, but I wanted to weigh the idea. I had limited exposure to CIA case officers in the field, but those I worked with had not impressed me, often causing me to wonder whether anybody above them in their organization even knew the things they talked and suggested. I was also aware there was a necessary procedure before Army soldiers were committed to certain "unusual" missions. I saw no evidence of that here.

I gave the Leica to Sergeant Roberts and told him it was a replacement for our faulty camera. He was glad to get it. I mentioned nothing else about its use. Over the next few days, I thought about the reported supply movements around Chu Pong Mountain and the possible new airstrip to the northwest. Chu Pong was mostly inside Vietnam, but its western quarter crossed the international border, sloping into Cambodia. It rose south of the slow-flowing Ia Drang, which bent a little to the northwest and west as it passed north of the large massif, called Chu Pong, with three or four prominent hills within its terrain.

I picked a small team to lead in the search of Chu Pong. I estimated it would take ten to fourteen days to do a decent search of such a large area. I weighed taking a larger force. We could search the area much more quickly, with a full company of CIDG soldiers, but I had another possible task in mind, and it would call for a small team. I decided to take no CIDG soldiers, but one of the Mountain Scout sections of thirteen men. And I would include the leader of the program, the man who had brought us the report on the probable fortune of the village population forty kilometers north of where we would be going. Phillipe had confidence in the head Mountain Scout, who picked each of the scouts. Aided by a small team of mountain ponies, a mountain scout team routinely stayed in the jungle stretches along the border for as many as forty days. They wore no prescribed uniform, and other than an interest in their health, we left their hygiene up to the scout team leader and the individual. They were the closest to what the SAS folks had told me was the best way to defeat insurgents. Get into their backyard and stay there, avoiding contact until you have learned most of their secrets. Of course, I did not regard our Mountain Scouts as in the league with the SAS, but it was a much more professional group than our CIDG.

I added Phillipe, of course. By this time, it was clear that both Phillipe and George Manuel considered Phillipe my bodyguard, not just an interpreter, and there was no one else I would prefer to have at my back and at my side. But I had to accept the same risks as each of my men, so I emphasized that I kept him at my side as an interpreter—which he was, and because he was a fighter—which we, by now, knew. I guessed he was the bravest among us, with Sasser as a close second, maybe Manuel, but I had not yet seen Sasser at his best. I wanted to take Sasser out again on this patrol, but he was going out on nearly every patrol or raid, and I did not want to overexpose him to danger, although I knew he would want to go if he knew what we were about to do. But nobody other than I knew that. I picked Sergeant Wallace, the junior commo man. His boss, Sergeant Crook was just back from a patrol where he was the lead adviser, and they had made good contact with the enemy. I would let him rest, for now. Wallace was excellent on the radios, and I needed to make sure we had sound commo on this operation. I would have liked to take Manuel, but he was the actual leader of the team in my absence, and I needed him here at the camp. I picked Roberts again. This mission was about intelligence and he had seen combat in Korea. Also, I had found him cool after the VC ambushed his column southeast of our camp. That was the team: the scout team with the overall leader of the program, Phillipe, and myself and two more Americans.

I briefed the four key people in the patrol, leaving the briefing of the scouts to their leader, but I asked Phillipe to be present at that briefing of the scouts to make sure they understood my key points. I covered only our reconnaissance mission on Chu Pong and what we were looking for in the way of supply routes, and more importantly, cache sites of supplies. If something happened to me, the other part of the patrol that I had in mind would not take place. I surprised Roberts when I asked him to carry the camera. I knew he would be carrying a load of equipment and rations, since we'd be out for thirteen days, but I was not yet ready to explain the purpose of the camera, even to him.

The Ia Drang, or Drang River, flows from the northeast to the southwest into Cambodia, turning slightly northwest and west, its course influenced in that manner as it passes north of Chu Pong Mountain. We took a half day to walk to the north bank of the river, stopping briefly near the Old French Fort, reportedly encircled with anti-personnel mines some dozen years old. The Vietnamese had abandoned the fort after the war with France. It was much closer to the border than even the hamlet of Thanh Duc, just two kilometers west of Duc Co. Thanh Duc was manned by a militia platoon under a lieutenant who reported to the District Chief. The French Fort would be a good location for the District Chief to strengthen the security of his region. It would make a statement to the VC, since it was nearer the border and closer to the Ia Drang. I made a mental note of it.

The terrain immediately south of the river was flat for a good distance before it began to rise on the lower slopes of Chu Pong. Our search plan was based on a map inspection and the aid of a few, poor quality aerial photos the "case officer" had given me. The absence of any indication on the photos of work on an airstrip was explained by the case officer: the photos had pre-dated the earliest reports of the airfield construction. We would inspect the likely routes out of Cambodia running along the border; then look for west to east paths south of the river. Finally, I wanted to look for poorly disguised disturbance of earth or foliage that might remain from the digging of cache holes or possibly tunnels.

We were looking for footprints of men, wheel marks of bicycles or carts, hoof marks of pack ponies or burros, and the padded, probably wrapped, hoof marks of elephants, the hardest of the tracks for the enemy to disguise.

We spent four days flirting with the Cambodian border as we moved south. I told my men that, since it was impossible to know exactly where the international boundary was, we would not worry about that too much. It was likely that anyone we ran into would be VC, I told them.

"Or NVA," Roberts said, meaning the army of North Vietnam. I had thought of that, even as our "case officer" talked to me, but I knew he would not discuss that possibility. Everyone knew the party line out of Washington and Saigon: They won't come in. I had first heard that back in the Counterinsurgency Course. It reminded me of MacArthur's confident, and incorrect, reassurances to President Truman back in the days of the Korean War—and MacArthur had apparently believed what he said about the Chinese not entering the war. I wondered if people in Saigon and Washington truly believed that the NVA would not come south, or whether it was part of that attitude that dominated in the Pentagon and the top ranks of the United States Army. Be positive—always be positive, and never criticize the war effort, for that is to criticize and undermine the troops. For a commander on the battlefield, that was wise advice. But many men of America's Army and Marine Corps died in the aftermath of the Chinese invasion of South Korea.

I was sure many would have liked to hear someone back in Washington speak up and question the patriotic, arrogant, and flat wrong pronouncement by General MacArthur.

Now, it was wise for the small, seventeen-man patrol, maybe three steps inside Cambodia, to think that if we found the enemy, it wouldn't make much difference if they were VC or NVA. Sergeant Crook's last patrol had come back with sketches they had made of soldiers who wore distinct insignia, different from any we had seen in our studies of the Viet Cong. We had still heard nothing from our "case officer" or from our B Detachment about Sergeant Crook's report and sketches of the distinct belt buckles. Both Crook and Roberts offered the guess the men were Chinese. They were larger men than the typical Vietnamese male, and they seemed to have a more self-assuming manner than the more recognizable Viet Cong officers Crook identified among them. That operation, completed three weeks earlier, had also dealt with the troubling border with Cambodia.

Our intelligence, from the District Chief, had reported a frequently used crossing point on the border in northwest Le Thanh District. Crook was my senior man on the patrol that went into the area with a reconnaissance mission. After they detected what appeared to be a temporary base of an estimated Viet Cong company, Crook set up multiple observation posts, and in late afternoon, my men were surprised the VC posted no security on the Vietnam side of the river as upwards of twenty men at a time, most naked, washed and played in the river. That was when they noticed the two larger men who limited their bathing to removing their tunics only and washing off their upper bodies with a cloth. By nightfall, Crook had fashioned a plan, and he broke radio silence to call in to get approval. His plan was to take the camp under mortar and machinegun fire the next morning, and then withdraw back to the Le Thanh District town. Neither of us mentioned the border. I approved the plan.

We had little to show for that action. There, of course, had been no effort to determine the damages to the Viet Cong, and we had not, and were not to receive any reply from higher level intelligence to our report. I later, months after our tour was completed, concluded that the force engaged was most likely a unit of the North Vietnamese Army, or NVA. As for the men with the distinct insignia, it is hard to say. Possibly Chinese, possibly NVA officers, of larger build than the average. This was not the only example of intelligence reports my team filed to which we never received any response, such as a shared report that reinforced the validity of our information. It was a one-way street. We were about to experience the same thing with the report we would send forward on this patrol I was leading into the Ia Drang.

That was troubling to me two years later when Captain Tony Nadal, as part of Lieutenant Colonel Hal Moore's big battle with the NVA in this same area, would find bunkers and tunnels that suggested an enemy presence of many, many months. At the time that Moore's battalion went into the Chu Pong Mountain area, there were multiple intelligence reports of significant use of the area by the Viet Cong. Unfortunately, our contribution to the information of that nature, based on my current patrol in late '63, was to prove limited.

We had found in our north to south search along the border, two places that held more promise than any other, areas of hard ground swept clean by the wind or, possibly, swept by man. We had not found any obvious signs, but I decided to stay with our search plan and turn back north, paralleling our route south but about a kilometer to the east. The terrain would be a little more difficult, but I hoped we could accomplish this route in three days. But, if we didn't find some evidence of west to east supply tracks or trails, I was not confident we would find much at the base or on the mountain at points to the east.

After two days, we found tracks of elephants. There was no pattern of a west to east movement, and little north to south. The tracks meandered, but Roberts, Phillipe, and I agreed, that could be an effective way to cover or confuse a trail. What little evidence we found suggested the animals might have come from the west. We were not discouraged—not yet.

On our northern route this time, having found no signs otherwise, I decided to go all the way to the river. There, we found a few tracks of elephants, but none of men or bike tires. The elephants' feet had not been wrapped or padded. We followed a few elephant tracks about six kilometers to the east, north of Chu Pong, but no more than three elephants had moved along the path. Phillipe's only comment about the tracks was, "Not VC."

We headed back west. Eight days and no sure sign of VC or NVA activity. I then decided to skip a part of the search plan and go well south into two low, cove-like valleys, shaped by three fingers of small ridgelines coming off one of the few tall hills on Chu Pong. Our thought had been the VC might favor a flat approach to a tunnel to move and store large loads, or even to run carts right into a tunnel. While we were searching the small valleys, Phillipe took two men to look on the higher ground for air holes for a tunnel. We spent two more days at this effort, with no success.

I then told the leaders on the patrol that we were going to go a little deeper into Cambodia and a bit farther north. I showed them on the map how I proposed to move, never more than three kilometers west of where we believed the boundary to be. Roberts looked at me with surprise, and I would guess a little resentment that I had not seen fit to tell him earlier of the report I had gotten from our visitor and of my intent to look for the airstrip. Phillipe showed something in his expression that I had not before observed. I couldn't read it. I was not sure. Possibly he did not think it was a good idea. Possibly he was sure, I thought at the time, that such an airfield did not exist. But by the time I finished my short explanation, they all appeared ready to go. Possibly, I thought, I was thinking too much, and neither Roberts nor Phillipe had any problem, or, if they did, maybe I surprised them by my decision to cross the boundary.

Our movement was quite slow, guiding on the pace of the mountain scout leader who had started three two-man teams out, to the front, right front and left front. Also, he had one team in the rear, watching our trail. We had nearly as many men providing the security as the number they were securing. On the other hand, it was a movement formation the scout team would have used, even if they had been on the move alone. Our only signaling or communication plan was, if a team of two spotted the enemy, one would continue watching and the other would come back to their leader. There was one other signal, firing weapons, meaning the number of enemy or their position kept our men from coming back. Soon, the vegetation became thicker, and the scout leader pulled in all but the lead and trailing teams.

Phillipe, Roberts, and I checked the map. I focused on the "X" I had drawn that morning. It marked the general location, I explained, where we might pick up the sounds or sight of construction work on a runway. We had moved about a half hour when Phillipe hurried ahead and talked with the head scout. The scout looked our way and then made a sound, which I later learned from Phillipe, was the call of a local bird. After maybe five seconds, he repeated it, at which point Phillipe walked back toward me, his hand up, palm toward me, the signal to stop. He explained that this was as far as we should go, which surprised me until he said, "Let me have camera. I will take two men I walk with now and go and find the airfield and take pictures and come back. Wait here. I will be two hours, most. If I not, you go on back cross border."

This was a different Phillipe. He was showing little deference to anybody, including me. He had spoken up like this was his patrol, like he had some experience in leading men; not being an interpreter. With what I thought, and intended, was equal command and finality, I said, "I can't do that Phillipe. We took this risk together, except that I didn't tell any of you. If only one goes with the two scouts, it has to be me."

He smiled. The Cowboy was back.

"*Dai Uy*," he said. It was a term he seldom used in addressing me, but he did so now with respect and sincerity. Sincerity absent when men spoke of *Dai Uy* Minh. "You are our adviser, our Tiger," he said and smiled again, "but too much risk for you here. Let me be soldier. Let me find if your man with money bag is true."

"I agree, sir," Roberts said, "but I want to go with Phillipe. I know how to use the camera. It's almost exactly like ours, just a newer model."

"No," Phillipe said. "We move too fast for you." Phillipe looked at Roberts' large body, similar to Sergeant Manuel's, but a bit softer.

"Okay," I said. "Phillipe goes with two scouts. We remain here. You need more weapons?"

"No, and I trade carbine for that camera. I need this," he said, referring to the .45 caliber pistol holstered on his hip. "Scouts have AK-47." He smiled again, highlighting the mountain scouts' preference for a VC weapon over any American weapon we could offer. We had two new, experimental Armalite, AR 15's, but we were not sure how good they were going to be. One of my men dropped one from the back of a jeep and the trailing jeep ran over it, smashing the stock like the plastic Mattel toy Sasser joked it to be. Sasser preferred the BAR. I missed him at times like this.

We waited after Phillipe and the two scouts disappeared into the foliage. The head scout pulled some of his men in a bit to set up a tighter security, but with men still out for early warning.

Phillipe and the two scouts were back so soon that I suspected something had gone wrong. Phillipe walked directly to me and said. "It's there, and we got it." He handed the camera to Roberts and took his carbine. I nodded.

"We need to get back across the border," I said, and asked Phillipe to tell the head scout to take the most direct route east that he felt best.

"I tell him how to go," Phillipe said and turned and walked to the head scout. We moved at a little faster pace than I preferred, and I signaled the scout to slow the pace, which he did. Phillipe looked at me as if he was going to say something, but he didn't. Once we were, in my judgment, at least a kilometer beyond the border, into Vietnam, I signaled for an even slower pace and there was another bird signal from our head Mountain Scout. About half an hour later, I called a halt and we took a break. Roberts and Wallace pulled close as Phillipe gave me a quick rundown, with all the politeness and sirs typical of a Cowboy performance. A smile every other sentence. All had gone well. There were three bulldozers and two or three hundred men working with mattocks, shovels and hand pulled carts. There were also buffalos pulling large timbers out of the cleared area. Phillipe could only say, "longer than Duc Co," referring to our airstrip, in response to Roberts' question of how long the strip would likely be.

As we started out again on a trail I directed, different from the one we had come down almost two weeks earlier, Phillipe drew closer and walked at my side. "We get pictures quick. We surprise guard. He led us to air strip."

"Where is he now?" I asked.

"He dead," Phillipe said in a low tone. He looked down at the big K-Bar knife he always wore on patrols. The Cowboy look was gone again. If I had to describe the look now, the same that puzzled me earlier, it was a look of command, of authority. I had for some time felt that Phillipe often knew more about some things than he shared with me or even with Sergeant Manuel. I shook off the thought. I was as confident of Phillipe's commitment against the Viet Cong as any of my Americans. But there was something about him. Maybe it was simply he showed that he had more experience fighting the Viet Cong than I had, as team leader. Maybe that was it. But I didn't doubt his loyalty, to our effort, or to me personally.

◆   ◆   ◆

Two weeks later, we were back near the border and nearer the Drang River. Sasser, Combs, Conklin, Crook, and Phillipe were with me.

We were at the Old French Fort, with the District Chief's Lieutenant Huan and a half company of men for security and hard work. I had spoken to the District Chief and suggested they reopen the old fort. He would not say that he would, and I was about to raise it again with him when he sent the lieutenant to see me with the message the District Chief had decided to reopen the fort. He had left it to the lieutenant to ask for my help, and that was okay with me. We had spent the time from our arrival at midmorning until mid afternoon probing the fields all around the fort, and up to the walls for mines. The reports of many mines had been exaggerated, but we had found seven, and Combs had blown them in place. Now, the soldiers were inside the fort and atop the walls carrying out debris and putting it in a big pile in front of the gate for later burning. They had started to remove the broken glass on top of the walls when the lieutenant told them to stop, saying the glass was part of the defense provided by the walls. He had gotten the approval of the District Chief to man the fort all right, but only during the daylight hours. I found that irritating, but it was a start.

Thirty to forty locals, mostly women and children, were watching our work, mostly enjoying the explosions when we blew a mine. They had come down from Thanh Duc hamlet where the lieutenant manned the westernmost security post in the district. We had held up blowing a mine twice while the lieutenant pushed the civilians back farther away from the explosion area. Finally, we had relaxed once we had cleared all the marked-off areas.

The explosion occurred behind me, and when I turned, I saw Sergeant Sasser rushing toward the wall of the fort. Some women shrieked, and children began crying. A mine, I thought. We missed a mine. Sasser. Be careful I thought. I stepped in his direction. He was lifting her off the ground. He looked at me and shook his head. Was she dead?

I stopped and turned to see Sergeant Combs moving toward me.

"Everybody stay back," I said, looking first at Combs and then the Vietnamese Lieutenant. There might be more mines. Sasser was slowly carrying the girl away from the fort wall. I guessed he was trying to recall where he had stepped, or maybe he could see where he had stepped. But, I knew he couldn't. The damp grass was rumpled by the prints of feet and knees where men had used bayonets to probe, looking for mines. At least one mine had eluded us. The grass was pressed down, the imprint of knees and feet like a carpet design. Sasser could not possibly make out his own tracks walking in to get to the girl. I moved to my left, as did Sergeant Combs, to intercept Sasser. I was not sure how far from the fort wall our probing might have missed a mine, but Combs and I had stepped toward the wall, and we needed to get to Sasser and the girl as soon as we could. When we met Sasser, the girl's foot was dangling by some skin and tissue. She was bleeding badly. His look told me he did not want to stop here. He walked on, farther from the fort, and then he bent low and placed her on the ground. I took her ankle with one hand and held the foot up against the ankle with the other. I nodded at Combs, who unfastened his first aid pouch and unwrapped it and encircled her ankle with it. As he tied a knot in the bandage, I knew this was not nearly the aid the girl needed. In the short distance of Sasser's carry, she had stopped crying and had passed out. Someone brought a poncho blanket; and before I could ask, three more personal first aid pouches were at my side. With one, Combs wrapped another compress around the ankle. With another compress and a stick, he applied a tourniquet just below her knee, and the bleeding slowed.

Command responsibility, or assumed responsibility, is a funny thing. Even as Combs worked the tourniquet, I faulted myself for having brought neither of my medical specialists on this mission. There was only one course of action. Since there would be too much red tape and delay trying to get a helicopter in from Pleiku, we would put her in the truck and take her back to Duc Co. Sergeant Miller, an experienced field paramedic, could care for her there. One of the lieutenant's soldiers took over the tourniquet and another cradled her ankle and foot. I was not sure the compress would do any good, except that it might keep the tissues free of dirt or bacteria. We would need to adjust the tourniquet. I decided to go back with the truck, leaving Sasser in charge with the jeep, which had a mounted radio. Combs clearly wanted to accompany the girl, but I told him to stay to help Sasser, and he nodded. The lieutenant appeared relieved that I was not taking all my team members back with me. He would stay and finish the work, he said. Combs looked at me. This meant more probing for mines. I told Combs to oversee the recheck and not worry about stepping on the Lieutenant's toes. He clearly welcomed the directions. I told Lieutenant Huan that he must rely on Combs' expertise. Huan looked relieved, which was not my intent, but is often the result when you have to take charge as an advisor. How much of the area would have to be rechecked would be Combs' call. Probably most of the area around the fort.

I rode in the front seat of the truck, looking back out the rear window where the two soldiers and a security team sat with the girl. Phillipe was sitting high on the back of the seat of the lieutenant's jeep ahead of us. He had again borrowed Sasser's BAR.

When we got to Duc Co, Miller, alerted by radio, was ready, a sparse, inadequate operating room set up in his small building for sick calls and immunizations. Still, I felt better once we were there and I could turn the task over to Miller and his assistant. But as I started to leave, he asked, "Sir, could you stay and help me?" I remembered: our junior medic, Collier, and my exec, Lieutenant Conrad, were both on a sick call at the Le Thanh District offices. Obviously, they were not yet back.

"Yes," I said.

Twice I looked away from the nearly severed ankle in my thinly gloved hands. I held the foot against the ankle as Miller sweated with the difficulty of finding and clamping the ends of all the human sinews and vessels he needed to sew back together. It was a long time, past dark, when Collier arrived and took over my chore. I walked outside. Even in the limited light Manuel said, "You all right sir?" I was glad to give way to Collier. I was sure the sewn-on foot wouldn't work, even if redone soon by a doctor. A cripple, I thought. A pretty little girl, a cripple. Not the right word, I thought, but the image in my mind did not change, regardless of the words. Manuel rushed back up. I had not noticed his departure.

"Here, sir," he said. It was a glass with a couple fingers of his bourbon, all the way from the team house. I didn't like the thought that the experience with the girl had shaken me that much. I drank it, and it burned going down and bounced on my stomach and I thought it was coming back up, but it didn't. Manuel nudged me toward the team house, but I turned and went back into the improvised operating room.

"How is she?" I asked.

"Pain killer is working. Breathing and pulse are good," Collier said.

"We won't know on the foot for a long time, but she has to have the right surgery—and soon," Miller said. Behind me, Manuel said that Conrad was on the radio arranging for a helicopter to pick her up tomorrow morning and fly her to a hospital. Then he added that Sasser had called in. They had rechecked for mines and found none. They were all set for the night, security out, and the lieutenant had taken the girl's family and others home in another truck. Sasser was where I needed him.

I went to the team house, sat, and Sergeant Manuel said something like he hoped the girl would be okay.

I leaned back, closed my eyes. No wonder advisory teams tended to take command of the units they were supposed to advise. So many bad things can be avoided when experienced soldiers are allowed to use their judgment.

I had damned good men.

Late the next afternoon, Sergeant Combs came to see me. He was dejected about the severe injury to the girl. By then I was rested, unlike him, as he had spent the night at the fort and, I could look at him and tell, he had not had much sleep. I pointed out that the girl was now with competent medical personnel in Pleiku, or possibly on the coast. I recalled what had taken place in our procedure of mine clearing, and remembered aloud to Combs how he had asked if one area had been completely probed, and our district lieutenant friend, Lieutenant Huan, said that it had. The lieutenant had given his firm, yes, when Combs asked him again, and the lieutenant was a man we had found reliable. I reminded Sergeant Combs of that process and sequence, but it did not seem to help much.

"That is the frustrating nature of being an adviser at times, Sergeant Combs. You were not in authority, you could not have had total responsibility. If so, that would have been mine. We trusted his judgment." I did not think that comforted him, or me either. I went on. "Sometimes, as an adviser, you can only give your best judgment and instruction, then you have to trust those you are advising to function. Sometimes they respond well; sometimes they don't. When they don't, sometimes we have to step in and do it ourselves, and sometimes all we can do is get some rest and try to do more the next time. Get some sleep."

He turned and walked out. He was a fairly tall and slender man, a little stooped of posture, but on this afternoon, his slouch was more pronounced. Only time would straighten him again. He thought he could have checked all the probing and clearing himself, and at such times most of us tend to fault our judgment—especially when the casualty is a pretty girl, about the age of Combs' children.

Chapter Five

Nightingales in White

Shortly after Sergeant Sasser bravely carried the Vietnamese girl from the minefield, an act for which the Army later awarded him The Soldier's Medal, *Dai Uy* Minh announced there was to be a new medical dispensary in Camp Duc Co. He should have discussed that with me first and gotten my agreement. Sergeant Miller, who was the first man in my team to learn of the *Dai Uy's* decision, came to me and told me about it with enthusiasm. He clearly had not recognized that Minh had done this unilaterally, and I decided it was not a matter to quarrel with Minh about. We needed a dispensary nearer the main gate to treat local Montagnards, including family members of our soldiers. I sent Miller to talk to the administrative officer and propose a planning meeting between Minh and me and whatever staff we needed. I suggested it be in the new team house that had just been completed. Still the same type construction materials as the old one, it was much nearer our operations center bunker, and included sandbagged walls up to four feet in the sleeping rooms. It was also air-conditioned. Someone had sprayed the roof, from inside, with a .45 caliber automatic weapon. One of my team suggested that maybe it was a "yard" as some called the Montagnard soldiers. I did not care for the term, and never used it, but members of our B Detachment headquarters often used the word. I asked Manuel what had happened, and he asked if I really had to know, and I asked if one of our men had done it. He said no, but one of our team was conducting the training when it happened. I said I needed no more information, but I told him to take action to make sure it didn't happen again. I guessed it was a Montagnard who had pulled the trigger of a grease gun. There were eight holes that we didn't need in that roof.

So we had our meeting in the new team house. Minh looked up and laughed at the holes when he came in. He probably knew who had fired the weapon, and his laughter further indicated it was a Montagnard. It was a good meeting. My two medics and the medic of the Vietnamese Special Forces team had drawn up the plans for the building. Miller had told me before the meeting, that it was a good design and would not be expensive. After the briefing, Minh asked that we add a small annex, a two-bunk sleeping space for the medical personnel, "just for private place" was Phillipe's translation of Minh's added suggestion. I agreed. It had been a good lunch and, somewhere, someone had found some ice and the *Ba Moi Ba* beer was cold. My men did not like the taste of this "Thirty-three" beer, nor did I, but it was what we had. As I left the meeting, I thought, too bad I hadn't shaped such good cooperation from Minh on our raids to kill VC.

Within days after we completed the dispensary, the *Dai Uy* invited me to the opening ceremony. What next, I thought.

We assembled for the ceremony two days later and waited. Then two Vietnamese women in flowing white *ao dai* costume exited an automobile, which two Duc Co jeeps escorted through the gate. The automobile looked like one I had seen that served as a taxi in Pleiku City. The common *ao dai*, pronounced "*ao zai*," were of various colors, mostly colorful pastels. But these two were white, both the high necked tunic that was calf length and split on each side up to the waist and the white pants that touched the ground and hid their feet as they walked. The material was silk. There was a murmur among the Vietnamese troops who had assembled at the order of *Dai Uy* Minh to great these women. The women, I learned, were our new medical personnel—nurses. The joke among my team members for days was who Sergeant Manuel would let go on sick call today.

The two women stepped into the camp routine with ease. Within ten days, Sergeant Miller swore theirs was the best-equipped and stocked dispensary in Vietnam, and he should know, for he gave that dispensary his personal attention. The *Dai Uy* addressed both of the women nurses as Co, Vietnamese for Miss, and one, Co Vong, clearly the spokesperson, was more confident and more given to smile. I soon detected that the Montagnards did not look directly at either of the women who, although represented by Co Vong, were equally beautiful. "It is not allowed," was Phillipe's explanation when asked why the Montagnards did not openly admire the two women as the Vietnamese soldiers did.

It was a long walk from their dispensary to the small eating space that *Dai Uy* Minh reserved for his key people in his modest headquarters. It was built, as all of our buildings were, of bamboo matting attached to wood poles and covered with a tin roof. The nurses walked to their meals there three times a day, on schedule, and the men of Duc Co—except for the Montagnards—positioned themselves to watch. I noticed that Phillipe joined in watching these two flowing, white nightingales (I think that Specialist

Collier came up with the names, but I am not sure.) as they moved to and fro. Of course, Phillipe was half-French. His wife, the Jarai princess, was also beautiful. She twice visited us at Duc Co wearing a colored *ao dai*. They had one child, but I never saw her. His wife and the child lived with her father well south of Pleiku City. The two nurses were welcome additions to our medical staff and improved the medical attention to the Jarai women who came to us in increasing numbers after Co Vong and her friend arrived. Their great contribution, however, would come two years after my team and I left Duc Co.

In the 1966 Viet Cong offensive in the Highlands, the VC targeted several key installations for destruction. One, the Le Thanh District Headquarters, the VC overran in June. In July they began an encirclement movement that eventually cut Duc Co off from all contacts other than radio. Duc Co was under siege, and it was the last of the surviving installations that the Province Chief could point to in the western part of the province. The Vietnamese military commanders, also headquartered in Pleiku City, wanted desperately to break the siege and restore the strength of Duc Co and Le Thanh District Town.

Before ground forces, Vietnamese and American, could break the siege, resupply of the camp was by airdrop, bundles attached to parachutes. When the VC cut off movement to and from the camp, Co Vong was in Pleiku City. The province chief denied her request for transport to return to the camp to meet her responsibilities. When she learned that one of the resupply drops was medical supplies, she insisted on parachuting into Duc Co with those supplies.

My wife and I heard of her brave descent into Duc Co while watching television news in the visitors' quarters at Fort Hamilton, New York, having just returned to America following a one-year tour in Germany.

Later, I learned that Major Norm Schwarzkopf was the senior adviser to a Vietnamese Ranger battalion that played an important role in lifting that siege. He later, as a lieutenant general, was my corps commander when I took command of the 6th Infantry Division in Alaska in 1987.

In all the many weeks before we left Vietnam, Sergeant Miller and I were unable to discover what happened to the young girl who, we hoped, lived to enjoy a sound foot again. I think that *Dai Uy* Minh, whom I faulted in many ways, brought Co Vong and the dispensary to Duc Co, moved by the incident of the exploding mine at the Old French Fort. That fort fell early in the spring of '66, deserted, I understand, as not defendable.

Chapter Six

Honor in Small Things

Looking back at that largely unsuccessful reconnaissance of Chu Pong Mountain, it is hard to accept that we missed extensive tunneling, even if the Viet Cong had not yet placed supplies and equipment in the tunnels. Some recent reports suggest, however, the VC dug the tunnels from the west, inside Cambodia, and when we searched the mountain, detection might have been dependent on the smallest of air holes. I limited our search, both in area and in time. Two years later Lieutenant Colonel Hal Moore and Captain Tony Nadal found themselves in the battle of their lives in the eastern shadows of the mountain. The VC supplied, supported and commanded their units from inside the tunnels that either they had not yet dug or, more likely, we had missed in late '63. My guess is they were there—at least largely underway by that time—because the VC built those tunnels by hand, a time-consuming project. That thought only adds to the conclusion I offered in my report as we left country in January of '64.

I wrote it in a spiral notebook, in longhand, although I hand printed a small portion. I discussed with Sergeants Manuel and Sasser what I later wrote, but no other member of the team helped directly or indirectly in its preparation. While it covered a chronology of events, only two matters warrant sharing now. First was my description of the practice that I had found a few weeks after I arrived at Duc Co and later found reason to think that it happened in some other camps. The books of the detachment that we replaced, the financial books that reflected income from the "case officer" and distributions in the form of check stubs, revealed improper use of funds. Put simply, by my calculations, the books reflected far greater payments in Vietnamese piasters for construction materials for the camp than I could see in the buildings standing or unused materials in the camp. I laid this out for my executive officer, to whom I assigned responsibility as bookkeeper, a common practice of deployed A Teams. I then inserted into his books a statement of audit reflecting the building materials and cash we inherited in taking responsibility for the camp. In another spiral notebook, I reflected the audit in detail, describing all, but keeping the receipts and check stubs in our books and under the control of my exec. I visited my B Detachment commander about thirty days after we arrived at Duc Co. He listened intently to my summary of what I had found and concluded, and he asked that I go over the contents with his executive officer, which I did. The exec asked that I leave the book and allow him to study it until I returned in a week to talk about it with the commander. On my return, the exec suggested I drop the matter, pointing out that we were in a war. I would do myself no favors getting us off track on a trivial matter such as this. In that and a later visit, the commander told me he had not read my report yet, but that he would. When I, still later, asked the commander for the return of my report if he was not going to read it, he brushed it off and again referred me to the executive officer. The exec told me the book had been accidentally destroyed—burned. I saw it best to drop it, for now. I did not share that I had a second copy I had written before I offered the original to my boss.

Two weeks before we were to leave Duc Co for the states, I went to Nha Trang. It was my only visit there during our tour, other than our arrival and departure from Vietnam. My executive officer, Don Conrad, had accidentally discharged his pistol while preparing to clean it and wounded his hand. While there, I visited him and the office of the commanding general and asked the adjutant to provide the booklet to the commander prior to my call on him the next week. Although I gave no details at the time, I had discussed in the report our efforts to prompt more aggressive action by the camp commander and the District Chief, and named the improvements by the District Chief and our improved sightings of the VC by our Mountain Scouts on the border. I added the number of soldiers trained in our CIDG program, our greatest accomplishment, on paper, and I said that we had made little progress compared to the outlay of American dollars for personnel and equipment. I recommended a change of focus to efforts similar to the Mountain Scouts, and a large increase in the presence of U. S. Special Forces detachments in the field, on patrol for periods of four to six weeks at least. I suggested we could train soldiers in the CIDG program with small cadre teams out of stateside Army training centers, not with an elite force of Green Berets or Rangers. I finished the report with the conclusion that we should make major changes in the way we were carrying out the Special Forces mission or we should leave.

I wanted the commander to have the report and to read it, hopefully, before the departure visit. Each A and B Detachment commander called on the group commander as he left country. I understood it would be brief, a verbal report to the commander. There would likely be some question as to my procedure of a full, hand written report. The adjutant seemed uneasy with my approach, and said he would have other staff look it over.

I learned when I went to see the commander that I would be seeing the Deputy Commander, the same Colonel Viney who had visited my camp months earlier. He wasted no time after I saluted and took the seat he offered to pull the report to the center of his desk. He leafed through it and I was disappointed, guessing he had not read it

Viney said he had taken the liberty to have the report brought to him when he heard about it and he then directed the staff review it and give him comments. He began with a criticism—that it was a bit late to be bringing some of this to his or the commander's attention. I did not defend myself. He was right, but I was hoping not to get into criticizing my chain of command. I was on thin enough ice as it was, having not surfaced this final, full report at B Detachment level as I processed out. I had given a shorter, typed brief that did not include matters about the information that had been accidentally burned months earlier at that same headquarters. I knew that would be the next criticism—jumping the chain of command, and probably the end of the discussion.

I was wrong.

He sat with my open spiral notebook and a sheet of typewritten notes to his front. The notes, I assume by a staff officer, were annotated with handwritten scribbling. I guessed someone had keyed the typed notes to the pages of my report, which I had numbered. He showed no interest in names of individuals involved. I think he asked questions only to clarify the nature of the asserted unbecoming conduct. He seemed more interested in my ideas on how our Special Forces should perform like the SAS in Malaysia.

I didn't know much about Colonel Viney's background, but I had heard he had spent time in the 82nd Airborne Division. I didn't know how long he had been around Special Forces. At times, he would pause and look at me, and I felt uncomfortable. I did not like doing this, they have names in the Army and elsewhere for men who report such matters when, by some standards, they don't have to. I tried to shake that thought. I guessed his looks had to do with me and my motives. If he faulted me in any way, I thought my report would go in a trashcan as I walked out his door.

Finally, I must have answered all the questions he needed to ask, and I thought I had answered them well, growing more comfortable and confident as we talked. He stood and said that he wanted to thank me. He said the report would be handled only as a basis to make inquiries, not to take action or to make any charges. Finally, he said that he had long thought the concept I offered on employment of forces had a lot of merit. However, he said that making such a change could be difficult in the short term, especially considering our constraints as only advisers. I guessed that meant the employment of A Teams was not likely to change. That change was far more important, I thought, than the misconduct in handling funds.

A few months later, I was at my desk as the training officer of Company B, 7th Special Forces Group, at Fort Bragg, where we were training A Detachments to prepare them for deployment to Vietnam. Captain Roger H. C. Donlon commanded one of the detachments for which I directed training. He would later earn the Medal of Honor for his bravery in Vietnam. A captain strode into my office, ignoring the clerk and my training sergeant, Master Sergeant Shevshenko. Shevshenko stood as the man breezed by him, and he looked around at me. I waved to him it was okay, and he sat back down. The man stopped before my desk. He raised his fisted hand in front of me, unfolded it, and dropped its contents on my desk.

"Here," he said. "You can have these. I won't be needing them." He paused. "They have blood on them." He turned and walked out. He had dropped two leaves, insignia of rank of an Army major.

He was the captain I had replaced at Duc Co nine months earlier. I had heard nothing about my report to Colonel Viney. I had no idea what had happened, if anything, or how it had worked. Now I assumed that Viney had caused some questions to be asked, and conclusions had been drawn. I picked up the two leaves, and walked around the side of my desk and stood. I could see Shevshenko looking in at me. He looked away. He was old SF. He had been around Smoke Bomb Hill and on deployments for several years. I admired and respected him greatly. I wondered if he knew, and if he did, what he thought of all of this and of me. I never asked. I thought of Colonel Viney. He was the kind of officer I had been looking for. A man of integrity who believed that an officer signs up to do his duty and expects no more money than his base pay and allowances. A man who believed that no position of Army trust is a license to seek or accept "extra" income simply because you are operating in a system of loose controls, where windfall gains are available. And, by the way, "everyone is doing it."

I dropped the insignia into the wastebasket. I didn't feel good about it. I would have preferred never to have met the captain. I wished my report had prompted the release of Green Beret detachments into the forests and jungles of Vietnam. Meeting and beating the guerrilla on his own terms was what we needed to do. Not the continued fortified bases of our counterinsurgency effort. I did not know then that within a year we would magnify this concept of war from base camps in committing hundreds of thousands of conventional U. S. soldiers to Vietnam.

Maybe some of the old hands were right, preventing a few hundred illegal piasters under the table was not going to go far in promoting the freedom of the people of the Republic of Vietnam. But what if we are not successful, I thought. What if, in the end, the government of those people falls, and a government from the north comes in to replace it and we all go home. What will we—each of us—have then, if not our honor? And honor does not rank deeds by their monetary value or their scale of impact on an individual, an institution, or a society. Honor is Honor.

When Carol and the kids and I left Fort Bragg a few weeks later, we stayed in the guesthouse, where Charlie Beckwith was waiting with his family to complete the process of leaving post. We were both on the way to Army schooling, he to the Staff Officer Course at Fort Leavenworth and I to the Infantry Officer Advance Course at Fort Benning. I would not see Charlie again until he was a colonel—mid '70s. I was serving in the Office of the Chief of Staff of the Army when Colonel Beckwith came by to see me. Showing much gray now, and carrying an extra twenty pounds, he was, however, still smiling and aggressive. Elated. He had just gotten approval on a major additional step in developing his latest project. I knew, and he knew that I knew, it was Delta Force, the most elite special operations unit the Army had yet fielded.

In 1994, retired and doing a little work for my old boss, Carl Vuono, also retired, I attended a review of the 25th Light Infantry Division at Schofield Barracks. After the ceremony, I was saying hello to many friends I had known when I served in Hawaii several months before. A young woman walked up, put out her hand, and offered her name.

"I am Colonel Beckwith's daughter, and he told me, if I ever saw you, to tell you hello because he considered you among the most honorable men he ever knew." I thanked her. We talked briefly of her family and parted, others pushing in to say hello.

"Chargin Charlie" had died just weeks before at the age of sixty-five. Fourteen years earlier, on his dream mission, on the sands of a place named, Desert One, in Iran, he had watched his Operation Eagle Claw go up in flames in an accidental collision of two aircraft. His Delta Force had gone on to many successful missions since that searing failure. He was tough—of mind and body—surviving severe wounds in two wars and slaying bureaucrats who stood in the way of soldiers' needs. He was "old SF," and he was an honorable man.

Chapter Seven

A Truck and a Letter

In the last month or so of our tour at Duc Co, *Dai Uy* Minh pushed me to do something about Phillipe Drouin. After our reconnaissance patrol into the Ia Drang Valley, which accomplished little, and our search for the airfield, in which we were successful, I recognized that Phillipe had gained an extraordinary status in our camp and operations. In taking the airfield pictures, he had appeared ready to assume authority well beyond his position. I admired his initiative, as usual, but I found myself thinking, as I had before, that Phillipe Drouin was more than his position as my interpreter and his assumed role as my bodyguard. He did not hide his contempt for the Vietnamese Special Forces soldiers in Duc Co. The rare times I saw his Jarai princess wife reminded me of his other life, his father-in-law, a tribal chief, a life that appeared on hold. There was mystery about the man, and more than his penchant for the dramatic could explain. He often described a person or a situation with some line out of an American western movie, normally John Wayne. He liked best, "That'll be the day," and said it often. Another was "Sorry don't get it done, Dude." He proudly told us after a few beers that his very latest was, "Out here a man settles his own problems." I recognized it from *The Man Who Shot Liberty Valance*, a recent film. He lacked the stature of John Wayne, but he didn't seem to mind. At times, he would show his version of the Duke's walk. It was good. But Phillipe had his own swagger. He seemed most at home in camp with the Jarai Mountain Scouts, whose leader had told us about the fate of the hundreds of villagers, taken by the Viet Cong across the international border. This same man had disappeared. When he was gone for over a month, *Dai Uy* Minh's administrative officer said Saigon said he was with the Viet Cong; and that all along, he had been a double agent. I had not known what to make of that. He had been one of Phillipe's closest friends.

When I asked Phillipe about the administrative officer's story, he shook his head and said he did not know, but then he added, "My friend not VC."

Captain Minh came to see me on short notice, asking that we use his interpreter to discuss a matter about Phillipe Drouin. He did not think Phillipe should be present. It was not my best judgment to rely on the administrative officer for interpreting, but Phillipe was on an informal leave that had now lasted five days. I decided I would grant Minh's request, because I had learned that he understood English well, although he did not speak it so well. It was mid-December, and, as it turned out, Minh's problem was in two parts.

First, he expressed concern that Phillipe had been using property of the camp, a three-quarter ton truck, for over six weeks, and he doubted Phillipe was using the truck for only official reasons. I waited for a statement or request for action on my part, but there was none. He then said that he had information that Phillipe had visited another Special Forces Camp and he wondered if I knew that. I asked him if he had something specific he wanted from me. That seemed to irritate him slightly.

He said that he just wanted to make sure I knew about Phillipe. I asked him what he wanted me to know, and he replied, through the admin officer interpreter, that he wanted me to know about the truck. I told him I did know about the truck, that Sergeant Manuel had talked to me about the truck, which was then little more than a carcass we used for spare parts. I approved the use of parts for Phillipe to repair the truck and to use it on business for the camp or our team. As far as I know, I said, he has not used the truck improperly.

"What about taking the truck to look for another job?" He asked me in English. I replied the trip was in the best interests of our American advisory role in Vietnam, and I considered it proper. Through the interpreter, he then asked if I knew that Phillipe had made some trouble with high-level officials in Saigon, and I asked what trouble. I could see I was frustrating Minh, but that did not bother me. I had known for a long time of the dislike between Minh and Phillipe, and Sergeant Manuel had told me that Phillipe had said he believed he would have to get a job somewhere else because of *Dai Uy* Minh. Manuel said Phillipe had told him he wanted the previous weekend off to visit a new Special Forces commander and apply for a job. I had raised no objection to that. Somehow, I sensed that Phillipe bothered Minh with something more than the trip to apply for a job and the truck. I waited.

Dai Uy Minh took a single sheet of paper from a folder and slid it across the table to me. It was a letter, a poor copy of a letter. It read:

To Whom It May Concern:
This letter is to introduce Mister Phillip Drouin. He has worked for me

at Camp Chu Dron for the past six months. During this time his work has been exemplary. Mister Drouin has displayed an excellent grasp of the English Language. In addition he speaks and writes French, Jarai, and Rhade. He has a small understanding of Thai, Cambodian, and Cantonese. He has an excellent grasp of tactics.

His three quarter ton truck is a salvage vehicle from this camp. The vehicle has been released from the books of the United States Government and was given by me to Mister Drouin only after he had repaired it himself.

Any assistance you may give in the registration of this vehicle will be appreciated.

I recommend him to the employ of anyone requiring the services of a superior interpreter-translator with a thorough knowledge of tactics.

Sincerely,

Johnnie A. Corn
Captain, Armor

I read the letter and slid it back to him. He said, "You keep. Your copy."

"Thank you," I said, thinking as fast as I could and hoping my face was as deadpan as I wanted it to be.

I hadn't seen the letter, but it contained nothing that I would not have approved if someone had asked me to do so. I didn't think Phillipe wrote the letter. I had never seen his name written without the "e" on the end, never heard his name pronounced in the English form. His English was good, but not this good. I suspected my Team Sergeant, George Manuel, might have had a hand in the letter, but George knew my name and my branch of the Army. I was Johnnie H., not A, and my name ended with an s, Corns. And George damn well knew I was Infantry, not Armor.

As we sat there, Minh's face slowly reddened. He got to his second point.

"You know, Phillipe could be in much bad trouble. He should come back here, now," Minh said.

"I'm sure he will, after he finishes the business he's doing now," I said. I actually was now not so sure he would return—or should.

At the time of the meeting with Minh, I had heard only innuendo around the staff at Pleiku that the Montagnards could get out of hand. They worried that at a single camp, if we were not careful, the Vietnamese Special Forces cadre might incite the Montagnards with excessive treatment. That was not likely at Duc Co. If anything, we were more likely to incite the Vietnamese by our preference for the Jarai people, which was, in part, behind this visit from

Minh. To jump months ahead and look back, I certainly had no thoughts the Montagnards might conduct what the Vietnamese would call an uprising against the government. I don't know how much Captain Minh knew right then, but I'm sure he, and others, suspected and feared these people with whom American soldiers easily built such strong rapport.

At the time, I simply had chosen sides between Phillipe and Minh, and Minh had lost. I viewed Phillipe as the finest soldier in the Duc Co Camp, and I take nothing away from my men in saying that. I viewed Minh as a little bureaucrat, caught up in the urgency to keep his bosses in Saigon content to keep his job and ensure his future.

A few days later, Minh was suddenly gone, and the District Chief confirmed rumors I had heard that Minh was in trouble and probably would not be back. I had written a criticism of his performance to my boss at Pleiku several weeks earlier, seeking his replacement by a more aggressive officer. But, just after Christmas, the Christmas by which General Paul Harkins told the *Stars and Stripes* and the whole world we would be out of Vietnam, Minh was back, wearing a swagger and smile of victory. He and I hardly spoke in my remaining two weeks at Duc Co.

Phillipe Drouin did not come back, and following my conversation with Sergeant Manuel, I am sure what was said was passed to Phillipe, including words about the copy of the letter Minh had given to me. I never asked George Manuel about the letter, and he never brought it up to me.

I am not the one to tell the rest of Phillipe's story. Another Green Beret captain has already done that. In his 1979 book, Jim Morris, the Commander to whom Phillipe presented the letter above, writes how he served with Phillipe on into '64, and went back to Phillipe's old stomping grounds three years later to find him. In his excellent book, *War Story*, Morris, speaking of Phillipe, writes:

◆　◆　◆

"At the same time his political enemies were getting together and forming their forces to chase Phillip around the city (Ban Me Thout) and try to assassinate him.

"Unfortunately, his guys were on bicycles and their guys were on the famous FULRO gray Honda 90's. So they caught him first.

"All these details, I was able to confirm.

"But I never talked to anybody who had seen the body."

◆　◆　◆

In his book, Morris tells of his colorful times with Phillipe and his discovery that Phillipe Drouin, in the days of the unsuccessful Montagnard revolt against the Vietnamese Government and afterwards, was a Colonel, commanding a Montagnard division.

Chapter Eight

A Reflection

In that long delay on the airstrip, waiting to leave Vietnam in January '64, I had, for a time, slipped into something of a reflection. It was not a specific, or even concrete, set of thoughts, or emotions. I felt apart, away from the men in the solid-walled plane, and the last six months seemed unreal, without much meaning, without the hard results one expects following a raid, even a long deployment. Our mission in all that time had been split, unfocused, and the Army, more correctly, the CIA, had not budgeted us adequately for even one of the missions. My personal missions, there being five, were: Lead and promote the success and safety of my eleven American Green Berets. Advise the CIDG battalion commander in his security and offensive operations. Advise the same captain in his mission to train soldiers for security roles in western Pleiku Province. Advise the same captain in his operational task of screening the international border using the mountain scouts. Advise the District Chief in his military operations to provide security to his district.

I did not give my team or me a high score, and it was not mainly the fault of my Green Berets or me. No honor is greater than to be allowed to lead fellow citizens in the battlefield pursuit of the values of our society. When the major national issues of economics and geopolitics are lifted away, such an endeavor becomes a personal and deeply felt, shared experience among a small group of men. For me, that was eleven other Americans, hardly a squad in size, but with missions of broad scope and affecting thousands of people. Each man is subject to scrutiny by the others, and he too looks closely at those whose home, food, security, and danger he shares. The months of shared training at home near our families contrast with the months of shared deployment far away from those families. Even on the quietest of days in the shadow of the people you seek to help and under the distant eye of those who would harm you, there is an intensity. There is an awareness. You are alive in a way that all objects can loom near and bold as if under a giant magnifying glass. Each gesture, each unique twirl of speech or tint of laughter of each man is registered more deeply and more permanently. Despite the threat that any one of them can be gone in a day, gone with finality and chilling speed, there is a warmth there the evening before. There is a shared line from a letter or the brief description of a sure way to kill—or to survive. There is no routine. Only a pretense at routine—a curtain that hides some degree of concern, anxiety, uncertainty, or a practiced confidence that denies the uncertainty as if it were not present. And yet, each man knows those realities about himself and respects them in the others and goes on to do what is right, what he has been trained to do. On some days, only that training and inner discipline drive one on under stress and danger as they drove Roberts in the ambush or Sasser in the minefield. And after a night's rest, the pretense at routine returns and soothes the intensity of the training and discipline of the day before. And each man is aware of each of the other men, and each sees the other without looking; is aware without speech or hearing.

It is an arena of honesty. Not necessarily of honesty expressed, but of honesty known, one man about the other. It is an arena of judgments made, not out of adherence to some social play, but out of living necessity. And the judgments seldom pass the test for sharing, they remain in the thoughts of the observer, eventually to fade before the press of other intensity. And we learn of each other. We know. We live. We are alive.

And when it is over, we are drained.

In such an arena, progress and success depend on the game that those in charge select, and the rules they announce and impose. As I thought of Vietnam of 1963/64, I doubted the merits of the game selected and the integrity of the rules imposed. I doubted those in charge who had fashioned the game.

I did not doubt the players.

But, what about me—the leader? I thought I should have spoken out more strongly. I doubted that anything would ever come from my report to Colonel Viney. If I were going to make a difference, I should have taken on the B Team Commander directly and consistently. I thought of the men our sister detachments had lost. I thought of the huge expense of dollars in fielding all the teams of advisers, even of the Green Berets alone, in Vietnam. On paper, we were a powerful force, even limited to the advisory role, and I hoped that many teams had been able to accomplish more than I had. But then there was the "passive accommodation." Surely they had run into the same thing. A policy that was informal, unofficial, and grew out of the reality of Viet Cong welcomed access at night into the very villages the men of *Dai Uy* Minh and the District Chief patrolled during daylight. I had been not so subtly encouraged to assassinate the same District Chief who had driven a jeep load of his men into the flanks of a Viet Cong ambush, and nearly died. These people, these district chiefs and officers and soldiers of the Republic of South Vietnam had tired of war, and I feared they saw little difference between us Americans and the defeated French of ten years earlier.

Right before the shrill and metallic sounds told me the engines were finally firing up for our takeoff, I thought of the numbers. My losses had been two, Sergeant Sieg and Lieutenant Conrad, both injured and recovering from accidents that should never have occurred. To me, they were my losses, my responsibility, but fortunately, for their families, the men were safe at home. The heavy losses were those Americans who had died in this conflict. It was said that, since 1956, we had lost just under 200 men in the Indo China area overall; of which about 85 were advisers lost in just the last few years in Vietnam. All killed as part of a group of advisers who could not fire on the enemy until the enemy fired on them. What ethic is that? As opposed to the ethic of the young commander who says, protect yourself, fire if needed, before they kill you?

No, I would spend the hours over the Pacific thinking of these eleven men with whom I had come to war. This had been our days in combat, our time in Vietnam. I would relive every memory about and shared with each man. I would savor the worthiness of each of them. I would try to weigh, no, sense, the total worth of all of them—all twelve of us. We were worthy.

Laughter engulfed the passenger area. What? I had missed it, but I smiled. The laughter continued, and I laughed. What were we laughing at?

What did it matter?

We were rolling. We were rising.

As we lifted higher in a stiff climb to avoid ground fire, I smiled again. All eleven of my men were sound of limb and mind. I only wished that they, and I, had some sense of victory, some sense of progress, in our little war.

The laughter became deafening.

We were going home.

Your Green Berets
by
John H. Corns

Portrayed in movies
Serenaded in song
We jumped into Hell
To right someone's wrong

Hid in the jungle
Moved only at night
Took the sentinel
With only a knife

Rappelled from choppers
Rolled out of the boats
Shocked the unwary
With hands at their throats

We were asked to teach
By our boss, JFK
Show love and patience
Win in a new way

Oh, what they did ask
Why didn't they know
That to do this task
Meant to die, so slow

How do you explain
The urge to revolt
When bound by a rope
Like a year old colt

Could we not do it
Of course, and we did
We gave all the shots
And consoled the kid

But while we aided
And fed old and weak
The guerilla foe
Close by us did sneak

And we joined others
In our mild surprise
As they burned the homes
Right before our eyes

Our men should have been
Out there close to them
Absorbing their smell
And matching their skin

We should have muddied
And worn the same clothes
Took back the jungle
And disarmed their nose

Said no to cool Kents
And no to a chew
Our numbers still small
A tough, elite few

Walked on in the rain
Slept out in a roll
Dried off in the sun
Ate live crawfish whole

Slept while on the move
With one eye alert
Stepped over their wires
Saw none of us hurt

Ahead of their thoughts
We, already there
When they came back home
To their unsafe lair

What all did we learn?
What all can we share?
To tell our story
To all those who care

There are many things
The SF is not
Just to show and teach
Is hardly our lot

The trainers supreme
Our huge Army holds
And the healers too
With pills for the colds

There are so many
To fill that key role
One that is not small
For it soothes the soul

But we are unique
So recall our ways
When you call on us
Your own Green Berets

PART II
The Cloud Above Snoopy's Nose

Introduction

Three Captains and a Colonel

Dick Sharp and I met in Vietnam in early 1967, and we worked, lived, and fought together for nearly a year in combat. We survived, continued to serve in the United States Army, and rose to the rank of general officer. We shared close professional and personal friendships with others who served in the Army and Navy Mobile Riverine Force in the Mekong Delta. One of those common friends was a captain when Dick and I met him in the days of the Second Battle of Ap Bac in Dinh Tuong Province. His unlikely name was "Clancy" Matsuda. He was, and is, a man of passion and strong loyalties. He knew Dick and me increasingly well as the years after Vietnam passed. He is a special and unique man, and, in this story, represents many officers with whom Dick Sharp and I served. I cannot properly tell the stories of all those fine men; and Clancy would protest singling him out. But Clancy Matsuda was my and Dick's friend. He served with us. He watched us separately. He watched us together. He, better than anyone, knew how we were alike and how we were different. Of all the men I knew in the Army, the man I would most want not to disappoint in matters of integrity and honor, was Clancy. I think Dick felt the same.

An Army colonel brought Dick and me together. He was seeking to staff his brigade headquarters with men he thought would fit into a team. A fighting team he would forge in America and test and bloody, if necessary, early in combat in Vietnam. A team that could find and defeat the enemy with minimum loss of soldiers. His name was Bill Fulton. In the years following Vietnam, Dick and I had parallel and similar assignments. One such assignment was serving as battalion commander concurrently at Fort Lewis, Washington, in the 1970s. Another was his arrival in '76 as I was departing as a student at the Army War College. And, at the end of that decade, I passed to him the command of the 2nd Brigade of the 2nd Infantry Division in Korea. Most of those years Bill Fulton was still on active duty, retiring in 1977 as a lieutenant general in the key post of Director of the Army Staff in the Pentagon. When he had managed to pull Dick and me together again at Fort Lewis, Washington, Fulton commanded the 9th Infantry Division, and he also brought, now Major, Clarence "Clancy" Matsuda there as well. We had all discovered Clancy the same day in early May of 1967 in Dinh Tuong Province, Vietnam. Matsuda sat on a log and modestly, matter-of-factly, told of his unit's heroic role in the just completed Second Battle of Ap Bac. The victory followed by four years an operation in this same location, north of Highway 4 and west of the provincial capital city of My Tho. Now, at Fort Lewis, Clancy, as I, was a major in the division G3, or operations, section. He and I would have preferred to be serving as the S3, or operations officer, of an infantry battalion.

Three years earlier, we were instructing offensive tactics in the Attack Committee of the Infantry School in Georgia. Dick visited the post briefly, and the three of us shared a beer at the aviators' officer's club. Dick was his energetic and ebullient self, chomping on his cigar and revealing his pleasure with his recent selection for promotion to lieutenant colonel, a list that I had missed. This was a list for the early promotion of a few selected officers in that year group who merited to be advanced ahead of their peers. If they had been filming John Wayne's *Green Berets* right then at Fort Benning, as they had just months earlier, Dick might have stolen either of the leading roles. That of the rugged Mike Kirby, played by Wayne, or the handsome, cynical news reporter, portrayed by David Janssen. Dick, like the two actors, was a hero type, not only in appearance, but also by proven performance. He was one of the few men I ever met who tended to be "larger than life." I smiled, but winced a little when Dick, looking seriously and sincerely at Clancy and me said, "Wherever I am going, I will want the two of you with me." His sincerity was unquestionable, but I thought, although I did not say aloud, I'll be right behind you, friend. I suspect that Dick—and Clancy—knew what I was thinking.

Fulton's touch was present in other assignments for Dick and me. We both were fortunate in attaining our long-shot hope in an Army career—to lead the soldiers of an Infantry brigade, in our case the All Infantry Brigade at Camp Hovey, Korea. The night before our change of command ceremony, Dick chewed the end of his cigar and watched me as I gave my rationale for turning down a coveted job. I had opted to go home to my family rather than respond positively to a career-enhancing invitation that would have kept me in Korea for another year. The glint in his eye suggested what I already knew— he would have made the same choice. We had talked of our families years before, a dozen years before, in the steamy heat of Dinh Tuong Province. It was what we talked about most when we were not talking about the last battle or the emerging plan for the next. Most of those days, I was the intelligence and then the operations officer for the Army's Riverine Brigade. Dick was the plans officer and then a battalion S3. That was before we knew that he would take the brigade operations officer position I held when I left Vietnam. We talked about what mattered most to us—personal and professional.

Our bond was strong, requiring neither explanation nor embellishment. The bond was finally forged to steel hardness in one day of battle. He was directing the fight of a battalion from a damaged, spinning boat in the Rach Ba Rai canal. I was directing the larger operation of the brigade of which his battalion was a part; our cooperation in the shared mission complicated by *The Cloud Above Snoopy's Nose.*

Chapter Nine

A Chance Meeting

The Cold War with the Soviet Union was the underlying reality of over thirty years of my life as an Army officer. The reality that made the broader national policy of containment within that Cold War personal and raw was Vietnam. I had left the Ia Drang region of Pleiku Province in the Central Highlands in early 1964. I held the notion that if we broke our Special Operations Forces, particularly the Green Berets, free from the training bases, we could be far more effective. We needed to put them out in the guerilla's back yard with indigenous counter guerrilla soldiers, rather than tying them to the broader counterinsurgency mission. In their places in the bases should be training teams from our stateside training centers to teach and train the Civilian Irregular Defense Group soldiers and others. And I believed two good American Infantry Divisions in each corps were needed. They would deter the doctrinal strategy of the North Vietnamese to grow eventually their supported insurgency to conventional force level. They would give us the right mix of forces to provide the example and to advise and lead the Vietnamese military and paramilitary.

I have often thought over the years of that gross underestimate of the task on my part, although our policy never included large-scale guerrilla-like operations against the VC guerrillas. Instead, we gave priority to our conventional forces, often led by generals who openly ridiculed and discounted our counter guerrilla potential and the meager counter guerrilla forces we did put in Vietnam. Meager, not so much in totals put in Vietnam, but in their numbers in the field in a continuing fight on the ground, soldiers seldom seeing the comforts of a static base camp. When I think of the statements of Army men years later, some my leaders, some peers, who say they had already discovered back then the steady course of failure that we were on, I can make no such claim. I was aware, when I left Vietnam that first time in '64, that the efforts of my own detachment produced little results, a conclusion I shared in a report to my chain of command. I favored greater emphasis on continuing counter guerrilla operations by teams advised by Green Berets, not in the training bases, but in the jungle. But then I watched the steady growth in dependence on and numbers of conventional forces. As I left Vietnam in early '64, the Americans killed was somewhere under 200, fewer than 100 of them in recent Vietnam operations. Maybe, in fairness, it was too soon for most Army officers to see the long-term course of the war. Maybe those who saw the eventual failure of policy came to that view in assignments in later years, not in that 1964 period. In '64, our killed in Vietnam doubled, to somewhere around 400. Later events showed that two divisions per corps were not enough; there never seemed to be enough.

Following that six months on the north slopes of the Ia Drang Valley in Vietnam, I returned to Fort Bragg. I shared some of my experiences as I directed the training of other A Detachments going to Vietnam from the 7th Special Forces Group. I was then assigned to Europe, stopping for nine months at Fort Benning for the Infantry Officer Advance Course, a program to prepare officers for company command and lower staff assignments.

The assignment to Europe pleased Carol and me. We were uncertain of what to expect, living not on post, but out on the German economy for most of our tour. I was first the assistant and then the operations officer for the 2nd Brigade of the 3d Infantry Division at Kitzingen on the Main River. In that year of '65, half of which we lived in Georgia and half in Germany, about 1800 Americans died in South Vietnam. Nearly a year after our arrival and only two weeks after we finally moved to government housing on post—a most welcome development—I received orders assigning me to the newly activated 9th Infantry Division at Fort Riley, Kansas. The orders were in response to my request to leave Europe and go back to Vietnam with enough time to get my family settled in my and Carol's hometown of South Charleston, West Virginia.

Her chin had quivered just a little when I had told her several weeks earlier that I did not want to remain in Europe. The Army was pulling officers out of Europe for duty in Vietnam. I was one of very few captains remaining in our division because I was about the only captain who had already served in Vietnam. Lieutenant Colonels commanded the three battalions in our brigade. They had only second lieutenants to help them lead their units. That did not strike me as the top priority of the President of the Unites States. By the end of '65, 6,000 would have died in Vietnam. This followed the buildup ordered by the Commander in Chief following the Tonkin Gulf incident. By the time our division would leave Fort Riley at the end of '66, about 8,000 men had already died in the Vietnam area over a ten-year period.

Today, I marvel at Carol's response in Germany, despite the quivering jaw: "I'll support what you think your duty calls you to do." Of course, at that time, her words were what I hoped for, and expected. I had to live a bit more of life to learn just who showed the courage in that moment and for nearly two years thereafter. Still, we took it in stride. Thousands of others did the same. What depths of patriotism and sense of duty lie there to be plumbed by commanders in chief in times of national need. They say—the commanders in chief, they have all said—that they know what they have asked. We hope they did—and do. But looking back, over the span of forty years, you must wonder: particularly about the string of commanders in chief that now have known no real military combat service. How could they know? Yet the many fine, young families think their top leaders do know. The leaders say they do. They said they did then. And we believed them.

What would I have said if Carol had replied, "John, do you know there is a National Intelligence Estimate that projects there will be well over 50,000 American military killed in Vietnam before it is all over?"

Of course, she did not say that. She had not heard of a National Intelligence Estimate of the projected loss of American life in Vietnam. There was none. Or if there were, no commander in chief would want to share it with the American people, share what he would likely call a stark and irresponsible error if such a prediction were to "leak."

I have learned over the years that America does not usually make good National Intelligence Estimates before sending men and women into a war. Who would make it? Who would endorse it? What person could President Polk have gotten to lay out precisely the purposes and objectives of the war with Mexico over 150 years ago? Would he have wanted to tell the American people up front that his aim was not limited to the question of the southern boundary of Texas on the Neuces or Rio Grand Rivers? He would probably not have allowed the estimate to address the lands that America later demanded with the defeat of the Mexican Army: places we now call California, Arizona, New Mexico, and more. He would not have wanted to speak of possible gold in those far western reaches. That gold, it would have been said, was little more than a rumor.

There is something I would call National Intent. It lies in a gray land between the imperative to plan efficiently and effectively to assure the accomplishment of the mission with minimum loss of life and treasure, and the imperative to lead at the National level in a manner that will promote an admirable legacy for the commander in chief and the continued success of his political party.

Once in war, the costs can be extremely great before victory is won or declared. The National Intent of a commander in chief before war has a companion once war begins that can best be expressed simply, "We shall not lose a war on my watch." Such an outward display of courage and leadership in no way promotes wise and honorable decisions in the best interests of Americans, either those dying in combat or waiting at home.

◆   ◆   ◆

Leaving Germany in the summer of 1966, Carol and I visited Fort Riley, Kansas, dropping Mike and Lisa off with our parents in West Virginia.

I reported in to the division headquarters and they told me that I was going down (a phrase referring to echelons in the Army) to 1st Brigade. I would tentatively be a battalion operations officer, the position I had requested in my letters to the command before I left Germany. I was pleased.

Later, at the post Officers Club swimming pool, by chance, I ran into and introduced Carol to Major Clyde Tate, an officer I had worked with in Korea during my first assignment as a lieutenant in 1959. Clyde and I filled each other in on what we had been doing the six years since we had last seen each other. I told him of my pleasure that I was to be a battalion operations officer. Clyde's greatest interest, however, was in my prior service with Special Forces in Vietnam. He asked me many questions about the Viet Cong. Two weeks later, when Carol and the children and I returned to Fort Riley, the same people at Division Headquarters told me they had changed my assignment. I was to go, not to 1st Brigade, but to 2nd Brigade. The commander there would tell me what I would be doing. They told me that Colonel William B. Fulton would be my boss.

When I arrived, I told the brigade personnel officer, a major, and the executive officer, a lieutenant colonel, there had been a mistake; that I had been all set to go to a battalion, not to a brigade headquarters. They were polite, but of no help, telling me the brigade commander was expecting me and was looking forward to my arrival. At the appointed time, I knocked and entered the commander's office. Two things caught my attention and distracted me as I saluted and reported. He was darkly tanned, accented by his bald head, and that head, with him sitting, seemed to come to the level of mine. He retuned my salute, but did not invite me to sit, inquired about my family, and seemed pleased that I had brought them with me, considering that the brigade was to deploy in less than six months. He asked a little about my background and while not impatient, he apparently already knew all that I told him. I paused in an answer, sensing that his interest had moved on.

"Have you thought about being an S-2, an Intelligence Officer?" He asked.

I did not hesitate, and went a little too far. "No sir," I said. "I've tried to avoid that job. My preference has always been operations."

He stood, and I guessed his height at six feet, eight, but I later learned he was one or two inches shorter than that. He did not rise abruptly, but seemed to uncoil as he rose.

"You're going to be my S-2. Sit down and we'll talk about it."

My thoughts were about getting off on the wrong foot or something, and I think he was prepared to put me further in my place if I criticized the intelligence business. I wondered if he had been an S-2, maybe in combat in Korea, or even World War II. I had never heard any Army combat arms officer in the field speak of the central role of intelligence in planning and conducting combat operations. Of course, intelligence should be given such a role, but often was not, mostly because it just was not good enough to stake total planning on it. But, I liked what he said, particularly with my own views of the close relationship of intelligence and police work to military action in counterinsurgency and counter terrorism situations. As he talked, I became convinced he had thought this out. He had turned down other officers offered as his S-2 because he wanted a combat arms officer, preferably infantry, with an intelligence background. I was about to tell him, to keep the record straight, that I had no intelligence experience, when he said that Major Tate had told him of my background in Special Forces, and my tour of duty in Vietnam.

"You've been there. You know the land, you know the people, and you know the enemy. That is what intelligence is all about."

He had taken his seat again shortly as did I, and now he rose again. I still believe he did it that slowly to give emphasis to his stature. Maybe not. But I stood too.

"You will decide where this brigade fights, and it will be a fighting brigade, and you will continue to direct and redirect the brigade during the fight. I am going to fight this brigade, and you are going to be my eyes."

I couldn't recall anything he said after that when I left his office, and still can't. I had gone in concerned that my qualifications to direct operations as a staff officer for a battalion commander were being ignored, and I was about, for the third time, to be an assistant operations officer at brigade level. I left concerned that this tall colonel—Big Bill I was to learn his staff and subordinate commanders called him—wanted far more than I had the experience to provide as an intelligence officer. I also later learned that he had never been an intelligence officer, and would have likely sought to avoid such a job, and would have likely succeeded where I had acquiesced and failed.

As soon as I finished my administrative processing with the brigade adjutant, I found the brigade S-2 shop. I was lucky. The man running the office was a Sergeant Buckalew. He had one assistant, a specialist, who was soon to do more typing for us on planning and operations matters than on Intelligence. Buckalew talked and acted as if he knew what he was doing, and he had what he called a full library of manuals on intelligence. I took them, one by one, back to the Wildcat Apartments, and on weekends, while Carol and the kids enjoyed the lighted swimming pool, I began my first real cramming since my days at Marshall College. The reading matter was boring, showing none of the dash and decisiveness of the Fort Benning Handbook on operations. Long after the kids were asleep, I sat at the kitchen table, scribbling on a yellow legal pad. Sergeant Buck had a handout from one of the Army schools that contained a discussion and how-to examples of something called pattern analysis. It was the first item I took home and read, and I converted it in my notes to the stilted language of the traditional staff intelligence estimate. I felt like I was getting somewhere.

I didn't see the brigade commander for two days and then I was called in with the S-3, Clyde Tate, to talk about Command and Staff Training. Colonel Fulton asked me if I was familiar with pattern analysis. I told him yes and recited a bit of what I had learned two nights before. He nodded approvingly. I was indebted to Sergeant Buckalew. He turned to Clyde and they talked about preparations for the next command and staff session. I paid attention, but I knew that I would deal only with the intelligence portion; the bulk of the work would be Clyde's.

"Captain Corns, I'd like you to work closely with Clyde on this session. It will be your first. After this, I'm putting you in charge of the program. Clyde has his hands full with the tactical training program. I think you can do this and bring our intelligence training program into shape at the same time."

What could I say? He was right. Clyde did have a full plate, and I would have time available. I had kept a large box of materials handed out by instructors while I was attending the Infantry School Advance Course. One of the items was called an Operations Handbook that had been developed at Fort Benning with primary input from a colonel instructor who was now the 1st Brigade Commander, Colonel Maurice Kendall. It would serve as an excellent guide for the situation and requirements I would pose for the battalion commanders and their staffs. I was to learn that the command and staff training program was universally unpopular. The three infantry and one artillery battalion commanders were not impressed by a newcomer who threw himself into the entire undertaking as if the battalion leaders and staffs did not already have a full day and week of work. Readying their individual soldiers, platoons, and companies for combat demanded all their time. I dug myself a hole with all three commanders with the heightened expectations in the situational folders and requirements that I prepared for them. Lieutenant

Colonel "Blackie" Bolduc clued me in, and nicely. He was a man of high intelligence and unsurpassed energy. When he suggested the sessions could be less time consuming both in preparation requirements and in the duration of the evening classes, I knew it was not an excuse for lack of smarts or will to work. It simply needed to take a little less prominent place in their priorities. I thought that we backed it off a good deal, but it did not raise the popularity of the sessions. The one man who knew best that unpopularity I believe was Colonel Fulton, and I made the changes by originating less in the way of suggestions and requirements. I think that our clerk and Sergeant Buckalew appreciated that change more than anybody else—less typing and less time away from my basic duties as intelligence officer.

I think what was most disliked about the Command and Staff Training was simply the show and tell nature of the sessions. That was well suited to an Army service school environment, but a bit intimidating when the man who critiqued your presentation was the man who would command you in combat. Only one of the three battalion commanders ever told me the sessions were worth the valuable time committed to them, but I think all three came to see them—later, in Vietnam—as highly valuable. I believe they were. They introduced many important considerations of operations, particularly in the Mekong Delta environment, that did not come as a surprise to those commanders and their staffs once deployed.

If any one of the battalion commanders had been the brigade commander, he would not have introduced such a command and staff training program. Neither would I, but we should have. Colonel Fulton, the brigade commander, was a teacher and innovator.

This was the Bill Fulton who, over the years, would sit back, smile, and say to Carol and me, "I remember when we put Carol and those kiddies in that little Volkswagen on Custer Hill. I watched them drive off, on their way from Kansas to West Virginia in December of '66." I remember it too. Another of the special responsibilities that Carol accepted or suggested that accommodated my "duty." In those days, it was considered safe for a seven-year-old, like Mike, to ride in the front of the car while his five-year-old sister, Lisa, slept on the backseat.

Carol later told me that southwest of Chicago, she had missed a turn on the Interstate. Mike advised her, looking at his large-scale, picture-puzzle map of North America, she should not turn left or she would be in Canada. The next day, a state patrolman took the time to ask her where she was heading and then told her of the nasty weather coming in and suggested she stay put in the town another day. The next morning the Volkswagen was not maneuverable. A service station attendant came by long enough to tell her the wintry road slosh had frozen the steering linkage. She could not turn the wheels until later in the day when the thaw came. I learned none of this until many months later, well after my tour with Colonel Fulton's brigade in the Mekong Delta. What I did not know, I would not worry about, was Carol's approach. It was probably right, but it resulted in many belated "thank you's" over three and a half decades of military service. It hasn't stopped in retirement, although I have tried to be more involved in family matters, poor compensation for the years before if nothing else. I have learned, however, not to praise her too much for such actions in the presence of the younger generation. Many young adults are not positively impressed by my actions back then, or hers. So I don't bring it up a lot. I just privately thank her again, and point out that, given the chance, I would do some of those things, only some, differently. She does not agree. Revision she says is not called for. She still admires the many stories of the contribution of women to the families in the Conestoga wagon caravans that opened up the western United States in the last half of the nineteenth century. If we had lived then, we would have taken a wagon west.

Still, changes were called for. No longer are you likely to find Army supply sergeants or commanders saying, "If the Army wanted you to have a wife (spouse), they would have issued you one." But my admiration of the women of the days of the covered wagons and of our National involvement in Vietnam is not reduced by implied, present-day criticism of them or of the men of those days. The new roles of women in our society and our Army today are necessary and largely beneficial. But I do not like to see the new roles promoted by strident criticism of the many fine men and women who served our society in earlier times.

My family's brief time together at Fort Riley, from mid-July to mid-December of '66, had few uproariously happy occasions, but every day was special and precious to each of us over the following year. We made the most of the limited days and the limited hours that I was at home with them. They never questioned my time away, what I was doing, or what I was about to do. It was a dedicated family and, thanks to Carol, it was quietly, without great flag-waving, an intensely patriotic family, and still is.

My days through September were filled with directing and monitoring the combat intelligence training in the brigade, and directing special training such as the crack-thump course, which each soldier in the brigade was required, thanks to Colonel Fulton, to undergo. It consisted, as it had for years in the Army, of positioning soldiers in protected trenches, in our case the pits on the Fort Riley known-distance, rifle qualification range. In their protected position, the officers and their men heard the rounds of various weapons used by the Viet Cong crack as they passed over their heads. My assistant, Lieutenant Bob Reeves, announced the name of the weapon firing each round before and after it was fired. The thump that followed the crack of the weapon's round flashing by was the sound of the bullet leaving the muzzle of the rifle or other weapon. We taught the men the cadence to count and gain an appreciation of how far away the weapon was and the direction to it. It was a safe training exercise that relied on the proven protection of the trenches of the firing range. Knowing the weapons were the type they would confront in Vietnam, soldiers showed great motivation to learn how to determine how far away, in what direction, and with what weapon the enemy was firing on them. Additionally, our own weapons were fired, hoping to lay a base for recognition of endangering friendly fire that unfortunately occurs in some battles of any war. Of course, unlike the frontlines of World War II and Korea, the wars of counterinsurgency introduce the paramilitary who often, by force of the origins of the conflict, or by design, arm themselves with the weapons of their opponents.

Bob Reeves was an Air Force Academy graduate who had been medically precluded from piloting. He had decided he would prefer to see and fight the war from the perspective of the Army infantry. He was a serious, smart, and motivated officer whom I was pleased to have join our little S-2 team despite my preference for a lieutenant who had seen duty at the platoon level first. Generally, the Army agrees with that view, but it is hard to do when new divisions are being created all over the Army and almost none of the lieutenants has prior platoon experience or has seen combat. Bob also preferred line duty and was disappointed with his assignment. I committed myself then to working to get him into an infantry battalion at the earliest opportunity. He and I made that effort, but when we deployed to Vietnam, Bob was still my assistant. He was already a first lieutenant. He might not see a rifle company until he was a captain.

It was just after the crack-thump training that I was called to the tall brigade commander's office again.

"Johnnie," Fulton said, "We have the opportunity to be the 9th Division's brigade that will be part of a new command in Vietnam, the Mobile Riverine Force. But, we have to convince the Division Commander that he should choose us for the mission. You now have the added duty as the Brigade Liaison Officer for Riverine Planning. Your first step is to go through these classified papers and draft a briefing to get the decision we want from the Commanding General. I want to see your draft in two days. Remember, you can have an excellent command, but whether you are the unit your commander turns to when the chips are down depends on what he thinks about you as well as your brigade. Until he can see you in a fight, what he finally thinks may largely be based on how you present yourself and tell your story."

I don't know if he made the last comment recognizing my own tendency toward understatement or merely sharing what he had learned and practiced, but it aided me. We were a new command with no combat experience. What else could the division commander use to select the right brigade but to consider all the facts and judge the man who was to command. We would not be able to argue we were the best prepared, that would be the role of the division staff, but we could present our qualifications. Fulton and I had one thing in common. We had both played with the idea of being a lawyer in our pre-military days, and in this presentation, our brief was to be that of the advocate—not the judge. I was unaware that another brigade commander was already seeking the mission. What was most in our favor, and was emphasized in the briefing that was heavily influenced by Fulton, was that we were third in the heel-to-toe sequence of activation of the three maneuver brigades of the division. We had more, not much, but more, time left before we would deploy. Later, as we completed the briefing and left the office of the commanding general, I had the strong feeling that our brigade would be selected. It was largely because of the professional and energetic manner in which my commander had spoken, and his innovative ideas, well beyond the content of the concept papers the division staff had provided.

We were assigned the mission. My role as liaison for Riverine planning took me to Combat Developments Command (CDC) where I met Major Don Morelli, a man whom I later accompanied to San Diego, California. There we met with and discussed draft operational concepts and techniques with the officers of the United States Navy who were to staff River Flotilla One. That was to be the Navy side of the Mobile Riverine Force. Major Morelli was the action officer of the doctrine branch of CDC who had been charged by the Army staff to write a doctrine for Riverine Operations. Morelli was enthusiastic about the undertaking and openly spoke of his intent to work to be assigned to the 9th Division and hopefully to what we were now calling the Riverine Brigade. Don would later be my successor, twice removed, as the operations officer of the brigade in Vietnam, a tribute to his dedication to the mission and intimate knowledge of the historical background of Riverine warfare. His assignment was all the more remarkable in that he was an engineer officer, inserted in a long line of infantry officers. Still later, as a major general, I moved into the quarters at Fort Monroe where Don had only recently lived before he lost his battle to cancer. He had also been a major general. He and I, over time, shared the benefits of working for and great respect for two superb shapers of Army doctrine and organization—Generals Bill Richardson and Carl Vuono.

Don's energies led to the publication of the draft doctrine manual, FM (for Field Manual) 70-32, *Riverine Operations*, in 1967. Others played important roles in producing the manual, but it was mostly the work of Major Don Morelli.

Meanwhile the United States Marine Corps, whom I and others thought would have been the likely military service to join with the Navy in the Mekong Delta, came out with their own doctrine manual in 1967. Much later, the Army and Marine Corps cooperated in the production of a manual that kept the Marine Corps solidly in the Riverine game by doctrine. Other commitments and considerations in Vietnam kept them from pursuing the role of the ground element of the Mobile Riverine Force. The Marine Corps, however, responded with an officer of fine professionalism and joint thinking when Colonel Fulton asked for a Marine Liaison Officer to the Brigade. His name was Jim Turner, a lieutenant colonel, and he was a major help to the commanders and staffs of the Mobile Riverine Force, Army and Navy alike. Colonel Fulton joked, but with some acceptance of the truth of it, that Jim was on board to teach the Army how you get along with and hopefully get what we wanted from the Navy. If that was Colonel Turner's role, he accomplished it with such professionalism and good humor there were no feathers ruffled. I suspect that Jim offered just as much insight about the Army's peculiarities to the Navy Commodore as he offered knowledge of the Navy to the Army Brigade Commander.

How do I introduce Navy Captain Wade Wells, the Commodore, Commander of River Flotilla One? I first met him at Coronado, California, in January of 1967 when Colonel Fulton took his staff to meet with and conduct training discussions with the Commodore and his staff. But that is not the way for you to meet Captain Wade Wells. We have to jump ahead to the April 1967 period, and you must meet Captain Wells, the Commodore, in his short-sleeved, starched, white uniform, complete with walking shorts, strolling along the upper deck of his flagship, the APB Benewah. He is approaching the briefing deck on the fantail, an area shaded by an olive drab, vinyl awning, secured to support poles and the ship's railing by white, precisely knotted lines. He is coming to a briefing. Colonel Fulton is already there. All—except Colonel Fulton—rise as he approaches. But no one is looking at the commodore. Prancing smartly ahead of him are two miniature, one black and one tan, shorthaired Dachshunds—Linus and Lucy.

I imagine that scene now as a picture in a book, and the opposite page pictures the actor, Jimmy Cagney, watering his private miniature palm tree in a scene from the movie version of the play, "Mr. Roberts." At that point, in fairness to Captain Wells, the comparison ends. His competence and concern for his crew were at opposite ends of the spectrum from those depicted for the fictional, career-driven ship captain in "Mr. Roberts."

But as to the desired affect of the two tiny dogs, it may have well been to remind all that the Commodore was captain of his ship. Of course, the ship already had a captain. But when the command was underway to another anchorage for the flagship and associated boats, the commodore was commander of the entire Mobile Riverine Force. Keep the captain and the colonel in mind. Their association and relationship would be key to the success or failure of the Riverine operations in the Mekong Delta. We'll come back to them later.

Chapter Ten

A Place Called Dong Tam

The Mobile Riverine Force moved into Vietnam in pieces, largely determined by the timing of the equipping, or fitting out, of the boats, large and small, of River Assault Flotilla One. As it was, the infantry brigade deployed to Vietnam first, and the time was valuable in shaking out the units in relatively soft operational areas east and southeast of Saigon in the II Field Force area. In the Nhon Trach, we worked for the first time with the division's cavalry squadron. We banged around largely firm, dry ground, finding few Viet Cong (VC) but managing to lose our first soldier. Platoon Sergeant Claude Onley had been shot accidentally and killed by one of his own men. Onley was a fine infantry platoon sergeant whom I had watched in Kansas train his troops in the use of our Claymore mines. He had approached his listening post in darkness this first night in the field in Vietnam. The use of sign and countersign had not been enough to reassure a nervous young private. The sounds of movement were in the same direction as the correct reply, yet the raw soldier imagined it was Viet Cong.

Just the day before our first combat death, I watched for a few minutes a repeat telecast of the first American football Super Bowl in the small office of a Vietnamese District Chief. The walls were bamboo and the roof was thatch. I doubt the few Vietnamese militia and political figures in the room understood anything more than this was a big event in America. Carol and I were fans of the professional Baltimore Colts football team and their "Captain Who," Alex Hawkins, our South Charleston schoolmate. I had limited interest in the game and little time to linger. Obviously the Colts were not in that Super Bowl. Lombardi and the Green Bay Packers were, and they beat the Kansas City Chiefs. It had little meaning to me then, and no meaning a day later.

A few boats of a squadron of the River Flotilla became available for shakedown operations, and Fulton tapped our new battalion—3d Battalion,

60th Infantry—to begin the training with the Navy boats and their crews. In exchange for this battalion, we gave up 2nd Battalion, 47th Infantry, to 3d Brigade. Commanded by Lieutenant Colonel Bill Cronin, 2-47 would become a mechanized battalion, equipped with M-113 personnel carriers. 3-60th Infantry, commanded by Lieutenant Colonel Skip Chamberlain, was to play a central role in operations of the brigade in its first year in Vietnam. This was Clancy Matsuda's battalion, although I had not yet met him. Soon afterwards, Fulton chose Blackie Bolduc's 3d Battalion, 47th Infantry, to conduct the baptismal full-scale operations with the Navy. Both the squadron commander and Bolduc knew a great deal about the tides and difficult mud flats of the Rung Sat Special Zone (RSSZ) where the operations took place. Despite the advance knowledge, we found only a manufacturing site and antishipping and land mines, which we destroyed. A few of our leaders poorly sited company command posts that came under a foot of water at high tide, despite good predictions of tidal changes. A helicopter, supporting the operation and attempting to land, went into the main waterway that runs through the RSSZ, connecting the Yellow sea and the port of Saigon. We lost the crew.

In early March our brigade replaced the 3d Brigade headquarters at Dong Tam, where we joined the 3d Battalion, 60th Infantry. In those first weeks at Dong Tam, we had the task of marrying up our three infantry battalions with the few Navy craft available for training, while conducting modest operations in Dinh Tuong Province with the 3d Battalion, 60th Infantry, followed by the 3d Battalion, 47th Infantry. These latter operations were primarily to secure our base. During one of these modest operations, Colonel Fulton ended one of my briefings at a tented, field operations center west of Dong Tam to "chew me out" about the limited information in my briefing. I was surprised. And embarrassed. He rose to do that, turning his back to me. I quickly saw smiles on the face of our brigade executive officer and our personnel officer, Jimmy Smith. Fulton then turned to me, smiling, and promoted me to major. As Smith read the orders of promotion, I still felt the heat on my face. Perhaps it was because Fulton had chewed me out, in earnest and in private, just days before, but more about that later. This was not a reprimand, but a ruse to make me uncomfortable before giving me the good news. It worked. I don't know when the happiness overcame the discomfort, but it had by midnight, when I wrote Carol a short letter, telling her of my new rank. I would have liked for her to be there, and told her so. I did not know then, but at my next promotion, seven long years later, she would be at my side, as would our daughter, Lisa. The man pinning the other silver leaf on my dress uniform as Carol pinned one side would be Colonel Fulton, then a major general. He would make two ranks while I was gaining one. I spent by far more years as a major than in any other rank in my career. Time in rank, or grade, varies, based on many factors. Five years as a captain, seven years as a major, six years as a lieutenant colonel, only two years as a full colonel, four years as a brigadier general, two years as a major general and four years as a lieutenant general. But in early 1967, I was quite happy to be a major. Later, in my wildest dreams, I wanted to be a full colonel and command a brigade. In my commissioning as a lieutenant and in all promotions, Carol was there, except for two: to major in Vietnam and to full colonel in Korea. The promotions are milestones in a military career, second only to where we were living as a family as a means of recalling events in our lives and in the world around us.

Back to March '67 in Vietnam. The uniqueness of the Mobile Riverine Force was in the small watercraft, which could carry an infantry platoon or, with modifications made in the factory before shipment, provide fire support, command and communications, and minesweeping.

The Armored Troop Carrier, or ATC, manned by a Navy crew, transported an Army platoon of three dozen soldiers. Soldiers and sailors called them "Tango Boats." They were armed with .50 caliber machine guns, rapid-fire grenade launchers, and 20-millimeter canon. There were 26 of these in each of the two river squadrons that made up the River Assault Force, the tactical designation of Captain Wells' Flotilla.

Monitors, or Fire Support Boats, 5 in an assault force, were armed with .50 caliber machine guns, 40 and 20-millimeter (mm) guns, 40-mm grenade launchers and an 81-mm mortar.

The Command and Communications Boat, or CCB, was similarly armed as the Monitor, less the mortar, and equipped with an array of radios and antennae. It was used jointly for command and control by the Navy task group, formed from the River Assault Force, and an army battalion. Two or three such boats were in an Assault Force.

Minesweepers were ATCs equipped to detect waterborne mines. Over time, the Navy modified other ATCs as fuelers, aid boats with helicopter decks atop, flamethrowers, and high-powered water cannon that could break down sun-hardened earthen bunkers.

Assault Support Patrol Boat, or ASPB, was a boat of a different design, more sleek, and equipped with twin 12-cylinder diesel engines that gave it twice the speed of the ATC in its modified forms. This enabled us to use the ASPB much as an Army land scout vehicle. It provided security and fire support, front, flanks, and rear for a column of the slower, heavily armored boats on the move. It carried a machine gun and cannon, and was a welcomed addition although it did not join the MRF until late September.

Early operations using these craft in the Rung Sat were not a notable beginning, but not unlike those of other units of divisions new to operations in Vietnam. The initial operations were in areas of low VC threat because of the abbreviated train-up time common to most deploying units. Still, the incidents of friendly fire and accidents did occur. In our case, the cautious beginning did not preclude the loss of a good platoon sergeant or a helicopter crew.

The large benefit of a slow start was the developing of a degree of knowledge about and confidence between the Army and Navy components of the new force. There would be other accidents, but in time the force experienced impressive successes, for it came at the VC from a direction not commonly used by the forces of the Republic of Vietnam or United States Army. It came from the waterways, and as it did, it strangled the principal get-away method of the VC in the Delta—the sampan, an oriental canoe.

But it would be a while before enough of the command joined to launch large-scale operations. Meanwhile, in early March, the 2d Brigade relieved the 3d Brigade at Dong Tam, the emerging brigade base camp on the north bank of the My Tho River in Dinh Tuong Province. And emerging it was, slowly growing as sand dredged from the river was filling the rice paddies just west of My Tho City.

On our first orientation visit with the 3d Brigade Commander and his staff, Colonel Fulton's and my interest had been high on the vulnerability of the pipeline carrying the sand from the dredge ship to fill the rice paddies. It was only waterborne sand, but the schedule to complete the base as a support site for MRF operations depended on that flow. The VC had recently blown a section of the large pipeline through which the water and sand flowed, despite the efforts of our sister brigade to prevent such an attack. The dredge belonged to Brown and Root, a private contractor scooping the sand from the river at risk of life to their crew, both American and Vietnamese. I later learned something of the high pay scale of those American civilians compared to an Army sergeant or similar Navy grade. Years later, as I looked back on the Vietnam conflict, I saw few operational elements, military or civilian, as successful in their goal in Vietnam as that private company, seeking a handsome profit for its owners and investors. At that briefing, I concentrated on the essential role of the dredge. A private company had found men in civilian clothing ready to take the risk of running the dredge. Their contribution was impressive even considering the relatively high pay they received.

We set about revising, actually doing away with, the routine of the security guards. We put the infantry squads into unpredictable, varied surveillance techniques, using both electronics and human inspections of the dredge and pipeline that carried the sand. We used randomly dropped grenades and other explosives into the likely underwater approaches to the dredge and its line. The use of our own swimmers with some frequency reassured us. But still, weeks later, the VC, or their civilian supporters, blew the line again. This time our best reconstruction was that the Vietnamese employee of a contracted provider of produce for our mess halls had hidden the explosives, we knew not where—maybe in a couple of cabbages or a barrel of pickles. At any rate, we surmised he hid on the base when his truck left and, undetected, moved to the line at night by the route we least expected, the same walkway the crew and our security forces used. Fortunately, only the line and loss of time were casualties, but I felt no solace. It was an area that my boss had looked to me to provide the threat understanding that could ensure successful security operations by our troops. I vowed to do better, but I think the long-term lack of attacks that followed was more the result of the tireless and smart security troops than to any increased knowledge of the threat. We had always known we might be attacked from within, we just didn't believe we would. Once it happened, we did not have to be burned twice.

One outgrowth of the dredge attack was the notion to create our own network of spies to add to the security of Dong Tam. Colonel Fulton was enthusiastic about the endeavor. I took a long time to identify a key person, a Vietnamese, who could play the central role and manage a few source agents for us. It was hard to know where to go and whom to ask for help. After action reports for years in Vietnam told of compromised operations even as the ink was drying on plans and orders in the Army of Vietnam (ARVN) and political province and district headquarters. Through a trusted third party, we selected a central figure. I seldom saw him although I was the primary contact for him. The information he provided tended to confirm what we already had concluded about the towns and villages. Guarded by government militia and patrolled without incident by ARVN units by day, the villages were visited by Viet Cong with frequency at night. They collected taxes, and held village meetings of elders and instructed boys and girls to emplace mines or to turn our own Claymore Mines against us.

We were not getting the information we needed. An exception and our only clear success was an alert on the location of a VC mortar position that was to be occupied in the near future to fire on the base. Rather than visit the site, I asked our man to monitor and report, and I gave the artillery radar team, located at Dong Tam, information needed to scan the area at greater frequency. We did not prevent early rounds from falling inside the base, and although our artillery counter fire soon silenced their mortars, our man confirmed the VC had evacuated immediately after lobbing just three or four rounds. As far as he could tell, they took no casualties. Neither did we. It was a modest success only in the quick reaction of our artillery on a pre-registered site. A few weeks later one of our patrols found our man's body not too far from the west burm of Dong Tam. The VC had executed him. I wondered how his wife and new baby would get along now. We never learned the fate of the agents who worked for him. It would not be surprising that they were not harmed, but converted to double agency by the Viet Cong within days of being approached by our man at the beginning. I made no effort to reconstitute the abortive intelligence net. We continued to rely primarily on our own patrols, night ambushes, and information from the local militia and ARVN units to maintain security.

At times we received highly classified reports from Saigon of monitored radio communications of VC units long associated with operations in Dinh Tuong and Kien Hoa provinces. I visited the intelligence command in Saigon and set up a flow of information on such monitoring. Lieutenant Bob Reeves and I broke out our pattern analysis methodology and began to plot electronic reports of identifiable radio messages going back as much as a year. I found a specialist in aerial photography reading tons of photos in a dusty tent at division and gained his assignment to my S-2 shop. I knew that we had been, and were, operating on a shoestring, and some of our efforts had been amateurish to say the least. But now, laboriously plotting old and current electronic information on enemy communications, we sought to fix the location of temporary or long-term bases the VC had been and were using. Our concentration was on bases that were accessible from the matrix of waterways, rivers, streams and canals that cut through the hundreds of square miles or rice paddies and vegetation-cloaked banks of those waterways.

Maybe the failure of the dedicated, modest, human intelligence network around Dong Tam could be offset by successful use of communications intelligence. Maybe we could learn the places we wanted most to know— where were the Viet Cong when they were not ambushing or attacking ARVN or militia units or civilian produce trucks on Highway 4. I felt the pressure. We were close to going fully operational with the arrival of enough boats to put our brigade, less one infantry battalion, afloat. I needed to find solid information. The colonel had said I would tell him where to fight his brigade. Big words, and right then I had no better guess than the S-3 about where to launch an operation. And I was the S-2, the intelligence officer. I knew that Clyde Tate knew how to put together sound operations, but I also knew that

Bill Fulton was right. The best-trained brigade with the best of the United States Navy would still come up with dry holes and bad luck without timely and sound intelligence. I worked late with my three assistants into every night plotting the time and place of various categories of reported VC activities, based on their messages. I was mindful that information I used from the highly classified electronic intelligence had to be presented as if from some other, more routine, combination of sources and means of collection. This was to protect the means that our national intelligence collection community was employing.

Before the APB Benewah and accompanying support boats and tactical craft were to arrive at Dong Tam, there was the need to secure the Dong Tam base and eventual home anchorage of the MRF. That meant finding the Viet Cong by going into the jungles of Kien Hoa Province south of the My Tho River and into the rice paddies and swamp-like fields of grass north of the river. Highway 4 that ran east to west through most of Dinh Tuong Province was the most important land transportation route of the Mekong Delta. We would be running mostly land operations, relying heavily on helicopters and the cooperation of the ARVN 7th Infantry Division. That division had responsibility for two provinces in its area of operations and placed its headquarters in My Tho, a short distance from the slowly sprawling Dong Tam base.

We had a field hospital at Dong Tam, an impressive group of tent-like buildings with air-inflated walls that served as support as well as insulation for the air conditioning and barriers for the sanitized interiors. It was to be a life-saving facility for our soldiers in the coming months. One morning I noted in the daily report of the duty officer that a helicopter had made an emergency landing, an auto-rotation, just north of Dong Tam, and two officers had been admitted at the field hospital. One was a warrant officer; the other was my old friend, Captain Bill Maples, from my days at Fort Bragg. I visited him later in the day. After I said hello, I asked how he felt.

"John, they tell me I have no broken bones, but there's not a place in my body that doesn't feel all bruised up. Hurt like hell 'til they gave me some pain killer. Not bad now, but all I want to do is sleep." We talked about old friends and acquaintances in Special Forces and updated each other on what we had been doing in the past five years. We were both on our second tour in Vietnam and upbeat on how we were all doing, although I was getting impatient with our delays in getting the Mobile Riverine Force afloat and operating. Finally, I could tell that either Bill was fighting sleep, or his pain medicine was wearing off; so I told him to get well, said so long, and left. He was evacuated the next day to Saigon. I never saw him again, ever, although I know he went on to higher rank as a field grade officer. Such was the nature of the Army. Together for a while to share some training activity, or a few minutes rest from the field of combat, and then separated, never to see each other again. It is a mixed feeling to think back to the scores of men I knew in that way. Mixed in the good feeling and smile of shared fun, or pride in danger shared and remembered, or the sadness of the fate of some in the long years of conflict in Vietnam. My friend, Phillipe, the tiger, is a touchstone for me and all those faces and memories. I now keep a U. S. Army, Vietnam Veteran cap atop the tiger's head. It is black with bold, gold lettering and the Army eagle logo centered above the bill. I have seldom worn one of those, or any other outward display of my time in Vietnam. It is a matter of inward pride and regret with me. I need no display to others of what I remember and feel. I hope Phillipe doesn't mind the hat. He looks good in it.

By late April, we were coming to know better the officers and men of the 3d Battalion, 60th Infantry, the "Wild Ones." Another battalion that had trained under Colonel Fulton at Fort Riley, shipped with us and then passed to 3d Brigade. This unit, 2nd Battalion, 47th Infantry, was re-designated the 5th Battalion, 60th Infantry, Mechanized. The loss of the men of this unit had been hard felt in the Brigade headquarters. In April, we were saddened by the battlefield death of the commander. Lieutenant Colonel Bill Cronin. It may be that the impact of that death on our brigade commander and staff accentuated the fact that the 3d Battalion, 60th Infantry, commanded by Lieutenant Colonel Skip Chamberlain, had not trained with us or traveled with us to Vietnam. For some in that battalion, there was a question of just how this new brigade commander and staff knew enough to tell the more seasoned battalion how to operate. In my contacts with the battalion's intelligence and operations officers, I did not detect this attitude. But the suggestion seemed to emanate from our direct support Artillery battalion liaison officer and commander, whose unit had also been in Vietnam and operating in the Delta longer than any original unit of the 2nd Brigade.

Whatever questions may have existed between the newcomers and the old hands, they did not last long. We learned the target for our first major, two-battalion operation in cooperation with the 7th ARVN Division was Ap Bac 2, just north of Highway 4. We also learned we would be at the site of an earlier, significant engagement between the ARVN and the Viet Cong. It was in our version of the Battle of Ap Bac, May 2 and 3 of 1967, that our brigade truly became a "unit."

In planning for that operation, we were still on our land base at Dong Tam. It would be a month before we would move our headquarters aboard a large Navy boat. Dong Tam was new, coming more alive every day. It smelled new: the new canvas that covered the wood frames set over a wooden floor, the new sandbags that circled each "hut" to about three feet, and surrounded our bunker in the operations center. There was also the smell of brown sand from the bottom of the river and the stench of burning human waste that was pulled from beneath the seats of the enclosed toilets, doused with oil, and burned. That stench was always present and never overcome by any other aroma or smell. The toilets were on skids, pulled farther away from our sleeping and work huts as the sand base grew. We built the security bunkers also on skids—Fulton's idea—to move our security line out daily as the sand fill settled.

The ARVN 7th Division had a long history of conflict with the Viet Cong in Dinh Tuong Province. However, our review of ARVN operations over the last two years revealed little more than large walks in the sun or rides on the tides in sampans to discover a cache of weapons or a small operation that made mines. One such operation had been conducted just weeks before Fulton took his staff planning team to visit General Thanh, 7th ARVN division commander, and his staff. Our team consisted of Fulton, Major Tate, Major Dick Sharp, and me. It was not an encouraging session. However, we left with an agreement on an operation about 1 or 2 May. The objective was not to be set until a few days before by the General and Colonel Fulton, in coordination with the Senior Advisor to the ARVN Division Commander, a U. S. Army Colonel.

Just three days before the operation was to kick off, by General Thanh's preference, his senior advisor told Fulton the concept. Only the idea of getting Thanh to act allowed Fulton to accept the late notification and the limited involvement of his staff in the planning. However, once we learned the Vietnamese plan, we found there was no planning on what we would do, except to attack to the north from Highway 4 into the Ap Bac area. As it turned out, we had enough time. The Vietnamese division, while cooperating, would operate south of us and Highway 4. It was not lost on me that any enemy effort to evade or escape contact would be to our north, still farther north from Highway 4, not to the south. The area took its name from the small village on the southern edge. We would conduct essentially two, separate, land-locked operations and rely on dismounted, overland foot movement after deploying on Highway 4 in trucks and by helicopters. There were not yet enough Navy boats in the command to allow for movement by boat, even if enough waterways had existed. It appeared it would be an operation like the ARVN generally conducted in the overall area, although not often. In the specific area of Ap Bac, it would be the first in over four years. Principally, it would be a predictable entry into the area from the south by personnel carriers, trucks, and foot with limited helicopters. In short, despite the effort for secrecy, the enemy would see movement toward the operational area hours ahead of the attack. But, at least, Fulton's new U. S. Brigade in the

Mekong Delta had gotten the ARVN division commander to commit to a cooperative operation, even though the ARVN battalions would be operating in the relative safety south of Highway 4.

Dick Sharp and I agreed that the ease of enemy movement north and out of the area, especially at night, made blocking forces up there essential. The best way to get them there was by helicopters, far more helicopters than division had allocated. So Clyde Tate and Dick Sharp went to our 9th Division headquarters at Camp Bearcat, east of Saigon, and gained the promise of two full companies of "Huey" helicopters to help kick off the operation.

However, division withdrew half of those choppers the next day, the day prior to the operation, and we were left to try to get forces in the north by combined air shuttle and slow land movement. Fulton and Chamberlain decided to use Clancy Matsuda's Company A of the "Wild Ones" battalion to go deep by helicopter and set up the key blocking position essential to trapping most of the enemy in place—if they were there. The helicopters would later go to Bolduc to position one of his companies deep, farther to the east.

I did not see Bill Fulton in the time, which exceeded an hour, that we waited on the morning of our attack and worked contingencies as it appeared that even the one helicopter company would not show. In the operations center at Dong Tam, Dick Sharp and I fidgeted around and drank coffee. Over the tactical radio, you could hear that MacArthur-like baritone voice as Fulton leaned on Executive Officer Tom O'Connor to call on the landline and get more helicopters from division. In the brigade headquarters, we sensed we were the new kids on the block; that other brigades had the priority, and we were fast losing any claim to the remaining helicopters. Finally, the Division G3 himself told O'Connor there was a Tactical Emergency, a Tac-E, somewhere else in other divisions, and the helicopter support for us would be very limited, less than a company.

I did not envy the unflappable Tom O'Connor as he passed this word to Fulton on the Brigade command net. Masher 6 was Fulton's call sign, and he responded with an order that all his key commanders meet with him. There would be a "new" plan he said. Dick Sharp, the plans officer, looked at me. "I guess I won't be involved in that," he said. It is bad enough to see a plan go sour in execution, but it was worse still to see it unravel even before the execution began. I had worked closely with Dick on the plan, and we both believed it was sound—if we had the helicopters. I said as much to O'Connor who was in our operations center with us. I realized he could do no more. I turned to the map, revising my thoughts of the time it would take to move companies north on foot into blocking positions. I thought we would be pushing the VC out in front of us. They were not likely to stand and fight unless we could block their routes out. I turned to Dick, ready to share my estimate of movement times. He listened, smiled, and turned to top off his cup of coffee.

I went to the intelligence map on the wall where my enlisted assistant, Sergeant First Class Buckalew was recording a new number, 31, in red. He circled it with a red grease pencil and in the legend at the side of the map he wrote, "estimated fifty sampans-empty."

"Where did you get that?" I asked.

"From G2, but it's over twenty-four hours old."

"Yes," I said, "But it's a good sign. They could have moved a small battalion in with that many boats." He nodded in agreement.

"Plus," he added, "you have to think there are more up there, better camouflaged with fresh grass."

"What was the source for the report?" I asked

"They didn't say."

"Did you ask?"

"Sure."

Aerial reconnaissance, maybe, I thought. What kind of aerial vehicle, I wouldn't guess. I knew there was a capability, compartmented information, they called it, that might have seen the sampans. But we would never be told that. Some cover story about the sources would be employed. Giving no source was unusual. Probably very reliable, I thought. I looked at the location of the "31" Buck had written in. I walked over to Clyde Tate's operation map with multiple acetate covers. Each cover, or drop, held bold black and blue lines and multiple, circled numbers along tree lines, dikes, streams, and Highway 4. The 31 plotted out just three kilometers north of the location that Clancy Matsuda would have landed his company, if we had not lost the helicopter support.

Dick came back with a fresh cup of coffee, and one for me. "Thanks," I said.

"What have you got?" He asked. I told him about the sampans and the location where Matsuda's company would have landed.

"You know him? Matsuda?" He asked.

"No," I said, "But Chamberlain picked him for the air assault when Fulton asked for his best man, according to Clyde," I said. "You know him?"

"No." He sipped the coffee, touching the map where a tentative LZ had been greased in. "Hell, I don't know any of them," he said.

I shared the feeling. I felt far removed from the companies and battalions, and I knew that he did too. We both wanted to be a battalion S3. What good was it to be a major of infantry and not be an S3 of an infantry battalion—in combat? I wondered which of us would break out of the brigade staff first

104 Our Time in Vietnam

and get a battalion job. Dick was senior to me, but I had more experience in operations, but both at battle group and brigade level; not battalion. I had failed to get a battalion S3 job in Germany—got siphoned off at brigade level and never got out of there. Of course, I had been made the S3 as a captain in Germany when the major rotated back home, but that was brigade—just like this. I had worked with Dick for only three weeks. Basically, I had just met him, and I respected him. He was commissioned out of Officer Candidate School, a fact that gave him great pride, was Ranger qualified, and was ready to do all he could at brigade level until an opportunity at battalion opened up. He was two years older than I and had, like me, a son and a daughter. Later I would learn that Matsuda also had a son and a daughter. Our wives were Carol, Pat, and Connie. It would be months, even years, before each of us met the others' wives.

Dick had joined us at Dong Tam, and it was great to get him. Plans officer is a key role, and he was bright, thorough, and, most importantly, showed a common sense approach to everything. I liked him. I knew that Fulton did too, from their first meeting. He was easy to like: comfortable, good sense of humor, a good listener, and a fast learner. He wasted little time with any concept, zeroing in on the essentials.

Fulton's voice, Masher 6, boomed over the command net. Somebody… then I recalled the call sign—the artillery battalion commander, Skeeter Meek—had not yet arrived at the meeting place. Fulton sounded angry in a way I had never heard him. Not at Colonel Meek, really. He was probably seething at the poor support from Division. I felt left out. I knew Dick felt the same. It was frustrating. I knew I should be concentrating on the battlefield, mulling over all the information we had collected on the 514th Local Force Viet Cong Battalion. Should be making sure that Buck told me of every intel report that came in, before he wrote it on the map, or logged it into our journal. But I knew he tended to keep me well informed. He probably was going to tell me about the sampans, but I was talking with Major Sharp, and he would have told me just as soon as he made the journal entry. I was fretting. I didn't like to do that—ever.

What more was there to think about or mull over? I knew enough about the enemy battalion, except the most important—where was it right this minute? How was it set up on the ground?

I didn't know.

I wished I were out with a battalion, as the S3, or, if I were going to be here at brigade, out with Fulton as his S3. I would trade hats with Clyde Tate at the drop of a ….Damn, I needed to get back to work. I looked around. The operations center was dead. Men were standing or sitting motionless. There were a couple of radios squawking on low volume, and the assistant operations sergeant was talking, whispering, to someone on the telephone, his hand cupping the mouthpiece.

We were all waiting for the booming baritone voice on the command net. We were waiting for Fulton to tell us the new plan.

My thoughts ran to the U. S. Army Senior Adviser to the 7th ARVN Division Commander. He had spoken of the battle at Ap Bac that occurred six months before I had arrived in the Northern Highlands on my first tour in country. The Adviser, a full colonel, remarked that our attack, 2 May, would be four years and four months, to the day, since the big battle of 2 January 1963. I had heard talk of that battle at Fort Bragg in early '64, after my return from the Pleiku area and I had taken staff responsibility for training more A detachments for missions in Vietnam. Some debated whether the battle was a victory or defeat for the ARVN forces, which had been principally the 7th ARVN Division with some provincial and local units that were not under the control of the division commander. I recalled the loss of five American supporting helicopters, and the fact the Viet Cong had slipped away after both sides had lost many men, killed and wounded, although the numbers of wounded for the VC had been speculation. Around Smoke Bomb Hill, there was a consensus the battle was a defeat for the South Vietnamese, but the version pushed around the Pentagon and some conventional Army headquarters claimed it a victory for our Vietnamese allies.

I had noted the Senior Adviser to the 7th ARVN in the days before had not characterized the '63 battle as a loss or win. I suspected the suggestion for our operation, by the 7th ARVN Division commander, was in his mind linked to that earlier battle. A year later, at Fort Benning, I would learn the South Vietnamese losses in '63 were likely much higher than the VC losses. Three Americans died in the battle. The Viet Cong and the National Liberation Front of North Vietnam, had pronounced the battle as the first major defeat of the American sponsored, South Vietnamese forces, military and paramilitary.

I thought over our earlier plan, the one made unusable by the loss of helicopter support. In my intelligence estimate, I had identified the likely location of enemy bunkers that could afford the highest capability for resistance and likely routes of escape near the village. Fulton and Clyde Tate had decided to send Blackie Bolduc's 3d Battalion, 47th Infantry, straight into the objective area on the right and Chamberlain's battalion on the left, south to north. That plan had included two companies going to deep LZ's by helicopter and setting up blocking positions on the likely routes I had identified. We had monitored Fulton's adjustment of that plan to only a frontal attack with just Matsuda' company going deep by air.

Now we waited for the next revision. As it turned out, we in the operations center were unaware of the changes until the battalions were already executing Fulton's plan in the field. That we were slow in learning is not as important as the fact that Fulton, forward and on the ground with his commanders, was making things happen with direct consultations and orders. It was basic, simple battalion in the attack, as Clancy Matsuda would wind up teaching it at the Infantry School within a year. Or, brigade in the attack, as I would be teaching, alongside him, a few months later. But this was no academic exercise—especially for Clancy.

Fulton's new plan was classic brigade in the attack with two battalions on line. The line of departure (a control measure, mostly to make sure that supporting fires are timed to assist the attacking ground battalions at the right time) was Highway 4. As it turned out, it was Blackie Bolduc's battalion that made the costly first contact with the Viet Cong. He then held on to fix the enemy in place while Chamberlain's battalion, with Clancy Matsuda's company carrying the attack, assaulted and overran the enemy with major support by a mechanized infantry company.

It was rewarding to learn later the full role that Fulton played in planning and influencing that attack and final assault. He was tenacious. The attack would take place, and Fulton would pound the enemy with supporting artillery and Air Force close air support and then the assault by the infantry of his brigade. He was determined that no problem—and there were several— was to be allowed to preclude his attack, and it would be carried out before darkness, before the enemy could use the cover of night to escape American firepower.

I could have taken some satisfaction that Fulton's dogged determination that day was driven by his confidence the enemy was where I had told him they would be. And that I had told him they would attempt to apply as much damage to us as possible in the first few hours, even minutes, of contact, and then escape at night. He had been a good listener. As the battalions moved forward prior to Bolduc's contact, I began to think maybe the enemy was not there now, maybe had not been there at all in recent days. Fulton had decided that he needed intelligence to be successful on the battlefields of Vietnam, and he set out to gain the capability to acquire that intelligence months before at Fort Riley, Kansas. He had hammered me with the importance of intelligence, not the other way around. But on 2 May, Fulton, as leader and commander, knew only what I had told him about the enemy and acted with his own total awareness of "how to fight a brigade." I was like everyone else, a small but important player in his cast of players.

But as is always true with staff officers, I was not nearly as important a player as Clancy Matsuda and his infantrymen. Let us, finally, get to that.

Under the newest revision, Matsuda's company, which had been prepared to make the deep airmobile thrust to block the enemy, became relegated to battalion reserve. This meant ground movement by all available trucks to the area where Company A's two sister companies would begin their attack. Matsuda's company did not arrive in the reserve position until after the attack began. The two "Wild Ones" companies crossed the line of departure alone, because the 3d Battalion, 47th Infantry, could not be transported to the LD in time.

It was not a conspicuous beginning, but it introduced all of us to a commanding battlefield presence of an officer, who, while always imposing and assertive, we had seen only in the training and classroom environment: Big Bill.

The advance unfortunately required movement over several hundred yards of open, drained rice paddies. They were surrounded by dikes of various heights, a few quite high, and small, tree-laden banks of streams and irrigation canals. In the heart of the objective area lay an uncharacteristically wooded area along a pattern of streams. The lack of helicopter support and resulting truck movements delayed the movement north of Highway 4 by two hours. To compensate in part for the reduced mobility, a mechanized company equipped with M113 Armored Personnel Carriers, Company C, 5th Battalion, 60th Infantry, was placed under Skip Chamberlain. He sent it up the west, left, side of the attack to get into a position to block enemy forces trying to move out in that direction. Except for the streams and canals with deep banks in the area, the personnel carriers could move over the terrain with ease.

One of Bolduc's lead companies, Alpha, reported sniper fire well before noon, but had been unable to locate or eliminate it. I told Buck the shooting might be a couple of local VC, taking a shot and crawling away on the north side of one of the dikes designed to hold water that was now largely absent from the paddies. Still, reports from Bolduc of sniper fire persisted. Then came reports of some VC snipers being overrun and killed by infantry squads. This sounded to me more like a delay to permit other VC units, farther north, to get out of the area. But the land beyond the tree-lined streams near the village was mostly bare. It was going to be hard for them to get out, in daylight, without being seen by one of our command and control or fire support helicopters. I began to feel more encouraged that we would find the 514th at home.

After arriving at the departure location along Highway 4, Clancy Matsuda led his company north, staying behind the left, lead company of the battalion.

By half past noon, it looked as if the intelligence had been faulty, or any sizeable Viet Cong units had already moved out of the area. An artillery observer, the lone passenger in a small observation helicopter, was asked by our artillery liaison officer in the helicopter with Fulton and Tate, to look over the area of the reported sampans. He and the pilot could see no evidence of enemy presence or sampans in the area, or nearby.

We had relied heavily on the intelligence of the 7th ARVN Division, and I was beginning to think it mostly outdated. However, the sampans stayed on my mind. They may have moved in the night, or been hidden in the area, just off one of the two, parallel canals that diagonally ran out of the Ap Bac area into the southern edges of the Plain of Reeds.

In the operations center, the action involving Company A of Bolduc's battalion unfolded, it appeared, more slowly and with some confusion that later reviews of the action revealed. After advancing 1500 meters over rice paddies, Bolduc's left Company made heavy contact about 1300 hours. One of his advance squads drew flanking heavy machine gun fire from a weapon positioned to catch our soldiers as they took shelter up against a dike. The withering VC fire was right along the "friendly" side of the dike, and every member of the squad was soon a casualty. None would survive the battle, but the fight of the squad and other members of Company A and their sister Company B was to bring honor on the entire battalion. Along with Chamberlain's two companies on line, they held the Viet Cong in position while Chamberlain's other company, Clancy Matsuda's A Company, and the mechanized Charlie Company of the 5th Battalion, 60th Infantry, moved into a position of advantage. Clancy wound up to the right flank of the enemy defenses and forward of Chamberlain's other two companies and Bolduc's lead companies. From the time the squad of Company A of Bolduc's "Tiger" battalion made contact with the enemy, Bolduc called in supporting artillery fire that his forward leaders adjusted on the enemy behind the dikes. Still, in a violent exchange between the platoon, whose squad was pinned down and taking heavy casualties, and the VC, it was difficult to tell at brigade level the specific location of the enemy firing north of Bolduc's fight. Only a brief time elapsed, however, and Bolduc's advance squad was silent. Other members of the platoon became casualties in their efforts to support their fallen comrades. Chamberlain repositioned as best he could his two original attack companies so they could place their fires on the tree line, which he saw increasing their fires on Bolduc's lead platoon.

Colonel Bolduc's command group and the artillery forward observers kept up a steady barrage of artillery on the enemy position, and the brigade called Division for Air Force close air support. Well before all the supporting fires were adjusted onto the VC, the mechanized company made maximum use of the .50 caliber machine guns mounted atop each vehicle. Matsuda, likewise had shifted his company and oriented them to the east. He was hampered in moving east because of the location and fires of one of his sister companies, still oriented primarily to the north.

Fulton, early on, saw the potential for an envelopment of the enemy, using primarily Clancy's company and the mechanized company. But first, Fulton later explained, there had to be some sorting out and fire control measures put in place. In his mind, his attacking forces, Matsuda and Charlie Mech, would be coming across in front of other friendly units, and some units might converge. Over the years after the battle of 2 May, I sat often with Fulton and listened to his hard and well-learned lessons of how to use supporting artillery. "Keep it up close," he would say, "where you can see its effectiveness, and use any direct fire weapon, artillery or a tank, to knock out a single sniper. Snipers," he would say, "cannot be tolerated. You have to kill them and kill them quickly, or they undermine everything you need in a unit to fight effectively." He would be referring mostly to his World War II combat up the boot of Italy. But that was also his thought at Ap Bac. He saw the cal. .50 machine guns on top of the armored troop carriers of Charlie Mech as an answer to snipers. Before the attack was completed, Matsuda reported fragments of white phosphorous fired against the enemy falling close by and into his formation, "danger close" before he requested the fires to shift.

Some brigade commanders might have foregone that aggressive, time-consuming coordination to attack before darkness and held all units back and pounded the enemy with artillery and air right into and through the night. Such reaction was not uncommon in Vietnam. In that event, most of the Viet Cong would have infiltrated out during the darkness. That they did not in large numbers was reflected the next day by the large number of enemy bodies and the still hidden and unused sampans.

Bill Fulton willed the preparation for and coordinated assault that finally overran the Viet Cong defenses. He solved problems and brushed aside hesitancy that surfaced in his discussions with his commanders. He was of one thought: attack before dark.

We barely did so, but when we did, artillery and air firepower were being applied with greater precision. Also, supporting infantry fire from the south was hammering the enemy and being held up or adjusted to the east as Matsuda and the Mech company attacked. And markings for artillery support were, for the most part, adequately seen and understood.

Matsuda's company maneuvered into the assault position with the First Platoon on the right (east), the Second Platoon in the center, and the Third Platoon on the left (west). The First Platoon Leader, Lieutenant Joe Pilcher, reported the casualties of Bolduc's battalion adjacent to his sector. Charlie

Mech was deployed to the left (west) of Matsuda's company. Upon the command to assault, the supporting artillery, gunships, and air strikes were shifted to stop the VC effort to escape. Shortly after the commencement of the assault, the Third Platoon Leader of Clancey's company requested permission to pull back due to heavy automatic fire. Captain Matsuda denied his request and called for some of Charlie Mech's armored personnel carriers with their .50 caliber machine guns to be shifted east to support his rifle company. The strong firepower from the mechanized vehicles was instrumental in allowing the Third Platoon to continue the assault.

The First Platoon was held up by high caliber enemy machine gun and small arms fire from a cluster of bunkers in the tree line. These were the VC who had inflicted the heavy casualties on the soldiers of Bolduc's battalion. Two heroic soldiers spontaneously rushed the blazing bunkers. PFC Raymond Wright was armed with a M-16 rifle and grenades. The two soldiers mounted a large dike in full view of the enemy and charged, firing their weapons. Wright eliminated the enemy in the first bunker with a grenade. Keller then took the lead, and the two men alternated movements, closed with the enemy, and suppressed four bunkers. Lt Pilcher and the soldiers of First Platoon, inspired by the gallantry of Keller and Wright, successfully completed the assault under the excellent leadership of Lt Pilcher. Pilcher credited Keller and Wright for saving his life and the lives of the soldiers of First Platoon. He recommended Keller and Wright for the Congressional Medal of Honor (CMH) for their actions above and beyond the call of duty. Keller was promoted to Sergeant and Wright to Specialist First Class before the end of their tours of duty with the 9th Infantry Division. President Lyndon Johnson awarded Sergeant Keller and Specialist First Class Wright the CMH at an impressive ceremony at the White House on 18 September 1968. Matsuda's coolness and leadership in the battle were noted by both his battalion and brigade commanders.

Four events stand out for me after that battle. The first was a conversation between Fulton and me, sitting before a briefing map late that night. We were alone. He spoke of the thirteen men reported killed in Bolduc's battalion. He faulted himself for not using more "reconnaissance by fire" by artillery and gunships into the enemy position as his two battalions moved forward. Years later I listened to him speak of the use of that technique as he "fought his rifle company" up along the Italian ridgelines in World War II. He once told me that his regiment went through thirteen company commanders during the months he commanded his company. I learned how he had taken great pride in his leaders for their taking of objectives with minimal losses of men, compared to the overall regimental experience. But I had heard none of that at this point at Ap Bac, and I hurt for him as his eyes glistened with tears. I found myself consoling him. Me, who had never led more than a handful of special operations, or more precisely, counterinsurgency soldiers, advising and leading a small Vietnamese battalion. I have felt a little embarrassment over the years thinking back to my reminding him that casualties are going to come in offensive warfare. But even then, I could not bring myself to say anything about the number of our men killed. I knew that one was too many. Several years later when I felt free to raise that specific with him, he immediately thanked me for my words of comfort back there at Ap Bac. But I knew, what he was thanking me for was just being there and listening. I have long since decided that my clumsy effort was presumptions, and it is a comment on his professionalism and humaneness that he received what I said with such consideration for me, both at the time and years later.

The second recollection is my failure in policing the count of enemy killed. I had, with Fulton's strong support, set some hard rules to avoid our falling into a body count mentality that would cause us to lose our way by inflating those counts. During the battle and well after nightfall, my assistant, Buck, and I went over the reports of enemy killed and weapons captured, trying to avoid the count of the same bodies or weapons by two different units. Sometime near midnight, I went down for three hours sleep. After Sgt Buckalew woke me and I went back into the tent of our hastily thrown up forward tactical operations center, I was surprised at and questioned the count of enemy dead. It was double what the count had been just three hours earlier. Finally, Buck told me I should talk to Tom O'Connor, the brigade executive officer, if I was "upset" with the count. O'Connor, and Fulton, knew I would be upset. The short of the story was that, while I was asleep, a "general officer from higher headquarters" visited us and directed the doubling of the count. He said he believed our constraints on our count were unrealistic. Obviously, I have never forgotten that. That one incident immediately disarmed me when I was later back home in the states and talking with people like my much admired high school history teacher who asked me about the integrity of the military reporting on the war. She meant more than only body count, but in a way, I came to view the inflated body count as symptomatic of other ills in that conflict. It was, I believe, symbolic of other reports, projections, and predictions, even promises, based on wishful thinking and, worse, the apparent need to resort to unethical claims to gain support for a mission we still believed in. In other words, or more general terms, using the means of exaggerated claims to gain a good and honorable end—victory in Vietnam. At a point, we were to see finally the body count was a symptom of an effort that could not gain success by military victories alone.

The third recollection is one of pure professionalism: the pride of Lieutenant Colonel Skip Chamberlain as he stood before the assembled leadership and recapped the decisions and orders of his battalion. The Battle of Ap Bac buried any reservations about his battalion and, I believe, about any part of the force involved. The casualties, friend and foe in the battle, were quite uneven, even if one cuts, which I do, the enemy losses in half. But, even now, one strong recollection comes to mind about the Battle of Ap Bac 2. We lost thirteen good men. One of them, PFC William Fesken, of Bolduc's Alfa Company, was later awarded, posthumously, the Distinguished Service Cross.

And the fourth, my and Dick Sharp's friend, Clancy, commander of the lead attacking company of his "Wild Ones" battalion, sitting on that log and calmly covering his actions and orders in the attack. He rose but once; when he spoke of the valor of his two soldiers who had attacked and overcome several enemy bunkers, leading to a successful overall company attack. The two men earned the Medal of Honor later awarded. Their commander, Captain Clarence "Clancy" Matsuda, would depart the battalion and brigade shortly after the battle, hand-picked to command the 9th Infantry Division's Long Range Reconnaissance Company.

The Battle of Ap Bac was the first major operation in the Dinh Tuong region joining the efforts of the U. S. Army and the ARVN 7th Division. It was a classic success of the coordinated attack, meshing supporting preparatory fires and infantry maneuver, both mounted and dismounted. We had been blooded. We had fought far from the streams and rivers in which brigade elements would fight over the next couple of years. But it was a major step in preparing the 2nd Brigade for its role with the Riverine Assault Flotilla of Captain Wade Wells. For me, it was my first witnessing of the drive and determination, under fire, that no doubt "Big Bill" Fulton had developed and demonstrated on the boot of Italy nearly twenty-five years earlier. He showed it to us anew at Ap Bac 2.

Chapter Eleven

Cooperation and Coordination

When they refurbished the Benewah from a landing ship for tanks and heavy equipment to a Mobile Riverine Force APB command ship with accommodations for an Army Brigade and a Navy Flotilla headquarters, no facility on board was more important than the combined office and staterooms of the Navy Commodore and the Army Colonel. This was where the two men would sleep, relax and, most importantly, size up one another.

The Joint Staff in the Pentagon had made that sizing up a necessary and critical process, because they had failed to agree to make this Mobile Riverine Force a joint headquarters and joint command. That is, they had decided not to cite the command as one that would be guided by the established rules of how the forces of two military services—the Army and the Navy—would do everything together—joint operations. The Mobile Riverine Force, MRF, was not a joint force. Instead, they wrote that the command relationship would be one of cooperation and coordination. That meant, the two Services would get along just about as well as the two commanders did, and further, how they agreed for their subordinates to cooperate and coordinate. Complicating this was the Navy-driven decision during our shared training at Coronado, California, not to recognize the Army manual forged by Don Morelli as doctrine for how we would operate. Informally, Captain Chuck Black, Wells' operations officer, acknowledged the manual as a starting point from which we could build the operational techniques that we would make, in practice, the American doctrine for Riverine Operations. "Riverine," a word that still exists only in dictionaries of the military.

On the Benewah, each commander, Wells and Fulton, had his own private stateroom, with a large, for a boat or ship, common area between them featuring a big, round table. It was that table that was to be the site of the Battle of the Services, the surface on which pictures would be examined,

staff proposals read, maps interpreted, and fists pounded, figuratively, if need
be to gain agreement. The two men, the two commanders, were veterans of
their Services. The colonel was a combat veteran of World War II, a seasoned
company commander who had led and won battles and lost men all the way
up the Italian boot, a member of Douglas MacArthur's staff in Japan in
the Korean War, a seasoned, and not unscarred, warrior of the halls of the
Pentagon, and a reflective member of the faculty of the Army War College
just months before assuming command of his brigade. And he was a big man,
so tall that the bunk in his stateroom had to be remade and lengthened to
accommodate his tall, fit frame. He could tower over most every man he had
ever met, but he had worked for men whose stature lay not in height, but in
mental capacity, stamina, determination, imagination, and the ability to read,
and if necessary, to massage and entice other men to accomplish an Army
task. He was a highly respected Army leader with a shot at someday being a
general officer. But, his reputation was that he would get said what ought to
be said, and he would do what he ought to do. For some, it was known that
such an officer sometimes said or did what ought to be to the wrong boss
who was unmoved by the correctness of judgment, only its agreement with
his own preconceived notions.

The Navy captain, the commodore, might well fit the Old Salt tradition of
the Navy. He had served in World War II also and all over the Navy, mostly
in the ships of the fleet that get the dirty work done, the tasks that someone
had to do and had to do right or the aircraft launching carriers, the old
battleships, or the sleek submarines would go dead in the water, unsecured,
unfueled, unarmed, and unfed. It may be that he held no aspirations for flag
rank; possibly had at one time, but no longer did so. It was clear that whatever
the purpose of the Navy in naming him as commodore, he was not a man
who would compromise the integrity of his ships or his men. He was not a
man who would give in easily, maybe even one of those who enjoyed a fight,
encouraging the impression that he would never give an inch, when all along
he planned to give eventually, a little, but only in exchange for a lot.

Early meetings of the two men in Coronado, California, before the
force was joined, left some of us wary that the two men would—could—
give enough to make the command work smoothly. We, the staff members,
thought each man was quite proud and quite aware of the ground on which he
stood. And there were points at issue, sometimes seeming to spring up more
quickly in formal meetings where little was intended to be discussed, but each
man displaying readiness to assert the needs peculiar to his command, to his
Military Service. I think now that some of us younger officers who had not
yet witnessed the infighting in the Pentagon, the maneuvers between crusty
old colonels on war college staffs, and most importantly, the performance of

duty by such men as our colonel and commodore under the expectations of flag officers, were overly concerned. While the officers of the Joint Staff and the military services they represented had been unable to agree on a joint command, the service component commanders in Vietnam made it quite clear to each of our two leaders. You will cooperate and coordinate in whatever ways you devise, but you will do so, and you will be successful in your operations in the Mekong Delta against the Viet Cong forces, regular and guerrilla.

Still, how it played out between Bill Fulton and Wade Wells was a human story well worth watching and being a small part of the performance. It was a game, but a very serious game. At stake was the life of a sailor, pulled into unsafe waters by an Army operational concept foreign to the Navy way of mission accomplishment and welfare of crew, or the life of an Army soldier, put ashore one terrain feature too far east, not on the flank of, but looking head into a Viet Cong bunker, deadly manned and ready. Probably it was the Navy that was asked more to sail into uncharted waters. The Army troops would feel the tension, the dry mouth, as an armored troop carrier, a Navy boat, slowed to enter a small waterway, and then rammed the bank, lowering the ramp to expose the troops and the Navy crew to whatever the enemy had to offer. But for the soldier, this was akin to feeling the flying helicopter slow, hover and drop to let troops jump the one or two feet to hard dikes between or the soft, wet mud of rice paddies, waiting for the crack of rifle or machine gun rounds passing through the air to accentuate the screaming engines of the aircraft. The Navy assault boats were also a means of closing with the enemy, simply by a different mode of transportation.

For the Navy crewmen aboard the assault boats, this was not the norm for carrying the war to the enemy. Technology had long since allowed increasing standoff distances between Navy boat or ship and the enemy. The Navy had come to pride itself in protecting sailors from the cruelty of a neutral sea and the reach of enemy fire. But there was precedent for such small boat operations by the United States Navy, and sailor and soldier had been told about, and some had studied, the operations of Naval gunboats in the American Civil War, China, and Latin America in the early twentieth century. Still, the armament on the Naval boats, .50 caliber machine guns, 40 millimeter automatic rocket fire, had range and could permit the boats to stand off from the enemy and still support troops ashore. That is, except when they had to ram the shore to land or pick up soldiers. From the beginning, it was clear that an Army leader, platoon, company, battalion, or brigade, would need to offer good justification for a Navy boat to cruise up a small stream and put bow to bank in support of Army troop transfers. Such landings should take place not where the enemy was, but where they were not, and only after the bank had been prepared by boat fire, or artillery, or helicopter machine gun or rocket fire. There was no room for a rapid run up a river to gain surprise on an enemy. Such a route only made the Naval craft a target itself to a single or several Viet Cong hiding in the jungle canopy along the stream. Enemy recoilless rocket launcher or other weapon designed to kill an Army tank were fully capable of creating mass casualties in a boat with shrapnel or sinking the boat with a shot at the water line. From the beginning, the task fell to the Army commander to explain and justify why a Naval boat had to be taken into harms way. There was no hesitancy on the part of the Navy to do what was proper, prudent, and brave. There simply was a need to understand why the Army so easily accepted concepts that took men and craft into the range of enemy fire so quickly and brashly when there were other means, particularly helicopter, to gain more information on the location of the enemy and to avoid surprise by the enemy.

Out of all this there came, over time, a set of tactics and drills designed to deliver and deposit the Army troops with Naval assault craft, and to support the operations ashore with fires, medical aid and evacuation, and repositioning of ground forces. These tactics were judiciously applied with great prior knowledge of Viet Cong weaponry, tendencies, and vulnerabilities, and knowledge of the width, depth, and tidal flow of the waterways, the foliage ashore, and the interoperability with artillery within range and helicopter and high performance aircraft support.

Beyond what the two commanders had learned of their sister Service over the span of a military career, Wells and Fulton learned from each other, and out of this new understanding came the commodore's agreement to try the landing of helicopters on small assault craft, his suggestion that barges, AMMI barges, be pulled alongside the larger ships of the flotilla to accommodate gangways that eliminated the need to climb and descend rope ladders, his gradual allowance of authority to pass down to squadron commanders to determine the small waterways they would allow their boats to navigate, and his acceptance of a tempo of operations that initially he found unnecessarily too fast and unacceptable. But the commodore also educated the colonel on the soundness of the rotation of his assault craft through a cycle of operations, maintenance, and rest and recuperation. This cycle came to be adjusted at times, but for the most part, one third of the assault craft were routinely not available for daily operations, roughly a concept the entire U. S. Navy had learned during years of experience on the oceans—and rivers—of the world.

Bill Fulton and Wade Wells would years later acknowledge that what each gained of most value from their year of professional cooperation and coordination was their unusually close and perpetual friendship.

The story of the MRF during my year with it in Vietnam is told in the book, *Riverine Operations*, one of the Vietnamese Studies chartered by General Westmoreland in 1972 while he was Army Chief of Staff in the Pentagon. I was working there at the time for then Major General William B. Fulton, who was asked by Westmoreland to do a study on that subject. Fulton asked for my assistance in the research and drafting, which I did, along with input from many people, but particularly by Colonel "Blackie" Bolduc and his wife, Mary, who wrote the Background chapter. I am partial to the manner in which the story is told in that book, and will not retell it here in the same comprehensive or detailed manner. Further, there are other publications, particularly written by our Navy comrades, which tell the story with greater insight into the unique operations that our brown water Navy was asked to do, and did with gallantry and great success.

No operations, however, better depict the changes in the confidence with which we employed the MRF and in the Viet Cong tactical response to the force than those conducted in May and September of 1967 near and on the Rach Ba Rai River and Canal, or the Ba Rai River. Those two operations closed the loop for Dick Sharp and me. While in the May operation, I was the brigade intelligence officer and Dick was the plans officer, in the September operation, I was the operations officer at brigade level and he was the operations officer in the lead battalion that led our attack up the Rach Ba Rai. The September operation also brought Bill Fulton, the colonel and brigade commander in May, back to the MRF as the tactical boss of our new brigade commander, Colonel Bert David. The return visit by Brigadier Fulton was to remind me of his assertive leadership in the fog of battle, this time, heightened by low-lying clouds and radios unattended by commanders and staff officers fighting for their lives.

But let me tell you the happenings of the months that led to that battle of September 1967, the one that took place under the Cloud Above Snoopy's Nose.

The Ba Rai River, or, as the Vietnamese call it, the Rach Ba Rai, lay some sixteen kilometers west of Dong Tam and slightly farther from My Tho City. It meandered south to enter the My Tho River and, at a point four kilometers from the river, made a skewed-horseshoe turn to the east, curved slowly, and then swung back west; then south again, reminiscent of the linear outline of the nose in the Peanuts comic strip of Snoopy, the dog. The Navy Flotilla intelligence officer, Clyde Smith, came to refer to the geography of the stream as "Snoopy's Nose." Dick Sharp laughed easily and enjoyed the name when I told him of Clyde's reference. Dick joined in making it forever the name applied to the signature terrain feature in the target area of an operation suggested again by General Thanh for mid-May.

Chapter Twelve

Rach Ba Rai

When Dick Sharp and I had sat, looking over the map of the Rach Ba Rai, just after the Ap Bac 2 battle, the terrain was covered with clear plastic and red grease pencil markings. Our principal challenge was to decide what to make of the intelligence the markings depicted, provided by General Thanh's intelligence officer. My little Intel team was hard-pressed to meet the intelligence needs for planning for a force with the scope of movement and fighting that the MRF possessed. Later, even with the staff of Navy Lieutenant Commander Clyde Smith, we were a small group. As we pulled together what we knew about the Kien Hoa and Dinh Tuong Province areas, each of us was operating as if we were at a level two echelons above an Army Brigade. I still had Buckalew and Bob Reeves, who had come on board back at Fort Riley. We had added a photo interpreter specialist from the 9th Division staff at Camp Bear Cat. Together, and over time, we had plotted the individual ARVN reports of VC actions or sightings in the two provinces. We had not yet developed our steady flow of secretive raw material from the Combined Intelligence Center in Saigon. We would eventually lay out the raw reports of radio emanations by the Viet Cong and include them in our pattern analyses in late August.

The targeted area had gained some notoriety as a place in which the VC were reported to visit often, and the 7th ARVN Division did not visit at all. It was called the Cam Son Secret Zone. The unit most often rumored to be in the area was the Viet Cong 263d Main Force Battalion. Less often reported to visit the area was the Local Force 214th VC Battalion. I saw the lack of operations into the Cam Son as a reflection of ARVN commanders' survival depending as much on their avoidance of loss of men and weapons to the Viet Cong as the damage they did to the enemy.

Thanh's people could not tell us where in Cam Son we would most likely find the 263d. But they told us if we turned north into the Rach Ba Rai or the nearby Rach Tra Tan, we'd find Viet Cong. As Dick Sharp and I looked at the pattern of red marks, two areas stood out. The most dots fell heavily along the north shore of the Mekong River where the Rach Ba Rai and Rach Tra Tan entered the larger river. Another area of lesser, but significant, reports lay about six kilometers north of the My Tho and sat astride the Rach Ba Rai north of Snoopy's Nose. General Thanh showed confidence that we would make contact in the southern area near the My Tho when Fulton, Clyde Tate, and I had visited him to explore another operation following Ap Bac. I found it questionable that a VC commander would position an entire battalion, or even two companies, up against the My Tho River. On our way back to our base at Dong Tam, our discussion moved Fulton to go ahead and plan to hit the southern area. I reluctantly agreed. It was wise, not because it offered the biggest prize in terms of the size VC force we might find, for I thought the northern area more likely to do that, but I did recognize the uncertainties that still existed about how far up the streams Captain Wade Wells would send his boats. Equally strong with me was the question of how hard Colonel Fulton, at this early point in our organization and cooperation, would push him. Besides, I thought the caution wise until our boat crews and rifle platoons saw how one another would react to enemy fire.

The likely routes of escape by VC units found in the southern area depended on the principal direction from which they were attacked. Simply put, an attack from only one direction by a large force predictably causes an enemy to move in more or less the opposite direction, much as a person forces toothpaste from a tube. However, a land approach from the north would trap the VC up against the River, reason enough for me to doubt that we would find the VC there in strength when we attacked only from the My Tho River. Still, VC forces in Cam Son were likely to anticipate an attack, if one came, by ARVN ground forces using mechanized vehicles south from Highway 4. In that event their likely escape routes, I thought, would be to the west and then northwest. I shared General Thanh's view that our riverine attack from the water would likely surprise any VC in the area, and that they would flee to the north, but he emphasized their likely movement to the northeast and east. It seemed to me they would move toward the area that reports suggested they were often present, up the stream and north of Snoopy's Nose. As it turned out, it was likely where the enemy moved would not make a great deal of difference when we learned Thanh was not prepared to commit significant forces in the operation and few helicopters were to be available from our division. In the area north of Snoopy's nose, local villagers told the ARVN division soldiers there were earthen bunkers along the banks of the stream. A truly successful operation targeting the southern area from the river would require us at the start to position a force, preferably by airmobile means, to block their escape, quite likely north of the area above Snoopy's Nose. Without adequate air, we would have only the options of movement of watercraft up one or both of the streams, or movement of a land force in from the north. The land movement from the north would require their deployment by road along Highway 4 and could consume considerable time, allowing the VC to escape, I thought, to the west.

In a follow-up discussion, the planners at the ARVN division still showed no willingness to discuss the insertion of their battalions as a blocking force from the north, but spoke of a Vietnamese Ranger battalion that might be available, but only after we made good contact. Fulton seemed to judge that Wade Wells was not ready to run our watercraft far up the two streams. The N2 pointed out to me that we did not know much about the navigability of either stream beyond one or two kilometers. Finally, our inquiries again indicated no likelihood that our tentative operation would draw enough priority to get more than a few helicopter gun ships from our division. As Dick and I prepared a scheme of maneuver into the southern area only, I did not have high confidence that we would make major contact. Maybe some security forces that would fade back into the vegetation along the stream banks, or, maybe no contact at all, despite the words of General Thanh.

When we briefed him, Fulton listened closely and asked us to leave the map with him. The next day, Captain Chuck Black told us the Commodore had agreed, in principle, to the location for our operation. But first, we needed to work more formally and in detail with Wells' staff alongside our Army brigade staff. We had been coordinating informally with both the Flotilla intelligence and operations people, based on discussions of such cooperative efforts at Coronado months before. However, this would be the first real test of the cooperation of the two staffs. It would test the rather unusual relationship between our Colonel and our Commodore, and how they had guided us.

The plan was simple, and cautious. Following the limited intelligence I had developed, the operation was much like a reconnaissance in force, moving forward on a front with two battalions landed from the big river, and retaining company-size reserves to respond to contacts. Further, as Fulton had taught us in the staff studies back at Fort Riley, we identified, circled, and numbered significant terrain, such as junctures of streams and canals, and heavy concentrations of grassy and wooded areas. It was a system that cluttered a map overlay, but offered flexible naming of movement and attack objectives. Further, it provided points of reference to report locations, based on the distance from one or more of the circled numbers.

The planning by the two staffs, working together, went smoothly, thanks largely to the professional and friendly relationship between Major Tate and Navy Captain Chuck Black. Black and I shared a stateroom during my time on the Benewah. He was a steady professional, and I have often thought of him over the years with great respect. It was Clyde and Chuck who carried out the tone set by our top commanders. Clyde set a high standard, and I tried to meet that standard when I later replaced him as the operations officer.

We finally kicked the operation off just after 0800 on the morning of 15 May. We welcomed Guy Tutwiler's battalion, the 4th of the 47th Infantry, on board. He had been the last to take his battalion through the riverine training in the Rung Sat Special Zone, and he was itching to get into some action and prove his battalion. Our plan landed Tutwiler's battalion on the right, two companies landing at the mouth of the Rach Tra Tan. Bolduc landed his lead companies less than three kilometers to the west at the mouth of the Rach Ba Rai. The two battalions were close enough to move quickly to the assistance of each other. Both battalions used helicopter gun ships to scout the banks to the north. The flexibility of the command lay in the reserve companies in each battalion, supporting artillery, gun ships, and the reconnaissance platoon of Bolduc's battalion. Fulton pulled the platoon under brigade control, mainly as a means to respond to possible contacts on the flanks.

Tutwiler's third company was waiting beside a few helicopters at Dong Tam, prepared to shuttle into the area as needed, hopefully to intercept VC trying to escape.

About 1400 Tutwiler contacted a VC force that fired on his men with small arms, machine guns, and rocket launchers. He returned fire and advanced slowly. It appeared to members of one of his companies the VC were going north along the west bank of the Rach Tra Tan. Tutwiler then shuttled his other company in by helicopters and landed it to the north, west of the Rach Tra Tan. He placed the unit far enough north to intercept the VC, but close enough to reduce the enemy maneuver, either to the east, across the stream, or to the west. Under Fulton's operational control, Bolduc's recon platoon, led by Lieutenant Howard Kirk, preceded the 4th Battalion up the Rach Tra Tan in a Navy ATC supported by a Fire Support Boat. If this was Fulton's effort to push Wade Wells, in getting boats up the small stream, the Navy Squadron Commander did not hesitate. He sent the boats into the small waterway, but the low tide and the firing of a couple of rocket launchers by the VC caused the boat captains to turn back. Kirk's platoon was put briefly ashore and then recovered as the boats prepared to turn south. . Kirk made no contact, but penetrated less than a hundred yards from the bank of the stream before needing to return to the assault craft.

Tutwiler's eastern company reported sounds from the waterway indicating some enemy were crossing the stream to the east, but they could not determine precisely where or in what strength the enemy were, and observation helicopters were unable to find them . Movement to the bank of the stream by infantry resulted in no sightings and no contact. Shortly afterwards, the company Tutwiler had flown in contacted the enemy while moving south, closing on Tutwiler's other two companies. The fighting was light. We had a chance to trap the enemy between the companies of the 4th Battalion and the bank of the river. However, in jungle, I knew the Viet Cong did not require much space, often going to ground on all fours and literally "loping" out of danger. I feared they were doing this, but not to the northeast and the vulnerable crossing of the stream, but to the northwest, toward the Rach Ba Rai.

But Bolduc's battalion was to the west. They should make contact, I thought, with any sizable movement from VC forced west by Tutwiler. However, over the next two hours, they made no contact. Fulton ordered Bolduc to move one of his companies by helicopter to the right, or east, of Tutwiler's battalion, across the Rach Tra Tan to search the area where earlier crossings of the Rach Tra Tan were suspected and the direction General Thanh thought the enemy would try to flee. Tutwiler took operational control of Bolduc's company once the company commander reported his helicopter landings complete. By nightfall, this company's search was unable to contact VC soldiers east of the Rach Tra Tan.

The MRF took few superficial wounds, most from the VC RPG fire in Tutwiler's initial contact while our troops were still on board the ATCs. But the impact of fragmenting rockets launched at the ATCs in the Rach Tra Tan was enough to be on the minds of most of the men in the boats on the way back to base two days later. The number of recovered VC bodies was small, and introduced the continuing speculation the VC disposed of their killed soldiers in temporary graves in the waters of the Delta. The few bodies recovered from the water caused speculation there were more that we could not find. The murky waters and the tendency to expect more enemy casualties from your firepower than is generally the case led our platoons and companies to begin estimating body count as well as viewed bodies counted. My view was that we had contacted no more than a security element and that we might have killed most or all of them.

Later back at Dong Tam, sitting at a table with Bob Reeves, and our two enlisted specialists, I listened to their views on where they thought the Viet Cong had been and where they went once we made contact. There was no consensus. Also, we had no way of estimating the size of the VC unit we had contacted. I thought it obvious that we had not found any significant size force. I looked at the tip of Snoopy's nose, the round salient that protruded to the east based on the arcing flow of the stream to the south. I thought my earlier ideas on the likely route of escape by the Viet Cong might have been correct. Once Tutwiler's battalion contacted the enemy and reports came in suggesting the VC were trying to flee to the east and cross the Rach Tra Tan, Bolduc's battalion had slowed the move up the Rach Ba Rai. He then provided a company to airmobile all the way to the eastern bank of the Rach Tra Tan. That was the way we were thinking in the brigade operations center, based on the reports of the eastern company of Tutwiler's battalion.

I wondered if that noise—splashing of water—had been a distraction by the VC, as they in fact moved west and northwest. I knew I was invoking my experience in small unit operations in the Vietnam Highlands three years earlier. We were looking for bigger targets. The investment in the Mobile Riverine Force called out for finding and destroying significant Viet Cong forces. When we did, I knew, there would be little need to speculate on their strength and movement. But first, we needed better intelligence, and we had to be ready to throw our unique capability against the enemy.

The day following our contact Bolduc's battalion had confirmed reports of bunkers north of Snoopy's Nose, some large, new bunkers on both sides of the stream. I did not mention to my people at the time that I had done poorly in meeting Fulton's expectations on this, our first riverine operation. I had provided little precise information to target the brigade operation, and then, during the operation, I uncovered nothing to indicate the VC strength or if they were escaping to the east or west. I thought they had gone west and then up the banks of the Rach Ba Rai. But, I did not really know, and it was of little help now.

I did, however, think that if we were to go back into the Cam Son again, I would recommend we hit the Rach Ba Rai and go deep, beyond Snoopy's Nose, and fast. Use the unique watercraft capability of the MRF to put the cap on the escape route from the start. That was not the job of the intelligence officer, to fashion the scheme of maneuver of friendly forces. But Dick Sharp and I had quickly formed a working style that stood on no formalities of staff responsibilities or authorities. But to push such a plan, we had to be ready to go up those narrow streams and we needed the lift helicopters to react to contact quickly. Rapid attack into a likely enemy was a proven tactic, the attacking force gaining enhanced security by the speed and audacity of their forward progress. It was a risky maneuver, but the speed of movement and our great firepower would provide much added security. But, before we could do that, the commanders of the River Squadrons, or Rivrons, like Lieutenant Commanders Horowitz and Rhodes, would have to assure themselves of the navigability of streams and the survivability of their craft. There was valid concern about the recoilless rockets and RPG attacks. We would need to gain confidence in our boats and in our use of our weapons. It was something we would do over the next four months, but there would be casualties, and Horowitz would be one of the wounded in that learning process.

I knew that confidence could only come with better intelligence about the waterways: tidal affects, turning spaces, draft clearance and from more operational experience by the entire command. I talked to Lieutenant Commander Clyde Smith and suggested we get the photos and do some precise measurement of stream and canal widths. My specialist who I had stolen from the 9th Division Photo Interpretation Cell could do much of that. It had not been hard to steal him away. He was untidy, smoked constantly, hardly a military bone in his body, but he worked with little rest to find what he was looking for in aerial photographs. I offered his dedicated work for a time on doing the precise calculations. Clyde Smith agreed, pointing out we would need more details on water depth at various tide periods, as well as the points on each stream that the tidal influence stopped. He said he would go to the U. S. Naval Forces, Vietnam, and ask for help in our effort. It would take time and much work, but he agreed that is often what good intelligence is all about.

Chapter Thirteen

Battle of Can Giouc

On 19 June 1967 in Can Giuoc Province, I temporarily took over the role of brigade operations officer to spell my tired and sleepless friend, Clyde Tate. That would lead to Fulton reminding me of why he had not allowed any talk of my going to a battalion operations job when I had raised it in the past. More importantly, it was a day of major battle and heavy losses. It was the day the leader I admired most relieved one of my closest friends from command of troops.

Captain Robert L. Reeves, my staff assistant for many months, on that day commanded a rifle company in a battle with the Viet Cong that we called the Battle of Can Giuoc. It occurred just south of Saigon, as Bob pushed his company south in the rice paddies along the west side of a river, the Rach Gia, toward a smaller stream, the Rach Nui. There were other American rifle companies to Bob's right, also moving south. Another company was afloat in Armored Troop Carriers to his left rear, ready to land if needed. There was still another rifle company well to the south, prepared to load helicopters and to fly north to land wherever needed.

The companies were all searching for the 214th Viet Cong Battalion that I had concluded, by pattern analysis, was likely to be in this area around this time, and so we launched the operation on the morning of the 19th. When the brigade contacted the enemy, it was at the disadvantage of Captain Reeves and his lead platoon. The platoon was moving, slogging is a better term, through recently flooded rice paddies. The enemy opened with blazing, surprise, automatic rifles and machine guns. In less than fifteen minutes, nearly a platoon of thirty men was down in the paddies. Many were dead and others wounded. Medics reached only a few before they too went down and the medic and his wounded charge took repeated hits. The enemy fire grazed over the water of the paddies. Five of Bob's medics would die trying to aid the fallen—three of his lieutenants.

Bob's lead platoon had walked into a classic, Viet Cong, L-Shaped Ambush. His platoon leaders had been sloshing through the mud with their scouts-out for early warning, but there had been no early warning. The scouts had fallen with the men of the main body in the opening clatter of weapons fire. There had been a report less than an hour earlier that upwards of three companies of the Viet Cong battalion were resting with center of mass coordinates just south of the Rach Nui. With that report, all the attention of Captain Reeves, his battalion commander, Guy Tutwiler, and his brigade commander, Bill Fulton, focused on redirecting the movements of the platoons and companies. All attempted to converge on the reported location. For Bob Reeves, the strength of the enemy force that attacked his lead platoon from ambush was north of the creek, not south. Captain Reeves ordered his trailing platoon to close on what he judged was the left flank of the north to south leg of the ambush. The platoon was unable to advance beyond a dike that provided the last cover before reaching the VC position. Bob requested supporting fires, but confusion on the closeness of friendly units to the enemy delayed the fires.

Meanwhile, Colonel Fulton directed the continued movement of Bolduc's battalion from the south and Tutwiler's other companies from the northwest. All companies were converging on the Viet Cong position that we guessed lay along the north and south banks of the stream. Tutwiler's B Company was the first to get close and immediately took casualties in a forward platoon trying to negotiate an open paddy to get into better position to place fire on the VC. The platoons hunkered down behind dikes, as close to the enemy as the grazing fire would permit. The steady roar of artillery fire and air strikes and gun ships began, interrupted only to allow medical evacuation helicopters to land and depart. An Air Force strafing attack stopped after their rounds hit a friendly company. One medical evacuation helicopter went down, and medical, or aid, boats evacuated several of the wounded. But most of the wounded of Company A of Tutwiler's battalion were not recoverable. The enemy fire was too intense. Navy HMC Robert Malone would later receive a Silver Star for his exposure of himself to repeated danger to get Army casualties into his boat. A battalion of the 46th ARVN Regiment held a blocking position to the west. We made no effort to reposition the unit nearer the American battalions, although we knew the VC sometimes took advantage of breaks between units of the two armies.

The MRF and U.S. Air Force fire support pounded the Viet Cong, but as darkness came, we knew little about how much we had weakened the VC. They were still firing automatic weapons from bunkers, and our companies were holding back, scratching out some cover, and letting the supporting fires attack the enemy position. At this point, many of Bob Reeves' men were still lying in the rice paddy in front of the VC position. Most were under water, only their backs and shoulders visible above the water level that still splashed with the impact of enemy bullets.

At 1700 hours in Saigon, I later learned, the daily press briefing by the Military Assistance Command, Vietnam, started on time, covering the day's major happenings in the country. About halfway through, the briefer referred to an ambush by Viet Cong forces of a company of the 9th Infantry Division in the Delta, inflicting heavy casualties. No other information was then available, the briefer said. Within minutes, a reporter filed a story with his magazine in the United States. It began, "Mercifully, the American soldiers never knew what hit them," and it went downhill from there. Within minutes, the story was on the Associated Press wire service going to radio, TV and newspaper outlets throughout America.

Back in the rice paddies, the battle continued at a level that dropped to sporadic fire only after midnight.

Midmorning of the next day, a helicopter landed on the APB Benewah carrying Lieutenant General Fred Weyand, Commanding General of II Field Force, Vietnam, and Brigadier General G. G. O'Connor, the assistant division commander of the 9th Division. Colonel Fulton met Weyand and O'Connor and escorted them below deck to the combined stateroom office he shared with Captain Wells.

At this point, ground units of the brigade had taken up pursuit of enemy soldiers who had slipped out between the brigade companies and the ARVN battalion during the night. We reestablished contact later in the day, but with no major results. At the site of the ambush, other companies of Tutwiler's battalion had begun to push into the cratered and treeless positions of the Viet Cong. The VC fired on our men at times from small clusters of bunkers, which our squads then took out with rockets and grenades. Slowly the count of enemy killed and weapons recovered mounted. The count of kills would eventually exceed 250.

About thirty minutes after the generals arrived, Lieutenant Colonel Tom O'Connor came up to me in the operations center and said that Fulton wanted to see me in his stateroom. As I walked into the passageway, O'Connor added the generals were still in there with Fulton and Wells. I wondered if Fulton was calling me in because, as the Brigade Intelligence Officer, I had led us into this area, and, more importantly, my mobile intelligence team reported the location of the VC unit. Working out of the Can Giuoc District Headquarters, my men gave us the coordinates for the location of the 214th VC battalion. As it turned out, the center of mass of the enemy was three hundred yards north, and across the Rach Nui, from the reported location.

When I entered the room and reported to Colonel Fulton, there was no discussion of my intelligence. There was no discussion at all. He told me he was relieving Captain Reeves of command, and he wanted me to know because Bob had been my assistant intelligence officer for eight months before going down to a battalion and then into command of a company. I got out, "But Sir," before Fulton raised a big hand and added that he would wait until he could withdraw the company and then he would tell Captain Reeves he was no longer in command. I started again to say something and the other big hand shot up and Fulton said, "You're excused, Major," and I left.

Outside in the passageway I was angry and disappointed. Fulton had no doubt seen that on my face. This was not fair. Captain Reeves was not the only man who had made decisions the previous day, and there seemed to be no interest in the heavy Viet Cong losses that our soldiers were reporting as they got deeper into the enemy position. It was as if killing Viet Cong soldiers was not relevant and Westmoreland was bent on firing somebody. I thought the impetus for the relief of Captain Reeves had come not from a balanced review of the battle, but from the fragmentary report of a battlefield disaster. Early reports had allowed the press to tell the American people the American military had failed again on the battlefield in Vietnam. On the way back to the operations center, the full impact finally hit me. Although I struggled with the thought, thinking of Bob, that, "It's not fair, it's not fair," almost as soon, the reality struck. We still did not have a final count on the men killed in Bob's Company. I knew it was at least two dozen, and there were more from Company B. I realized Fulton could not keep him in command. I had been out early that morning with Fulton, acting as his S3. Despite all the efforts of the previous day and through the night, bodies were still in that large kill zone that Company A had entered. Among the dead, which I would later learn totaled forty-seven, there were six medics, of which five were Bob's, a stinging fact, and three lieutenants. It was the most staggering twenty-four hours of my military career. I could not imagine what my friend Bob was going through right now. We did not see him, but I learned he was well and was with Colonel Tutwiler. I knew his company was ineffective and essentially already off line. I knew his mind and soul would be with his men and their families back home.

Later when we were back in the command helicopter, looking over the situation, our men's bodies we were still recovering was an image burned into my mind. We decided to visit my team at the District Headquarters, hoping to get information that would help us regain contact with enemy elements that had evaded us in the night. As we made a wide and descending circle to land,

I felt more than heard the thud...thud...thud hit and rock the helicopter. The pilot said he was hit, but we quickly realized he was referring to the aircraft and not him personally. He made a second circle, and I saw the tracers of what turned out to be a 20-mm machine gun firing from a bunker below. I saw the tracers as the rounds were fired in the direction of a gun ship that was rapidly approaching us. I heard the chatter between the gun ship pilot and our copilot, and suddenly we broke away and swung back to the northeast, away from the bunker and the gun ship.

It took a while for local militia soldiers on the ground to confirm the rockets from the gun ship had silenced the two-man crew on the weapon in the bunker. Fulton insisted we go on in and land as we had planned, and the pilot hesitantly agreed, saying it would be a good chance to check the damage to the helicopter. Before we went into the headquarters, we looked at the only two impact points we could find from the 20-mm rounds. Both were fewer than six inches apart—on the heavy armored plate just to the left of the pilot's seat. Without the armor plate, the rounds would have struck the pilot high on his left shoulder and left arm. The young warrant officer turned after inspecting the two depressions made by the rounds in the thick, metal plate . His smile was weak, and he was pale.

We visited briefly with the District Chief and the liaison officer from the Vietnamese battalion that had been in the blocking position. That battalion was now leading the search to the south and would be the first to find the enemy later in the day. Fulton complimented my scrawny and unkempt specialist who had relayed us the coordinates of the enemy battalion the previous day. He was beaming. He obviously had not yet played with the idea, as I had, the degree to which the coordinates were off had proved significant. Further, I speculated the information on the enemy battalion location may have come from the battalion itself, in some indirect manner. It was a technique not unknown to the Viet Cong units I had studied and dealt with in the Pleiku area over three years earlier.

I had been working for Colonel Fulton for almost a year. Over the next few months, as the brigade operations officer, I would share pressures and dangers in the manner that two men, up close, learn things about each other that shape their relationship. In the pressures of the battlefield, there is no middle ground. There is respect or there is not. Fulton and I forged a professional and personal friendship that lasted forty years. We were like father and son, although he was only 18 years older than I. We kept that friendship over the years after we left the Army, right up to the time he passed away. In all that time, we never talked about the meeting in the Benewah stateroom or about the relief of Bob Reeves. My guess was that Bill Fulton did not regard it as one of his best days in the Army. It certainly was not one of mine.

Lieutenant Colonel O'Connor later told me that it was apparent to Fulton and Wells that before General Weyand left the Benewah that morning, someone would be relieved. The only question was would it be the company commander, the battalion commander, or the brigade commander. Still, O'Connor said, as Fulton and Wells explained how the operation had unfolded, it was clear that Weyand did not find it easy to identify who had acted in a manner to warrant relief. It had come down to what was best for the men left in the company, and who could best take those men and a platoon of replacements, and whip it into a confident fighting unit again. Clearly, the judgment was that it could not be Captain Bob Reeves.

Twenty-five years later, as a Lieutenant General in command of the U.S. Army, Pacific, I paid a courtesy call on retired General Fred Weyand. He was living with his wife in a penthouse atop the tallest building in Honolulu. The penthouse was the property of a bank in which Weyand had been a Senior Vice President and board member for most of the past 14 years since his retirement from the Army.

At a point in our conversation, I referred to that morning on the Benewah, and I told him that I had initially found it hard to accept the relief of Captain Reeves. He said he recalled something of that when Fulton told me of Bob's relief. I added there were other men, commanders and staff officers, who had made decisions that morning, not just Bob Reeves. I thought he would not reply, but then he said, "That was war, General." He then went to another subject, and I did not mention it again. After all, I thought, the relief had taken place 25 years earlier.

As the elevator lowered me down the core of the building, I thought of General Weyand, the veteran, one of the most respected and professional officers I knew in over 35 years of active Army duty. He was living well, and he had earned that quality of life in his service to the bank. But I guessed that for him too, there were days in the war it did little good to revisit. Then again, he may have viewed whatever he recalled of that day as I now did. Whatever went badly in the battle, the decision to relieve Bob was in the best interest of him and his men

Then I thought of Captain Bob Reeves, who, on 20 June 1967, knew the stigma of relief from command, where the act of a senior commander suggested he had fallen short of what was acceptable as a leader of soldiers. No judgment is more stinging to a professional leader. His relief had resulted not just from action on the battlefield, but from early fragmentary information about that action and the manner it had come to the attention of leaders and millions of American citizens sitting in their living rooms. My wife was one of those, and she had to fight off the worst of fears before my letters reached her, reflecting the nature of the battle.

There was a story—I thought—to complete: the impact on the Viet Cong on the dikes after the early, devastating losses in Bob's company. Of course, that did little to ease the pain of all of those fallen soldiers. The loss of one of your soldiers is never minimized, but while friendly losses drove all early considerations of higher headquarters and the media regarding the Battle of Can Giuoc, the losses of the enemy seemed irrelevant. I never found any indication the reporter bothered to file a follow-up story back in America on the battle.

Bob Reeves had to carry the scar of relief and implied failure in leading his soldiers for the rest of his life.

I wish I could say that Bob's story, while sad, ends there, but it doesn't.

In December, six months later, Lieutenant Colonel O'Connor told me that I was on the early drop list. That meant, instead of leaving Vietnam on 16 January 1968, my scheduled rotation date, I would be leaving 16 December. I would be home with my wife and two children for Christmas. I asked about the other officers, NCOs, and soldiers from our brigade cited in the orders, and he showed me the list. Tom O'Connor's date to leave was just three days away, 6 December. He had brought our advance party over, by boat, a long, hard cruise. He had been the perfect executive officer—smart, alert, decisive, tactful, but capable of taking a man's head off if needed, but most of all, he had been there for everybody else; not for himself. I congratulated him. Although Bob Reeves had been transferred out of our brigade and was assigned to division headquarters in July, I asked if he was on the division headquarters list. O'Connor said he did not know, but he would check.

On 16 December I sat in a civilian passenger aircraft on the taxiway at Tan Son Nhut Airport near Saigon, waiting for the takeoff that would start me home. I thought back to what O'Connor had learned the day after our conversation and shared with me: Reeves would not be on the early drop list. And he would not be going home in January—or February.

The load I felt was heavy. Bob had been assigned as my assistant intelligence officer at Fort Riley, Kansas, in August of 1966, five months before our brigade deployed to Vietnam. I had been given his file, thinking I had the option to okay or say no to his assignment. His lack of experience in a rifle company or even in an infantry battalion struck me. His assignments from the day of his graduation from the Air Force Academy, until he arrived at our brigade, except for basic, infantry officer training, reflected none of the normal growth pattern for an Infantry lieutenant. He was a senior first lieutenant who had never seen a rifle platoon, never served a day in an infantry company. That was where he needed to go now, not to a brigade staff. I took the file to Major Jimmy Smith, the brigade personnel officer, who said I should talk to the Exec. O'Connor told me I had no choice. Reeves was my assistant, and Fulton was the only brigade commander in the division who had an opening for him. O'Connor told me Fulton wanted me to oversee Reeves' on-the-job training, make up as best we could for the months he had lost in his training as an infantry officer. And I tried to do that. For five months before deployment and three months in Vietnam, we visited Infantry platoon and company training any time we could. I sent him on intelligence training inspections where little intelligence techniques were involved, and I required only that his training inspection report show the subject of the training and his time there. We spent hours late into the evening talking American infantry tactics and Viet Cong tendencies. I learned more about Bob's family, his upbringing, his last months at the Air Force Academy. I knew his life now with his wife featured the limited hours that our full, seven day a week schedule allowed and the counting of days until he left Fort Riley.

Following his relief from command, I had seen Bob three times, once at our land base at Dong Tam four days after his relief and twice at division headquarters in the months after he left our brigade. Both of the later times I was impressed with his upbeat, positive attitude and his constant references to what he was going to do in training and leading his next rifle company. I left him each time feeling that he was trying too hard, that he wanted command again to prove himself. He was a proud officer, and I worried that, underneath, his hurt was severe.

And as my airplane picked up speed on the runway and lifted me out of Vietnam, I thought of the last thing O'Connor had told me. Bob had extended for six months in Vietnam on condition that he would be assigned to command a rifle company once again.

Later I learned that he had assumed command of his company in mid-January, just in time for the huge Viet Cong Tet Offensive of February 1968.

His company was providing security for an artillery firebase in Dinh Tuong Province when the Viet Cong attacked. All night they probed his company defenses and each time his men held. At times VC mortar rounds dropped inside his position. Through the night, Captain Reeves made the rounds of his perimeter, stopping at each foxhole, asking about their ammo supply, if they had eaten, and then joking with them about their shared dislike of the Army food, the rations. With daylight, Reeves continued his rounds: smiling, laughing, walking erect and proud as if he were still on the Air Force Academy parade field. He didn't crouch, did not use the zig-zag trenches in moving from one small group of his men to another.

Two soldiers said he had just left them for maybe the fourth time since midnight, around 0800, when another enemy mortar round came in, not too close to them or to Captain Reeves, they thought. One of them said he watched as Reeves stood tall, not crouching or seeking any cover. Then the captain walked back toward them and stopped just three or four steps away. Then he pitched forward on the ground. It was just minutes before the medical evacuation helicopter came in and flew out with him on board. Somewhere between the firebase and the hospital Bob Reeves died of a shrapnel wound to his head.

The Army presented his wife the flag from his coffin and a medal for bravery.

From the day of 19 June, Bob Reeves had carried the scar of a veteran, a deep scar that he might accept, but he appeared determined to heal the original hurt that had caused it. Bob Reeves, the cadet who drew the questioning of his tactical advisor at the Air Force Academy because he insisted on an Army commission. Bob Reeves, who then would not agree with the Army on a commission until he was guaranteed he would be an infantry officer. Bob Reeves, who could not please his parents, as a sole surviving son, by accepting duty other than Vietnam. Bob Reeves, who boarded a bus at Fort Riley in late December leaving a wife who did not want him to go to Vietnam and who opposed the war itself.

Bob Reeves was a veteran who carried invisible scars and, unfortunately, carried them for only a few months until his death at age 26.

Many, many veterans carry the scars of military duty. I share this story of Bob Reeves to focus on happenings of the battlefield, some horrible, some unfair, some driving deep into what we call our pride, or our guilt or our wounded sense of humanity and decency. Veterans carry those wounds—the invisible as well as the visible ones.

Recently, I went on my computer to three web sites. At one, I read the names and hometowns of the forty seven soldiers killed on that day. Thirty-one from Bob's Company, one from battalion headquarters, and fifteen from Company B, which had maneuvered in and attacked to relieve pressure on the surviving members of Company A. I couldn't leave the site. I sat and wrote down the rank and name of all the Company A soldiers. They are listed at the end of this story. Another web site was the Vietnam Memorial in our Nation's capital. Bob's name, of course, is on that long, black wall, as are the names of all the fallen from his company and the other companies on 19 June. I recorded where to find his name on the wall: Panel 41 E, Line 43. At the final site on the internet reserved for Captain Robert Linwood Reeves was a single message, posted on November 9, 2004 by Manuel Pino, Jr., a fellow soldier. Just a simple notation that he was a fellow Vietnam Vet and a fellow Coloradoan of Captain Reeves.

It struck me: Here I was writing about him and I had never left a message there for Bob, not like Manuel had done. I knew I wanted to do that, although my bad timing added to my feeling that I had not done for Bob Reeves, in life, all that I should have. But for now, I decided to send an e-mail to Manuel. It read:

"Manuel, tonight I am giving a Veterans Day talk at my local Ruritan Club in Virginia. Captain Robert L. Reeves is the featured veteran of my comments. He was my assistant intelligence officer when I served as the S2 of the 2nd Brigade, 9th Infantry Division, at Fort Riley, Kansas, from early July of 1966 until our departure for Vietnam in early January of 1967. He remained my assistant for a time once we were in country and before he went down to the 4th Battalion, 47th Infantry, where he eventually took command of Alpha Company. Bob's story is his love for soldiers and the Army and the Infantry. It's his big Battle of Can Giuoc on 19 June 1967, his pain at the loss of men in that battle, something that never quite left him. It is his yearning to prove himself, something that for me was never necessary. It is his extension in Vietnam to lead troops again in combat. It is his bravery on the night of 25 and 26 February, 1968; and his death on the 26th. It is the Army's recognition of his courage and bravery, and his place on the wall. All of that story is ours.

"I was pleased to find you there when I searched the website of the memorial just today, a last check with Bob before making the only public talk I have ever made in his honor. I was pleased to see that he was not alone, that he had you there.

"I went on in the Army and retired in 1993 as a Lieutenant General and Commander of the United States Army, Pacific. I now live in retirement in the Shenandoah Valley of Virginia and write novels based on the history of our Nation. I have that freedom because of soldiers like Bob Reeves and his fallen men. He was a man of honor whom I think of with a heavy heart, and I am very pleased to extend a hand in brotherhood to another soldier who knew and admired him. Be well, and Thank you for being there for Bob. From: Johnnie H. Corns, Infantryman."

I later received an e-mail from Manuel. He had not known Bob. He had simply visited the wall on the internet, and left him a message.

◆   ◆   ◆

Shortly after the Battle of Can Giuoc, Fulton tapped me to become the operations officer of the brigade. The Division Chief of Staff was on a talent hunt for experienced officers to bring up to the division staff. Clyde Tate, a tribute to him, was caught in that web. The change caused me to recall the day, several weeks earlier, when Fulton explained why he had not permitted me to go down to be a battalion operations officer. I was in his land-based office at the time at Dong Tam, and he received a call from Brigadier General O'Connor. Fulton waved me to stay in the office and have a seat. I did so and waited. I could tell that he was getting some bad news. At a point he told O'Connor, "He's right here. Let me ask him."

He put his hand over the mouthpiece and explained to me the S3 of First Brigade had just been killed in action and that O'Connor was calling to get me released to take the major's place. Fulton asked me what I thought. I told him that if they wanted me to, I would go.

Fulton gripped the mouthpiece of the phone more tightly and held it off to his left and said, "I had in mind, whenever we lose Clyde, to put you in as my S-3." I felt small and disloyal, but that had not been something I thought might occur. Clyde had arrived in Vietnam when I did, and would leave Vietnam when I did. I assumed he'd be right here as operations officer for the duration. I was not sure what staying would mean: no battalion S-3 job, for sure, but the brigade S-3 job here … when? However, my hesitation was slight. I told him, "In that case, I'd rather stay here."

He pulled the phone close again and told O'Connor that he had plans for me to be his S-3, and that I wanted to stay where I was. They talked a little more and then Fulton said good-bye and cradled the phone. Fulton said, "He said it may not be over, but I think it is. Colonel Kendall has other options." We went back to our original subject and no more was said about when I might be the S-3. I never brought it up again. According to Tom O'Connor, Colonel Kendall had then taken the position that if Fulton would not give me up, he would have to accept losing Clyde. And so, I became the brigade S-3, my second time in such a position, the other having been in the 2nd Brigade of the 3d Infantry Division just over a year earlier in Germany. By this time, Dick Sharp had already left his plans job and was now the S-3 of 3d Battalion, 60th Infantry, Clancy's old battalion, now under command of Lieutenant Colonel Mercer Doty.

A couple of weeks later, I moved to the brigade S-3 job. Throughout the summer, our Mobile Riverine Force moved about the Mekong Delta, striking areas along the waterways that had long been sanctuaries of the Viet Cong. Over a few months, our operations had grown crisper and more effective as the Navy and Army team members built knowledge of one another. With that knowledge came trust and a readiness to extend the unique capabilities of each force to raise the combat power of the other. On the Fourth of July, at the height of our early success and shortly after I took over the operations officer job from Clyde Tate, we kicked off a search operation in Go Cong Province. Our intelligence showed consistent occupation of the area by supply and training activities in support of local Viet Cong who operated primarily out of this base. The base was on a peninsula that suited itself for attack by our forces coming off the waterways, complemented by helicopter lift and gun ships and by a local militia unit provided by the leaders of Go Cong Province. The gun ships set up a screen to the west side of the operation, while the local Vietnamese militia blocked the land routes off the peninsula.

The operation was a significant success because of the large numbers of trainers and supply personnel captured. Viet Cong losses in killed were small, but high in personnel captured, while our forces, American and Vietnamese, took no casualties. Further, the cooperation of the local government was complete and security before the attack was tight. A few days after the operation, I presented the details of the operation in a briefing to General Westmoreland, commander of all American forces in Vietnam. He was visiting the Benewah, and he was enthusiastic about the operation, or, more significantly, the potential of the MRF. It was not his first exposure to the concept of the force or of our operations, but it was the first time he had the opportunity to hear, as Fulton would have put it months earlier, us telling our story. Fulton took the opportunity to reinforce the need to speed up the movement of other Navy boats to Vietnam to allow the force to grow larger and more effective. Westmoreland seemed ready to push that with Washington.

A few weeks later, we had the opportunity to present our case, again on the fantail of the Benewah, and this time to Secretary of Defense Robert McNamara. He proved to be the most difficult of all visitors for me to brief, not because of questions or comments, but because of a seeming lack of interest or an impatience with spending the time listening. However, at the end, he was complimentary of the success of our operations. Still, he gave no signal the movement of more Navy boats would be accelerated. As it turned out, there was no early fielding, and we would not add the capability to lift a full, three-battalion brigade until the following year.

Those were the days, the summer of 1967, the MRF was entering smaller and smaller waterways and delivering heavy damage on the enemy with little damage to our boats. But, by early fall, that was changing, and in ways that were to change more dramatically in the following year. The Viet Cong were coming to recognize the placement of a few rounds of 57-mm recoilless rifle rounds and RPG-2 and RPG-7 anti-tank rockets in the hands of their Mekong Delta units could bring good results—for them. The VC had hit us with a few such rockets, fired at the canvas-covered troop area of an Armored Troop Carrier. The results had been a spray of shrapnel down into the bay, the rocket striking one of the metal support rods for the canopy. Sometimes casualties were numerous because a full platoon was packed in the area below.

Often, although wounded, men went right into battle, and a medic attended to them after the situation ashore was under control.

Late that summer, Colonel Fulton was promoted to brigadier general and was reassigned as the Assistant Division Commander of the 9th Infantry Division. Clyde had already left, weeks before, but most of the cast of officers and enlisted men I had trained with at Fort Riley and fought alongside for over six months, were still on the Benewah, or one of the other large boats that provided a home when the men were not out in the rice paddies. We all, however, felt the departure of Fulton from our daily life. Probably a couple dozen men, of all ranks, felt the same way that I did, that I was his best friend. There was no question with me. I knew he was my best friend, closer in a way that Dick Sharp could not be. Fulton was like a second father to me. In one dimension, he was more to me than my father: he had seen me perform in my chosen profession in a manner that my father never could. It was a bond that I came to learn was not just felt by me. It was shared.

Weeks before his departure, I accompanied him on a helicopter flight up to Vuong Tau to pay respects to some fine Australian soldiers. As we flew back south over the South China Sea, just the two of us in the troop compartment with the crew chief and door gunners, he flipped the intercom to private. He referred to the leave he had taken, called an R&R, for rest and recuperation, a few weeks earlier in Hawaii. He met his wife, Nan, there and as it turned out, I took my R&R such that we had several days in common there on Oahu. My wife, Carol, had arrived there just a day before I did and met me at the airport. During our brief stay, we saw the Fultons a couple of times and reminisced about the shared times at Fort Riley, preparing the brigade for war. Such talk of war and training was limited. The time was precious, but the fact that Bill and I would be going back to Vietnam in a few days was never far from his or my mind or the thoughts of our wives. Carol and I often over the years have reflected on the difficulties of those few days, not the least being the absence of our children, despite the beauty of paradise.

On the occasion of the flight south from Vung Tau, I mentioned our children, "the kiddies," as Bill liked to refer to them, and he spoke then the words that have proven the most cherished to me—and to Carol of all that he ever shared. "You know, Johnnie," he said. "There'll come a day, if you're lucky, that the kiddies will be grown and out on their own, the Army won't need us any more, and, if we're lucky, what we will have to go home to is the wife who has stood behind us through all the times like this." I didn't reply. He said no more. No reply or added words were needed.

Five years later, he and I would be back home with our families. Carol and I would arrive at Fort Lewis, Washington, to find a message. "When you get in, the CG wants to see, you, Carol and the kiddies, at his quarters, regardless of the time of day." Of course, we called first, but when we arrived, our two children were the center of attention. They completed the incomplete assembly of our families there in Hawaii. Bill and Nan's children were older than ours and already off in college or making lives for themselves. But, we had seen some of their children before, and would again, more than once.

I once shared Bill Fulton's words of wisdom over the South China Sea with Nan. I could see that she was touched. I'm glad I did. Later I put it in a poem, "Big Bill," that follows this story. I recall these things to emphasize that Colonel Fulton's departure from the Mobile Riverine Force was more than just "one commander leaves and another comes in." Ours was a shared experience that, for me, stands highest among all the extraordinary soldierly experiences I had with a handful of other fine officers and non commissioned officers. That he subsequently shaped my military career is a sizable understatement. All that flowed from the shared situations in those short months in Vietnam when, up close, he and I knew who and what, as individuals, we were, and who and what the other was, as a soldier and a man.

Chapter Fourteen

Planning for Snoopy

The MRF returned to the Rach Ba Rai in September, a quick reaction operation, growing out of successes in August and early September in Dinh Tuong Province, just east of the Cam Son Secret Zone. The operations had included limited contact near the mouth of the Rach Ba Rai, still reflected in our intelligence as a transient base for the 514th Local Force and 263d Main Force Viet Cong Battalions. Our capability to react swiftly to fresh intelligence resulted from months of confidence-building operational successes and a close confidence among all elements of the force. We received a report of the presence of the 263rd in the Cam Son area on 14 September, as we were returning to our anchorage base.

While reports by the 7th ARVN claimed the presence of the 263rd as well as the 514th in the Rach Ba Rai, such reports were not unusual. Earlier reports had been part of the information that had launched the operation from which we were returning on 14 September. What caught our attention at that precise time were reports directly from the Combined Intelligence Center in Saigon that reflected highly classified information indicating the current location of that battalion, the 263rd. Our intelligence staff, under Major Dick Jennings, had continued our pattern analysis technique, and what they now showed our new brigade commander, Colonel Bert David, left no doubt—we needed to turn around the next day and go back into the Cam Son Secret Zone.

On arrival on the Benewah, I joined immediately my plans officer, Major Dick Munsell, and the intelligence S-2/N-2 teams of Dick Jennings and Clyde Smith. I told them we had only thirty minutes for me to get back to our new brigade commander with a concept of operations, a process that often took as much as twenty-four hours; sometimes more. I listened and watched as the intelligence overlays dropped down over terrain with which I was now very familiar. Most of the accumulating indications of VC presence were precisely where we had seen them indicated before. What I was waiting for were the latest reports from General McChristian, commander of the Central Intelligence Command and Westmoreland's top intelligence man in Vietnam. I was looking for the reports that would tell me where the 263rd Battalion was now, or had been just hours earlier.

Well up the Rach Ba Rai, maybe four kilometers north of Snoopy's Nose, this special intelligence showed considerable activity, mostly on the east side of the Rach Ba Rai. I stared at the large number of highly classified interceptions of the communications of the enemy main force battalion and its supporting elements. Only one other person looking at the overlay, our S-2, Jennings, knew what these reports really were. He too knew that this was unusual. This was unlike the 263rd. There communications security was good, but they were likely on the run and mending their wounds. We had cornered them on 31 July some ten kilometers to the east of the Rach Ba Rai. We pounded them all afternoon and into the night with one Air Force strike after another, the greatest number of Air Force air strikes I had seen during both my tours in Vietnam. We had gotten multiple reports from agents and local villagers the 263rd had taken significant casualties. We found few as we made our way through the heavily cratered battlefield the day after the enemy battalion attacked in one direction and then infiltrated out of our encirclement in the opposite direction. They moved around a blocking battalion between them and the Cam Son zone. We had followed that up with air strikes into the zone, but with no land operation.

Then, again, on 12 and 13 September, we had found smaller units of the battalion in the same Ban Long area, just to the east. The "Wild Ones" of the 3d Battalion, 60th Infantry, had borne the brunt of that operation, inflicting significant casualties on the VC, but taking nine killed themselves. Just now closing back into base, they had to be tired. I knew that Colonel David knew that, and that Captain Saltzer, the commodore who had relieved the departing Wade Wells, knew that his sailors were tired as well, although the operations of the past fortnight had tended to be inland. But when the boats were not ferrying infantry or providing direct supporting fires, they were constantly patrolling the waterways nearby, large and small, to interdict the sampan movement that carried VC moving to the attack, repositioning, escaping or being re-supplied.

The multiple overlays of information on the enemy and the terrain reminded me how far we had come with knowledge of the navigability of the streams in the Delta. I dropped a clean layer of acetate over all the red-marked overlays. With a blue grease pencil, I drew one, long, bold arrow up the Rach Ba Rai, well past Snoopy's nose. I put a point on the arrow after a sharp right turn just beyond an equally sharp bend of the stream to the right. There, on the north side of a land salient that jutted from the east into the west, much like a reverse and smaller Snoopy's nose, I picked two of the feasible company size landing sites the intelligence team had identified. These would be two beaches, about eight hundred meters apart. This was where I visualized two companies of a battalion landing after a bold push up the Rach Ba Rai. I then drew a second arrow alongside the first, upriver, and beyond Snoopy's Nose, three kilometers south of the first two landing zones. I split the arrow and drew circles for two of the several potential landing areas. Those would be beaches for a second battalion. It was hardly a complex maneuver, on paper. One battalion would go all the way in to put a cap on the likely escape route of the 263rd to the north and northwest. Then the other would land and move north, catching the enemy between them. There would be more forces needed on the east to block movement in that direction and on the west bank of the Rach Ba Rai. Units already in the area would have to do. We had already held up the 5th Battalion, 60th Infantry, borrowed from the 3d Brigade, keeping them near Highway 4, north of both the operational area of the previous day and the one we were scoping out right now for tomorrow. A possibility for a blocking force to the west might be the Vietnamese Ranger Battalion in the area. We had not worked with them before, but their advisers had signaled a wish to do so. That was a detail I would have to work out later that evening. And, of course, there was the firepower, the fire support. The three batteries of our direct support artillery battalion, under our operational control, had proved a flexible and lethal force, but it was still only three batteries. At times we had the support of a battery or more of 155-MM artillery to augment our 105 MM guns, but that would not be the case the next day. There would be gun ships. We could rely on at least a team or two of helicopter gun ships. And there would be the U.S. Air Force on call. I had come to value their capability even more after their earlier operations in Ban Long at the end of July. Hunkered down behind a jeep and working from a map with our Air Force Liaison Officer, I had felt the heat of the battle in a way I had not experienced since three years earlier in the Vietnamese Highlands. We were coordinating fires in support of the attack by our battalions, but we also wanted to quiet the enemy ground fire that was plinking around our temporary command and communications site. The Air Force had done both, and I hoped we would need to call on multiple strikes by them tomorrow. Everything in the concept I had drawn relied on getting our lead battalion onto those northern beaches. It was risky, but it gave us the opportunity to cap early the best escape route the 263rd Battalion would have—if we found them at home.

I knew one person who would readily agree with the aggressive maneuver, the man who had sat with me and looked at maneuver options before the operation on 15 May—Dick Sharp. At that time, we had seen our options limited because of the few intrusions our Navy craft had then made into the small waterways, and the caution we shared in doing so. But by now, the shallow draft, armor protection, and armament of those boats had been proven. The crews were ready to go where the action took them, but with a high regard for available information on the antitank weapons which the VC had adapted to use against our waterborne vehicles. Dick and I had seen this confidence grow slowly and now knew the capabilities of the force. Still, this was a bold move, and I would need for Dick, now down in the fight, and his battalion commander to agree. Even though they had borne the main effort in the Dinh Tuong operation just completed, I was going to recommend to Colonel David that Dick and Colonel Doty's battalion lead the attack up the Rach Ba Rai. By Snoopy's Nose, all the way to Beaches we would designate White One and White Two.

Boldness as a planner is not the same as boldness as a commander; particularly the commander who will lead, on the ground, the bold maneuver. As a planner, you may convince yourself that it is the same if you know and understand and accept all the risks just as if you were to be the commander on the spot. The clear test of the difference, however, lies in executing the plan; particularly in the early stage of execution if enemy action is such as to threaten staggering losses on your command. Then, you yearn to be the decision maker; the leader on the spot who will quickly gain the advantage, inflict major losses on the enemy, and minimize the hurt and sacrifice of your soldiers. The farther you are from that decisive position, as a planner or a high-level commander, the greater the room for concern about the rightness of the plan you have helped put into action.

Colonel David approved the concept quickly with the concurrence of Captain Saltzer, whose relative newness might suggest some hesitation under the circumstances, but there was none. Preparations for the attack up the Rach Ba Rai went quickly and smoothly, although it meant for many of the sailors little or no sleep in order to turn the boats around in top fighting condition so quickly. Most of the planning at battalion and River Squadron level did not start with specifics from the MRF Headquarters until midnight. People were operating on warning orders and operating procedures that had become informally standard over the last four or five months. Anticipation in the boat crews and the infantry platoons was high. Mention of the 263rd Battalion suggested the best the Viet Cong had to offer in this area of the Delta. Within the 3d Battalion, 60th Infantry, it was greeted as another shot at the unit they had locked horns with just two days before. They had thought they had the VC cornered, only to learn the elite unit had slipped away in the darkness with moderate casualties. The "Wild Ones" wanted another try at the 263rd. They would get it.

They say, "Be careful, you may get what you ask for." Our success in finding the enemy the next day in the specific area we had estimated produced the kind of violent response the Viet Cong offered only when cornered.

In the weeks, months, and years following that battle on the Rach Ba Rai on 15 September, there have been many discussions, war stories, and accounts offered. I later reviewed my impressions and recollections and most of those offered by others about the battle. Recognizing that accounts differ during a battle, I recommend the article by John Albright, "Fight Along the Rach Ba Rai," in the booklet, *Seven Firefights in Vietnam*. Published by the Office of the Chief of Military History, United States Army in 1970. It reflects extensive study and interviews by John with many participants in the battle. I worked with John at the editorial offices of the Chief of Military History in the editing of Fulton's book, *Riverine Operations*, as I had shared with him, earlier, my impressions and account of the Rach Ba Rai battle. What follows tends to deal with some matters in more summary fashion than John's account, while providing a little more personal information on the battalion and brigade, perspectives.

I would add that Dick Sharp and I did not discuss in detail the concept of this operation before it was carried out, but at a point in the battle, I know he held the plan in low regard. He told me that less than two years later. But, let's not get too far ahead of the story.

Chapter Fifteen

The Cloud Above Snoopy's Nose

In several ways the operation on 15 September began as many had before. An early morning wakeup and breakfast, for many beginning at 0200, just two hours after they had gone to sleep because of the lateness of arrival of orders. Loading the Armored Troop Carriers with an infantry platoon was slow and dangerous. One hour was a good time for an experienced infantry battalion to load. A soldier walked slowly down the ladders to the barges lashed alongside the large boat; then handed his weapon to a man already on the ATC before he grasped a post for balance and stepped across into the assault craft. Earlier in our operations in May, a soldier radio operator had attempted this transfer with his radio strapped on his back. He lost his balance and fell into the river. He went down immediately and we did not see him again. The darkness, current, and muddy waters made his recovery impossible. After that, we passed the radio across before the soldier transferred from the barge to the craft, a procedure we regretted not setting up from the start. We did not recover the radio operator's body. Fortunately, there was not a repeated incident in the time I served with the MRF.

On this morning, the ATC's pulled away from the barge, moved out, and took up a position in the sequence assigned to its commander. The formation, once lined up and including all boats called for in the plan, moved farther along the river, awaiting the command for the entire formation to get underway.

Because such a move was easily seen by eyes on shore that we assumed included supporters of the Viet Cong, we would often send a smaller or equal size formation in a direction other than that of the planned attack. Later, once the force had entered the small waterways of the true destination, we would recover the deception formation and bring it into the area of the attack. Surprise was an advantage, both in catching the enemy unprepared and in

144

protecting our boats. If we could avoid the antitank weapons in well prepared, hidden positions, the deceptions were well worth the effort. We used such a deception on the morning of 15 December.

The boats of River Squadron 11, under command of Navy Lieutenant Commander Dusty Rhodes, a proven favorite of the Army soldiers of all ranks, began their run up the Rach Ba Rai around 0700. Our intelligence showed little presence of VC south of Snoopy's Nose, but that was of little reassurance to the boat crews or the infantry in the compartments of the ATC's. While many of the infantry had slept most of the three hours moving on the My Tho River, whispers about the Ba Rai River, and Snoopy's Nose soon had them alert. They fastened their helmets, secured flak jackets, and double-checked their, on safe, but ready, weapons. Navy crewmen manned the .50 caliber machine guns on the ATC's, and all weapons of the Fire Support Boats had the full attention of the Navy crews. Out front, two ATC's, equipped as minesweepers, moved slowly and cautiously. The floating or slightly submerged mine, remotely detonated, was the most-feared threat for the Navy boat commanders. More than a hit from an RPG missile or a recoilless rifle, a mine detonated at or below the waterline threatened to sink the boat quickly, possible blocking efforts to maneuver or escape the area in narrower streams.

Behind Colonel Doty and his battalion was Colonel Guy Tutwiler, now commanding the 3d Battalion, 47th Infantry. They too were aboard Navy craft and holding at the mouth of the Ba Rai River. Additional battalions of the U. S. 9th Infantry Division, 7th ARVN Division, and Dinh Tuong Province moved into the area as blocking forces, either as part of the initial maneuver or in response to the later contact with the enemy. For purposes of clarity, I will concentrate on the two battalions mentioned above, and the supporting Riv Ron 11, under Lieutenant Commander Rhodes.

To increase the likelihood of the Viet Cong units remaining in position and fighting, all helicopter overflights and preparatory supporting fires of artillery or close air support were withheld until after the first battalion cleared Snoopy's Nose. This was the opposite of what we often did in our operations, employing significant supporting fires to prepare the area. Our knowledge of the Viet Cong told us that they often reacted to these preparatory fires; especially when we did not place the fires directly on the enemy. They would rapidly move out of their temporary base on well-rehearsed escape routes. Our aim was to limit the time they had for such evasive movement, which had characterized most contacts the MRF had made with the enemy in the previous four months.

As operations officer for the overall command, I spent the first two hours of the morning of 15 September, 0400 to 0600, monitoring the early movement on the My Tho River. I reviewed the brief progress reports in the form of code words coming into the operations center aboard the APB Benewah. Shortly after 0600, I joined the Naval Operations Officer, Captain Chuck Black, in briefing Colonel David and Captain Saltzer on our status in their command stateroom. Colonel David agreed we should go airborne in our command and control helicopter at 0650 from the helipad on the APB. We would fly west along the river to our forward command post on a barge on the north bank of the river. There we would land and await the passing of the lead battalion around Snoopy's nose. Then we would be airborne again over the area of operations.

Just before we took off from the Benewah, I gave David a quick rundown as we walked out to the helipad. I renewed my comments once we were airborne and had on our communication equipment of integrated headphones and mouthpiece and a handheld push-to-talk switch. As usual, besides the helicopter crew, were Col David and I, sitting in facing positions, he with his back to the pilots and his left shoulder to the starboard side of the chopper. He was in an outboard seat, as was I. To my immediate left was our artillery fire support officer, and to his left, our Air Force Liaison Officer, or ALO. My briefing complete, we kept our silence as we flew west in the morning light. As predicted, we had scattered clouds, but large, cumulus clouds that could cover a large area for a time down to fifteen hundred or so feet. Weather should be favorable, I thought.

We landed at the forward barge without incident, and found our communications fully operational and a sense of anticipation within the small bunker, bristling with antennae. It was just after 0700, and Dick Sharp had come up on the net to report the code word for entering the mouth of the river at 0700, just before our helicopter landed. Dick was with Dusty Rhodes, who, among his several hats, such as commander of River Assault Squadron 11, was today the Commander of Task Force 117.1, or CTF 117.1. Simply, this was Rhodes' squadron and task force at the lowest level of his tactical command, Task Group 117.2. I will refer to him and his command on the Ba Rai River as the task group. His boat carried multiple radios and heavy armament. It was critical to have the battalion operations officer, if not the battalion commander, and the task group commander together on this one boat during a movement up a narrow river or stream where contact was thought imminent. Rhodes was in command until the battalion, or at least a company, was ashore. Then he would be supporting the ground commander. Until he passed that command authority down, Rhodes would decide how to respond to enemy fires on his boats and decide what actions to take. His guides, beyond his tactical and technical judgment, were in the operating procedures of his commander, Captain Saltzer. If the reaction that Rhodes chose could be assisted by supporting fires or ground maneuver by Army forces, Dick Sharp's presence gave authority to the link with artillery, gun ships, and Air Force close air support.

Rhodes and Sharp knew the risk. They had heard the briefing by our intelligence people. This time, they knew, the briefing officers were very confident the enemy was there—and in strength. They also knew that, if they could land the two infantry companies on White Beach ONE and TWO, the ground troops would be blocking the most likely escape route for the Viet Cong, to the north. They knew that, even with a friendly Vietnamese battalion inserted to the west of the Rach Ba Rai, it would fall to the firepower of the squadron to help prevent the Viet Cong from crossing the Ba Rai River and escaping. It was a mission the task group, and similar ones, had carried out before, but their success had come in restricting movement on and across waterways in daylight; not after darkness fell. They would need to fix the VC quickly and pound them in coordination with the two infantry battalions Rhodes was helping support and two other Army battalions that would be coming in from the northeast to block. All would have to close quickly, and the plan would depend a great deal on the artillery, gun ships, and close air support that could be placed on the enemy between the converging and blocking battalions. If they did not get the companies on White ONE and TWO, the enemy would have an easy escape route to the north, even in daylight. The entire plan depended a lot on his squadron, and Dusty Rhodes liked that.

Dick Sharp was comfortable with his dependence on Dusty Rhodes. Imagine you are there with him and Dusty as Dick tries to stay abreast of the reports of boat commanders on Rhodes's task force radio command net, while staying alert to reports of company commanders on the Army battalion command net. The roar of the boat engines at times made the use of headphones necessary, complicating the monitoring of the two radio nets. You are moving up the river. Ten of the task group boats are up ahead. Two minesweepers, a monitor, six armored troop carriers with two rifle companies in their open compartments, under only a vinyl canopy supported by metal poles, and one more monitor. You are looking out port and starboard, but you don't see much: high banks with heavy foliage and, above the foliage, the fronds of palm trees. There is little wind, from the north. The clouds are low but white, and off to the northwest you see a patch of blue. You round Snoopy's nose.

Any hope of surprise is gone now. The roar of the boat engines, you know, carries far over the waters. You continue the move up the stream, so far so good. Colonel Doty breaks the silence. He is overhead in a small helicopter, but indicates the column is not visible to him because of low clouds. You confirm the lead company boats are now well north of Snoopy's nose. They too report lower clouds. A little later, Doty is back on the net, confirming he can see at times through the opening in the clouds and tells you the lead minesweepers are not far from White Beach TWO, but still south of the sharp right turn in the stream.

It is 0730. You are holding one earpiece of the headset plugged into your battalion command net to one ear, listening with the other ear to Rhodes' net over the roar of the engine of the CCB. Little is said. No chatter. You can feel the tension.

The task group radio barks—an excited voice. It's the commander of one of the minesweepers. He has hit a mine. A mine. That could result in a quick sinking of one of the essential minesweepers.

How bad is it you want to ask, and then your B Company Commander, aboard ATC 111-6, Captain Wilbert Davis, reports enemy fire on a minesweeper. In quick succession the minesweeper commander reports a second explosion rocked his boat; he has casualties—men hit with shrapnel. Above the waterline hits you hope. Hit by rockets too, most likely the source of the shrapnel. The commander of Company A, Captain Gregg North, comes up on the battalion net, reporting that his boats are under enemy small arms and machinegun fire.

Then you hear the commander of the other lead minesweeper—his boat is under fire also: a mine, maybe rockets … yes, rocket fire.

You look to Dusty Rhodes. You hear the clank of machine gun bullets on the hull of the CCB.

The captain of the Monitor behind the minesweepers reports an explosion on board, and their steerage is ineffective.

Rhodes orders his boat captains to return fire with all weapons. He repeats his command, ordering fire on both banks of the river. Now you can't hear the task force radio because of the din of the weapons firing. You again pick up a headset connected to the task force command net and hold it to your other ear. You're standing, and you think to hunker down and then you sink to one knee. Doty tells you the artillery officer with him in the helicopter is shifting the planned artillery fires on Beach White TWO to the south, just east of the line of boats of Rhodes' task group. He asks about gun ships. You remove the headset of Rhodes' command net and let it dangle from the radio as you pull on another headset and call the brigade operations officer on the brigade command net. You request a helicopter gun ship team, two of them. You get a Roger, wait, out.

You feel the boat rock as if hit by a giant hammer, and it throws you to your left, up against the port bulkhead of the boat. You lose the headsets. Above and forward of you, Rhodes, still standing when the boat was apparently hit by a mine or rocket, slams against the bulkhead also and then drops to the deck. Your left shoulder hurts, but you are glad you were already on one knee with less distance to fall. You crawl quickly to Rhodes. He is unconscious. A crewman shakes the shoulder of his commander, looking for wounds of his upper body. You check his torso and legs. No wounds. Rhodes stirs. He looks around. The din of continued firing, VC as well as the boat weapons, continues. You are aware the boat is turning, spinning, on the river. Rhodes gets to one knee, shakes his head. "I'm okay," he says, but lets the crewman get him to his feet.

You look at the headsets dangling from the radios. There is a metal box nearby and you pull it back to starboard and sit on the box as you try to recall which headset is to which radio. The boat seems to be righted again, but hardly moving. You guess correctly and get the battalion command net first. You report to Doty the CCB has been hit, but appears to be operational again. You are glad the radio works. You check the task force radio; it too is working. Another boat reports a hit. The crewman is trying to tell Rhodes something. You step closer, and remove the headset from one ear. The first monitor, number 111-2 has beached and has taken another hit, and the second monitor has been hit too—two rockets—and one man is dead; two more wounded. Rockets, he says, we are being hit with rockets. The minesweeper has taken more hits. Several are wounded on the second minesweeper, similar to the first one.

Rhodes orders the first minesweeper to the rear. You put the battalion headset back to your ear. Over the battalion net you try to get a report from each company commander. No report from Captain Davis, Company B, but Company A commander, Captain North, reports he is still under fire and is returning fire, augmenting the fires of the Navy boat crews. He says he has several casualties, some of whom are still able to fire their weapons. From the other headset you hear the second monitor is now beached. ATC 111-12 reports taking fire from small arms. There are casualties to the infantry in the open hold. There is another man wounded on the second monitor that was hit. Another armored troop carrier reports a hit; then another reports two rounds impacting. At least four crewmen wounded; maybe more of the infantry.

At a point, you receive a call from Masher 3, call sign of John Corns, the brigade operations officer, offering the requested helicopter gun ship team. You tell him you can't control it. You pass it back to him. Then you hear Colonel Doty telling Masher 3 that he can control the gun team in coordination with the artillery liaison officer , also aloft in an observation helicopter.

You suddenly are aware again of the loud staccato of the boat's weapons firing. The radio says another ATC takes a hit. The fourth? Or fifth? What are the casualties to the infantry?

Rhodes repeats his order, now for both minesweepers to turn back, and he tells you both are now beached, but the captains think they can get underway. You ask if there are any boats sinking, and he says there is none, and you ask about mines. Rhodes shakes his head, as if he doesn't know for sure, but says, B-40 and B-50 rockets—that's what they say most of the hits are. You know that means the VC are firing the RPG rocket launchers, designed to take out armored land vehicles.

You know one of the cardinal rules of the entire Riverine Assault Force. You do not go up a stream without minesweepers in the lead. Rhodes doesn't know the status of all of his crews, but it sounds like nearly all the men on the two minesweepers have been wounded.

You call Doty and tell him it looks like they are going to have to turn back. Doty says that we need to get on in to Beaches White ONE and TWO; that one platoon is about to land at Beach TWO right now, ATC 111-6.

But you hear Rhodes order all boats to return to the vicinity of Red Beach TWO, three kilometers south of the White beaches. He tells you there can be no further movement up the Rach Ba Rai until he gets replacement minesweepers in, and possibly one or two monitors. You call Doty and advise him of Rhodes' decision. Doty does not reply. Then he rogers. You know your commander does not want to turn back. Apparently, Rhodes still has no commo with the captain of ATC 111-6.

You feel dejected. You look at Dusty Rhodes. He appears to feel the same, but right now, you know you both have the same worries: getting safely back down the river and reorganizing. You still have to get people on those northern beaches. You call Colonel Doty on the battalion command net. He does not reply. You wait, call again, and this time he replies and you advise him that the entire boat formation is turning and proceeding back south to Red Beach TWO. He acknowledges, and says he will continue to monitor the progress of ATC 111-6 and Captain Davis and his platoon. You roger and realize the Captain and ATC 111-6 will probably be making that run alone, behind the main formation.

All boats continue to fire as they make their turns and move rapidly down the river. You hear Rhodes call back to Saltzer's operation center, asking for assistance in fielding two replacement minesweepers. At least one will have to come from his sister river task group; maybe both, he tells them.

You monitor some of the talk with the Aid Boat on the battalion logistics net. There are casualties in the infantry too; maybe many casualties. Your head hurts. There is almost a smile on Dusty Rhodes' face. You look down. You are sitting on an Army hand grenade box. You don't know if you want the box to be full or empty. Somehow, you hope it is still full. You may still need them.

You shift your weight and chomp down again on your cigar. You have not lit it, but you have chewed it down. It is only a couple of inches long.

No rocket hits are reported on the move back down the river. Small arms and machine gun rounds crack in the air at times and slam up against the side of the CCB. The congestion is building around Red Beach TWO as your boat nestles up against one of the ATCs carrying the A Company commander. A few boats still have fires in their canopies and on deck, and the fires are getting priority attention. You monitor the crowding in on the aid boat and hear fragmented reports of the wounded and the dead. Two of the Navy crewmen are reported dead. All you get when asking for a firm count on your wounded and killed is a wait, out.

You speak to Rhodes briefly as he gives out instructions on reforming crews and rearming of the boats. He stops to call again and ask for the status on identifying replacement minesweepers and a monitor. He tells you he has over sixty crewmen wounded, but maybe half or more are still able to man their stations.

You inform him that one of his armored troop carriers, 111-6, with which he has no commo, is on the way down the river, now, after arriving at White Beach TWO, and landing a platoon, which was then recovered. You tell him that Colonel Doty has already called him and is asking to go back up the river ASAP. It is almost 0815. Rhodes says his task group is in no condition to make a run back up the river; not yet.

Shortly, ATC 111-6 arrives at Red Beach TWO, crowding in to the aid boat. There is one dead and four wounded in the Navy crew. The boat was hit again with a B-40 rocket on the run back down the river. Lieutenant Rogers' platoon has over a dozen casualties.

Surprisingly, no boats had floundered or sunk. Probably there had not been any mines, Rhodes' assistant commander tells you. The rockets were apparently mistaken for mines in the first several minutes. Except for one minesweeper and one Monitor, all of the mounts for the machine guns and 20 and 22-mm guns were still operable, despite damage. ATC 111-6 is one of the most damaged boats and has taken one of the three crew KIA's. As the time passes you are aware that Rhodes is getting reports, one after another, that his troop carrying boats, other than the two with inoperable gun mounts, are operable for another run up the Rach Ba Rai.

There is a lot of discussion about when another run can be made up the river. You talk with Colonel Doty and then with Major Corns about the possible use of 3rd Battalion, 47the Infantry, to take over your battalion's mission. You don't want that, and Corns says that is not likely; there is too much congestion on the river to allow a well coordinated passage. You agree, and push for approval, as Doty has already stressed with you, for 3-60 to make the run again on the upper beaches. Nobody wants to make that run again more than Dusty Rhodes, and he is not ready to turn that role over to the other task group supporting 3-47 Infantry. Rhodes stresses that you couldn't even get his sister task group through the area around Red Beach TWO. Still, he emphasizes that he will not order his boats up the river again until he has adequate crews, and he has rearmed all the boats. You pass that on to Colonel Doty.

You think: when Dusty's ready we'll go again, and this time you will insist, if needed, that all weapons on the boats and of the infantry on board are blazing as you go. Somehow, you doubt that Dusty Rhodes will need any encouragement to do that.

Nearly a half hour later, Colonel Doty, who has been off the net briefly and refueling his helicopter calls Colonel David on the brigade command net, asking that David approve his battalion to attack again. David agrees, saying the timing of the second attack will be based on the Navy saying they are ready. You begin to feel better. You call Corns again and ask about close air support and learn it has already been requested and approved. If the enemy is still there, Corns tells you, 9th Division is prepared to keep a flow of air strikes into the area. You think of the fight in the Ban Long area just days earlier. There were over twenty strikes that day. Still your battalion lost nine killed in the battle.

At any rate, when we go up the river this time, you tell Lieutenant Commander Rhodes, there will be lots more than just one battalion of artillery and some gun ships to support us. But as time passes, it becomes clear that two battalions from the 3d Brigade who are being positioned to the east to block VC escape routes will limit the fires of the Navy boats. You wonder whether the battalions there are worth the great decrease in firepower that Rhodes would be able to release on the starboard side of the formation. It will shut down the 20-mm guns for sure; maybe even the .50 caliber machine guns. Still, if the enemy is still there in force, you know they will fight. You check with Corns again on the timing of the positioning of those battalions. Maybe they will not be in position at the start to restrict the fires. After some delayed discussion with his people, Corns calls back and says the fire support limits on the 20-mm guns will be unavoidable, since both battalions were nearly in position right then. You are anxious. You want to get underway again. You are thankful and surprised that more men, soldiers and sailors, have not been killed. Maybe this run, we will lose nobody. Then you just hope the enemy is still there.

Still later, near 1030 hours, the task group is underway again with two new minesweepers, and one new Monitor. One of the original minesweepers, that had lost some sweep gear was still back at the end of the column in a support role. Gone for repairs were minesweeper T-91-4 and Monitor M-111-2. Over two dozen sailors and a similar number of soldiers have been evacuated. The Doc indicated most had superficial face and leg wounds from the shrapnel from rockets exploding against the metal frames above the troop well of ATCs. Including the three Navy crewmen, you know of six men killed in the first run.

Rhodes has just commented on the huge amount of ammunition taken aboard as a result of the heavy fires on the enemy during that 30-minute firefight. What you don't know is how much of it hit the VC or their bunkers, and how many of the rounds, even direct hits, penetrated the bunkers. You are going back up the river. Every man is leaning on the weapon he crews or individually mans. Army soldiers are nearby, ready to man, as you have been told they did without orders on the first run, gun mounts where the casualties among the vulnerable sailors have left the station unmanned. There was a stern determination among these men now, soldier and sailor alike. They felt they had given as good as they got on the first run, but on this one, if the Viet Cong were still there, the enemy would be getting a lot more than they could give out.

The preceding account is what you and I can imagine Dick Sharp was thinking. It is what happened to him, and as close as reports and my own conversations with him later allow with regard to his thoughts. Others in the battle, men like Colonel Doty, Dick's commander, had, in that same hot, half hour, a different point of view. Doty's was a pivotal role affecting the decision to make the second run up the river, and who would lead it.

Lieutenant Colonel Mercer Doty had been airborne before 0730, even as his lead company started up the Rach Ba Rai on Rhodes' boats. His view was from the area of the My Tho River and was soon limited as the boats came under some low clouds over Snoopy's Nose. Doty's view, once the fighting began and north of Snoopy, was through spotty openings in the clouds, but provided a clearer understanding than anyone could get listening to the tactical radios. In fact, early enemy contact radio reports within and external to Dusty Rhodes' task group, painted a picture more menacing and threatening than what Doty could see from the air.

Central to the initial impression was the report of mine detonations. These reports were found to be wrong, confused with the results of rocket fire. Reports did not reveal that as many as two-thirds of the wounded, Navy and Army, were able to continue their fighting throughout the day. Finally, reports of one boat sinking and three beached, added to the boats temporarily out of control, created a picture in the task group CCB of more severe loss of combat capability than was the case. This impression at brigade and flotilla headquarters was based upon reports from the site of the battle. Doty later said the confusion of reports on the battalion command net suggested far more damage to boats than he could see. However, he recognized that his view, initially clear as he looked north below Snoopy's Nose, soon became even cloudier as the boats responded to Dusty Rhodes' command to fire all weapons. This new cloud was man-made, and it soon smelled of the cordite of spent ammunition, even to a helicopter passenger at a thousand feet altitude. Directing his pilot to lower altitudes, always aware of the south to north gun target line of the supporting artillery, Doty was able to find holes and get views, at times, of the twisting and turning boats on the river. He noted some continued forward movement of the boats, their guns thundering and creating more smoky clouds, for the first eight or ten minutes after he was aware of the VC fires, or ambush. Dick Sharp reported the first hit to him, and he had seen one of the lead boats take a hit before Dick's message. After the first bursts of enemy fire, the column slowed and nearly halted except for boats seeming to keep moving to make the VC gunners' task more difficult. To Colonel Doty, the formation seemed to maintain its military control, despite the twisting and turning movements, to include two boats that spun in the channel that was over fifty meters wide, as if rudderless, or lacking a coxswain. One was the CCB and for a time, he got no response from Major Sharp on the radio. A couple of boats beached, but only briefly, and as the battle progressed, he became aware the minesweepers seemed to make no effort to continue north, although no longer under heavy fire, while the lead ATC 111-6 continued north, unprotected by minesweeper or fire support monitor. He confirmed their status with Dick Sharp and urged his S3 to get Commander Rhodes to continue north to the White beaches.

He saw an explosion behind one boat. A Boston Whaler's fuel tank burst in flames. He saw what he guessed was the outboard motor come hurtling up into the sky before it fell back to splash in the river. He got no reply on the battalion command net when he called Captain Davis, and Dick Sharp spoke up to tell him he had been unable to get Davis on the radio since the firing began. Doty contacted Davis on his company internal command net and told him to land. In just a few minutes, Davis informed him he had 3d Platoon ashore, and he was ready to land the other platoons, but his other ATCs had not yet rounded the point. He said the VC fire had knocked out the ATC radio package, and he had only one operational radio. Doty directed him to get a radio up on the battalion command net as soon as possible, but to give priority to the communications with Rogers on shore.

Doty watched as Lieutenant Rogers' ATC touched shore, bow machine guns blazing into the jungle foliage. The ramp lowered and Rogers' platoon poured into the jungle. Doty had contacted Captain North of Company A and had learned that his ATCs were not continuing north and that North understood they were withdrawing. Doty called Sharp only to learn about the task group commander's order to turn back. He asked Sharp if the commander would reconsider, and Sharp advised him that neither minesweeper had operable sweep gear and that Commander Rhodes had no alternative. Doty then returned to Davis' internal net and told him to reload the boat and to get back south. His company commander simply and calmly reported, "We're coming back now." In later years, after a couple o f beers, Dick Sharp would tell this story, and repeat those words. Doty told him they were some of the saddest he ever received in combat.

For Colonel Doty, the decision to turn back was difficult to accept, but he did so, in respect for the authority of the task group commander. Immediately, however, his thoughts were that they had to come back. He had monitored the call several minutes earlier that passed the brigade order to Tutwiler to prepare to take over the 3-60 mission. He had not thought it a practicable alternative, but had been too busy to discuss it with anyone. Now he wanted to come up on the net and make sure that did not happen. He did not know the number of casualties, but all seemed to be wounded with no deaths, and mostly in Company A. Company C, Captain Botelho's unit, was still in reserve and fresh, and Davis's company had taken few wounded.

He reflected on the action on the waterway as his pilot headed the helicopter south to refuel. The sky was opening more, just as the clouds of smoke was picking up again as the boats hurried south, many of the weapons firing openly. He heard no new reports of rocket hits, but he asked the pilot to make one more turn if he had the fuel. The pilot said he did have a little time, but not much. Doty wanted to check the progress of Captain Davis' ATC. He found the boat was maybe a half kilometer or more behind the last boat in Rhodes' line of retreating boats. Each boat had gotten underway as soon as it could following Rhodes' order. ATC 111-6 was not firing its weapons, and had not reported taking enemy fire. The pilot said he had to go, and Doty said okay, and they headed south again.

Colonel Doty did not learn of the B-40 hit that boat 6 had taken until after he refueled and took off from the fire support base. While at the base, he saw Brigadier General Fulton who shared Doty's belief that it was essential to get troops on Beaches White ONE and TWO. Fulton also shared Doty's view that it made sense to have his battalion lead again on a second run up the river. Neither officer questioned at the time a second run. It was just a matter of how soon they could do so, and both agreed the sooner the better. Fulton suggested that Doty, once airborne, contact the brigade commander and suggest to him what he had shared with the Assistant Division Commander. Doty did so, resulting in the decision and instructions that kept 3-60th Infantry as the lead battalion in the attack. The Navy would set the time to run the river again, based on the readiness of their boats and the transfer of wounded to boat or helicopter evacuation.

Doty would later say that from his perspective, the first attack was always doable, but he would bow to the group commander's decision to replace the minesweepers that Captain Saltzer wanted out in front of troop movements. He would add that from what he saw, boats that beached did so for only a few minutes, no boat was sinking, and Davis' lead platoons were not far from White Beach TWO when the VC opened fire. Doty had viewed the conditions of the boats with confidence. As he later said, they had found the enemy where the intelligence said they would be, and he had great confidence in the plan. The greatest risk, running the gauntlet as some would put it, had essentially worked. He wanted to press the action and get on with the plan.

Even the minesweepers that had taken, together, sixteen wounded, retained some capability and did not return to the rear immediately when so ordered early in the fight. He knew the reduced capability of those minesweepers was a major reason for Rhodes' decision to pull back to Red Beach TWO. It was Doty's intent to continue and land Davis' entire company as planned. Only after learning of Rhodes' decision did he back off.

Still, Doty and all concerned accepted the reorganization of Rhodes' task group, and the operation continued as planned with some change in lead maneuver units. The number of casualties among the infantry aboard the armored troop carriers was not known until the reorganization process at Red Beach TWO. Generally, there were more wounded than reported to Colonel Doty or to Major Sharp, but the wounds were less severe than many expected.

Colonel David's and my perspective, beginning about 0730, suffered more from a lack of information and a worst case sensing of that limited information than from what we knew. This was to impact the limited amount and nature of the directions and orders from brigade level during that brief time. Near 0730, our brigade command group, consisting again of Colonel David, myself, our artillery liaison officer, and our Air Force ALO, went airborne. Early reports of the contact after we were in the air were delayed by the confusion in the boats. The report of the boats hitting mines caused immediate concern and an urgent need for more information. Our pilot flew us west of the Rach Ba Rai and north, trying to get us into position to see the river, but the clouds were heavy along the river above Snoopy's Nose. There were two artillery spotting helicopters east of us, as well as Colonel Doty's helicopter. As was standard procedures, our command pilot gave priority to the airspace for those aircraft nearer the gun target line, which, in this case, meant also our waterborne formation on the Rach Ba Rai. Our efforts initially to get a good survey of the battle area was hampered by the cloud over Snoopy's Nose and, increasingly, the smoke rising from the friendly and enemy gunfire north of that signature turn in the river. It was not possible from our distance and visibility to gauge the intensity of the firefight or to confirm the reports of mined and sinking boats. The fires in the canopy and rear decks of a couple of lead ATCs were at times observable, and served to add to our concerns. Finally, Colonel David directed the pilot to make a south to north pass as close to the river as possible along the west bank. He asked the pilot to make it as low and close as he felt he could. The resulting pass was, in retrospect, at a bad time. As we turned away, our open interphone discussion by the four members of the command group, the copilot, and crew chief created a clear impression. One or two boats beached, one boat dead in the water, two careening about clearly out of control, and a report the CCB had taken a direct hit by a rocket.

Colonel David immediately ordered the pilot to return to the forward command post, where he said we would have better communications. Also, we had just talked briefly with General Fulton on the command net, and David had suggested they meet now at the forward command post. We flew south.

Fulton had called just before our pass along the river seeking a status report. Using my call sign, Masher 3, he called out, "Sitrep." It was our long-standing working procedure to respond to that call with a rundown on our status. It occurred to me he had not addressed Colonel David first, which I would have preferred. After assuring that he had a map with the overlay of our plan in front of him, I gave him a report, but interrupted it as Colonel David got my attention. I gave up the radio to him. As I listened, David tried to repeat a confusing report of new, multiple hits on our boats by B-40 rockets.

I switched to the 3d Battalion's operations net and contacted Sharp, who reported hits on several boats. There was clear concern in Dick's voice. He lacked information on the status of each platoon, and Rhodes wanted the condition of the minesweepers, which the crew reported had hit mines. Dick gave me a "wait, out," and for a time he was not available. Presumably, he was talking to Colonel Doty or one of his company commanders on one of his company nets.

When he came back on the battalion operations net, he seemed more settled. Once David and Fulton ended their conversation, David asked what I had learned from Sharp, and I told him close to what he said he had gotten from Doty. He said that we should take some action. I pointed out the two liaison officers were already coordinating the artillery that we had planned for Beaches White ONE ad TWO onto targets selected by Colonel Doty's artillery fire support officer. Further, our ALO was requesting close air support. The explosions on the ground east of the river had already confirmed for us that our artillery battalion was hard at work. That seemed to ease Colonel David for a time, but then there were more reports from our brigade operations center stating that at least two of Commander Rhodes' crewmen on the CCB had been killed. We learned later this was wrong, that the killed were aboard Rhodes's ATC'S.

Most striking were the reports that there were many wounded infantrymen aboard the ATC's in both of Doty's lead companies. Dick Sharp then confirmed the boats had stopped their progress, and that Rhodes was injured. At the same time, as I tried to pass a team of gun ships to Dick's control, he gave me a "Negative, negative, Masher 3, you handle them, I have my hands full."

Clearly, the situation on the CCB was not good. I think Colonel Doty listened to all of that and formed a similar judgment. He came up on the brigade net to tell me he could coordinate the gun ships, and I passed them to him. David then talked briefly with Colonel Doty while I switched to another net, and I did not know what they had said. Once we were both off the nets, David again told me that we had to do something. I knew he was waiting for me to recommend whatever that should be. We needed more information. I told him we should not continue back to the forward command post, but try to get into a position to see more from the air. At first he agreed, but before the pilot could begin a turn back north, David said we would continue to the forward command post. He had told Fulton he would meet him there. He looked at me and said, "What would you recommend?" I had no recommendation other than to get more information, which I had already said. I asked him what Colonel Doty had said. David told me that Doty was upbeat and thought they should press on in the operation. But David added that Doty didn't know just what the extent of the boat damage or casualties to Rhodes' group or his battalion was.

I suggested that we ask Doty to come to the forward command post also and see what his ideas were. David nodded his head agreeing, but then said, "We need to get the 3d Battalion, 47th Infantry, ready." I replied that they were already well up the river and to move them much farther, they would be at their assigned Red Beaches. I did not think we should order them to land at this point; not until Doty's situation was clearer. "Well, Tutwiler should know what our status is and be prepared to take over," David said. I thought that was correct, but that we needed to know the condition of Doty's battalion better before we could decide what to tell Tutwiler or how to use his battalion. "We need to tell him something, now," David said.

I hesitated, and then said, "We could tell him to move as close to the Red Beaches as he can, hold, but not to land until ordered, and be prepared to assist Doty's battalion." David's expression suggested that was not what he was thinking or looking for. "Or, we could tell him to be prepared to take over the mission of Doty's battalion," I said.

"Yes, tell him that," said Colonel David.

Even as I contacted Colonel Tutwiler on the command net, I knew that such an action would be difficult, if not impossible. If Doty's battalion and Rhodes' task group were in no condition to continue the mission, the route up the Rach Ba Rai could be too congested to get Tutwiler's battalion through. His soldiers were aboard the boats of the other Navy task group, not far to the south, but the question was, how to get Tutwiler's boats through the congestion of Dusty Rhodes's command. When I passed the "be prepared" order to Guy Tutwiler, I detected in his request for me to repeat it a degree of doubt, if not disagreement. I then added, "This is a contingency. We are working now to get further clarification of the situation, and will keep you informed." Tutwiler gave me a Roger, out. I didn't know what he thought of the order, but I was uneasy with it. I noted that Colonel David nodded as he monitored my added comment to Tutwiler. I guessed that he simply felt better that he had taken this precautionary step.

It did not take long for the warning order to Tutwiler to be questioned. Shortly after we landed at the forward command post, Brigadier General Fulton arrived. Colonel David gave him a general rundown and repeated the warning order I had issued to Colonel Tutwiler. "Yes, I heard that," Fulton said. I had worked with him long enough to know he had more to say about that, but he didn't say it … not then. Later, after I had given him a more detailed rundown, with which he showed some impatience, he pulled me aside and questioned why we were here and not in the air. I dodged the question, saying that we had been forward and I was sure the brigade commander would be going back up soon. He then asked why we had given the warning order to Guy Tutwilwer, and before I could answer he said that it wouldn't work. He then left me and rejoined Colonel David. I listened to the conversation as Fulton skillfully suggested that he thought that Colonel Doty would be able to sort out the boats and casualties and still take Beaches White ONE and TWO. He told David that he should press the Navy to make sure we didn't lose too much time before we went back up the river. We could lose the enemy if we took too long. He pointed out the essence of our whole plan was getting to those two White beaches.

"You have to put the cork in the bottle," he said. He never referred to the warning order to Tutwiler. When he left, he gave me a nod and a half wave. Had we been back in the command and staff training at Fort Riley, I think he would have told me that I had made a mistake. He would likely say that I should have simply told Colonel David the order to Tutwiler was not workable and that I should have just told him he should not give that order. At least, that is what I thought he might think, but maybe it was just my own honest critique of what I should have done.

I then renewed my suggestion to Colonel David that we meet with Colonel Doty and get a better feel for his battalion's status. He agreed. It was another fifteen minutes before we took off. It occurred to me to tell him he should rescind the "be prepared" order to Tutwiler. Then I told myself, we were not in a Fort Benning classroom dotting "i's" or crossing "t's" or at a command and staff training session at Fort Riley, Kansas. That choice, never a good one, was now dead anyway. We did not mention it again.

Shortly after we were airborne, Doty called David and told him he had just spoken with the Assistant Division Commander, and that he, Doty, believed he should continue the mission of his battalion. David agreed, but reminded his battalion commander that Commander Rhodes had ordered all boats back to Red Beach ONE and TWO. Once the Navy was ready to make another run up the river, David told Doty, his battalion would again have the mission to take those beaches.

When we renewed our attack up the Rach Ba Rai around 1030 hours, Colonel Doty put his fresh Company C in the lead and Company B in reserve. Enemy resistance remained strong, but our boats and the infantry aboard went into the original area of most effective VC fire, the ambush area, as we called it, with guns blazing and artillery and gun ships in full support. Air strikes hit the VC positions for hours, steadily. Only one armored troop carrier took a significant rocket hit, most of the VC small arms and machinegun fire bouncing off the armor protection. But that one hit nearly took out a platoon of Company A, wounding eighteen, of whom one soldier died. While nearly all the other seventeen men returned to action within days, when the platoon landed on its assigned Beach White ONE, only four men went ashore.

We never met with Colonel Doty until late that afternoon, well after all battalions had moved, by boat, helicopter, and overland into the positions they would occupy, essentially, for the night. Although we suffered one more soldier killed and the eighteen wounded in Captain North's run back up the river, losses for the rest of that day and the next were light. Despite our best efforts to tie together our forces around the enemy, the gaps were too large. We had experienced that before, especially large gaps between our American battalions and the Vietnamese Army battalions. The Vietnamese Ranger battalion had landed by helicopter northwest of 3-60th Infantry. They then moved by foot to block enemy escape west over the Rach Ba Rai. Whether because of approaching darkness or concern about getting too close to the firepower of our boats on the river, the Vietnamese battalion took up a position on a narrow front made narrower by its security orientation of 360 degrees.

VC probes and light contacts during the night suggested that, despite our efforts to secure the river with our boats, the enemy likely ex-filtrated west in the darkness over the Rach Ba Rai. Early morning searches west of the river by the Vietnamese battalion and by 3rd Battalion, 47th Infantry, supported that likelihood.

The battle had confirmed the capability of the MRF to move and fight on the waterways. The boats, more so than in any other operation so far, proved themselves survivable against enemy rockets, grenades, machine guns, and small arms. However, we had not confronted the dreaded floating land mines. We had proven to be vulnerable, especially the Navy gun crews, to both shrapnel of the rockets as well as machine gun and small arms fire. The boat gun mounts and crew stations had little metal armor, and sandbags added little protection above knee or thigh level. The vulnerability of the infantry in the canopy-covered wells, when attacked by the B-40 and B-50 rockets, was a major concern. While many rockets passed overhead or even ripped and passed through the vinyl canopy without exploding, causing no harm, their explosion when they hit the metal frames supporting the canopies showered the infantry with shrapnel.

The attack up the Rach Ba Rai was at the maximum speed the boats could make through the area of reported and assumed enemy presence. I had thought of the idea to attack in this manner on this same river after our attack there four months earlier. It was bold, but only in its determination to move infantry companies beyond the enemy to block likely escape routes to the north. The speed of the boat movement would not be rapid enough to keep the enemy from getting into fighting holes or bunkers that they usually prepared in any area they used for resting and training. Our conclusion was the Viet Cong used the Cam Son area to rest their men and retrain. We thought the bunkers, such as they might be, would face mainly to the northeast to defend from movement into the area by Vietnamese mechanized units along the road from Highway 4. That proved to be largely the case. There might be, we thought, surprise gained by the volume and effectiveness of the combined fires of all the boats, backed by artillery fires from guns pre-positioned and ready on the first request for fires from our companies. It is not clear that we gained surprise in terms of the enemy being denied time to prepare an effective gauntlet of fire along the right, east, bank of the river. The surprise was likely to have been limited to the attack from the My Tho River and the south—and the fact we attacked them at all.

Our intrusion in force into the Cam Son base, a base the Viet Cong for years had considered impenetrable was in our favor. Against a force the size we used in the Cam Son, the VC would usually try to avoid battle. On 15 September, they had to fight as our lead boats passed their location. They knew we would soon be able to land troops north of them—block their best route out. The relative loss of friendly and enemy forces was and is always important, at least viewed in the short term of battles lost or won. They are also important when the attrition of available soldiers is key to the capacity of either or both sides of the war to continue. In late 1967, we still believed we would defeat the Viet Cong if we lessened their strength enough. We would do that in the battles of TET five months later. Some claim we had beaten the VC by then. However, it had always been the published strategy of the North Vietnamese to raise the insurgency to conventional land warfare. The regiments and divisions that could wage such war were in North Vietnam. Their strategy suggested they would eventually engage us with those conventional units if they believed they could win. North Vietnam leaders such as General Giap have said since the Vietnam War that they believed they would get to the point they could bring their conventional forces into the fight, as they did in piecemeal fashion from TET onward.

But in late 1967, we still believed we could defeat the Viet Cong by attrition and thus win the war. In that context, our battle north of Snoopy's Nose was a victory. Of 123 friendly wounded, 77 of which were Navy crewmen, 23 needed evacuation beyond Dong Tam. Three sailors died and Army killed were 4, giving us 7 killed in action. In all, nearly three dozen wounded were evacuated from the area to Dong Tam. The next day, we counted 79 Viet Cong bodies on the battlefield. Our MRF combined enemy kills for the four days, 12-16 May was much higher, but in that four-day period, we lost 16 soldiers and sailors, killed in action.

I did not share with anyone the role that our Assistant Division Commander had played in the battle. It had been, in good measure, behind the scenes, most notably in agreeing with Colonel Doty's assessment and prodding him to press the early resumption of the attack by Doty's battalion. It was the same aggressive insistence on carrying the fight to the enemy that Fulton had displayed in the Battle of Ap Bac (2). He would say, he was only applying respected Army doctrine, what any graduate of the Army's Infantry School or the Command and General Staff College would know. That would be, in my judgment, quite true. But the difference on the battlefield is the leader who sees that reality in the smoke and clouds—the so-called, fog of war. And more, it is the leader who sees it, and acts, aggressively.

The day after we closed on the MRF afloat base offshore of Dong Tam, General Westmoreland visited us, escorting Senator Stuart Symington, of Missouri. I was especially proud to meet the Senator and to brief him and Westmoreland. Symington was one of my dad's favorite politicians. He proved himself to my dad and to thousands of school kids like me when he took on

Senator Joe McCarthy and his outlandish campaign of character assassination under a blind witch-hunt of anticommunism in the 1950s.

I found it interesting that General Westmoreland asked several questions that allowed me to highlight the close cooperation and bond that had developed between our sailors and soldiers at the platoon and boat level. I probably spent more time than I should have on our operation up the Rach Ba Rai. Colonel David summarized with comments on the cooperation at all levels as well as individual contributions by Army and Navy commanders at squadron and battalion levels. He complimented me and my Navy counterpart, as well as our S2, Major Dick Jennings, and our plans officer, Major Dick Munsell. He made special note that for this operation, I had suggested the scheme of maneuver as both planner and operator, based on our operation the previous May. The intended twenty-minute briefing took over forty-five, with questions and interruptions, but General Westmoreland was clearly pleased and upbeat as he and the Senator left the Benewah.

Possibly flowing from that visit by Westmoreland, there were requests from American advisers and Vietnamese officials for the presence of the MRF throughout the Delta in late September and all of October. We ranged from the Rung Sat Special Zone, in response to an attack on shipping on the channel going into Saigon, back to Kien Hoa and Dinh Tuong Provinces. We turned again north to the Can Giouc area south of Saigon to reinforce security for the conduct of early fall national elections.

On 30 October, our highest-ranking visitor, Vice President Hubert Humphrey, came aboard the Benewah. On 1 November, I wrote to Carol:

> I am enclosing one of those rare items of life. In February, Lisa met the Vice President at Charleston. On 30 October he visited the USS Benewah for a briefing. Just before I began the briefing with the Army portion, Col David, who learned of the newspaper clipping from Col O'Connor, interrupted. He said, Mr. Vice President, this is the major whose family you met in Charleston, West Virginia. The Vice President, whom I had already been introduced to, stood up, took the clipping and said, Oh yes. (I doubt if he recalled, but he might have.) He asked how all of you were, said that I had a fine family, and that this was a rare and delightful happening for him. Anyway, he said let me write something on it and you can keep it as a memento of the occasion. He did—with my pen—handed it back, and then I went on with the briefing. At a point he mentioned again the pretty girl, and I said yes sir, you have seen her since I have—Got a chuckle from him. He was easy to brief—very alert and curious. Anyway, it's a small world and the incident reminded me of my pride in my family.

The clipping, which Carol had sent to me in the mail, pictured our daughter, Lisa, in a black and white, checked raincoat with a matching scarf. Vice President Humphrey was holding her with Carol and a large group of people standing nearby. That was at the local airport, which was later named, Chuck Yeager Airport. Spotting this little girl in her mother's arms as he and his entourage walked by, Humphrey stopped. He turned, pointed back at them, and then led his group back where he ignored security and walked over to the fence and asked if he could borrow our daughter.

As he told the story there on the boat, anchored in the Mekong River, you would have thought he was on a street corner in a city in the United States, campaigning. Maybe, with the river as the street in this case, that was exactly what he was doing, considering his entry into the Presidential race the following year after President Johnson announced he would not run for reelection. Carol's dad had seemed unimpressed by the picture in the local *Charleston Gazette*. Probably all this did not impress him, since Hubert Humphrey was not one of his favorite politicians. He likely questioned why his granddaughter was up there at the airport in the first place. But, I think Mr. Cyrus was proud too, but as a staunch Republican, he couldn't say so.

Just a few days later, the MRF engaged in one of our largest battles. I wrote to Carol on 7 December, two days after the battle, referring to "a classic Riverine operation." Overstatement aside, I was referring to a battle on the Rach Ruong Canal, still west of Rach Ba Rai and Snoopy's Nose and on the western boundary of Dinh Tuong Province. It was our first operation with the newly arrived 5th Vietnamese Marine Battalion. It was similar to the Rach Ba Rai attack in September with a big exception. When hit by enemy fire going up the canal, Major Nam, the battalion commander, ordered a direct assault on the enemy, a right degree turn of the ATC's into the bank and the enemy. His was a decisive action, which the U. S. Navy task group commander, technically in overall command, immediately agreed to support, and the results were decisive. The VC casualties on this operation of 4 and 5 December were 266 killed, essentially destroying the Viet Cong 502d Local Force Battalion and heavily damaging the 267th Main Force Battalion. The primary reason for the high number of enemy killed was the attack the Marine battalion carried to them and never lessened. The VC were not free to flitter about and test our strength or make their escape quickly as we were calling in supporting fires. But the price was also high for Major Nam's battalion: 40 killed and 107 wounded.

Later, as an instructor of Riverine Operations at the Infantry School, I would analyze the battle using all available responses from participants to include an adviser to the battalion from the United States Marine Corps. The tactics of Major Nam, the enemy killed, and the friendly casualties taken were similar to results of some Marine amphibious operations during World War

II. The need for an island base in that war made a frontal assault essential against a predictable landing beach, since there often were no other beaches available. The Japanese forces put up stubborn defenses.

Dick Sharp, as S3, and the entire Mobile Riverine Force would carry the nature and results of the two battles, Rach Ba Rai and Rach Ruong, into 1968 and throughout the life of Riverine operations in Vietnam. The tendency of the men in the boats, soldier and sailor, was to favor the reaction to a canal ambush with a frontal assault. Commanders at higher levels tended to favor the same reaction as Army ground vehicle columns did in ambush. That is, to fire all weapons and run through the gauntlet to then land at a point of less resistance and turn on the flanks of the ambush force. In the time that this maneuver takes, the enemy has the opportunity to adjust also, and to begin to break contact, if that is his will. Which approach to take will always be a question for units involved in Riverine Operations, wherever they take place.

In a letter to Carol, I wrote, "Sorry you have to get the word on these big battles when we take losses like that, but it seems part of the state of things. I started to call, but was afraid I would scare you. I have never seen such a fine application of combat power in which I played (I think) a good part. Colonel David has named it the Corns Operation simply because it was the last one for me as S3. Dick Sharp will be in charge next time and I'll monitor from the Base.

"What a year. I miss you terribly, but you have a very proud husband who has achieved at 31 what we all strive for and many never realize."

A couple of days later, I had grown no more modest as I told her she should read my last efficiency report. The report came after I sat in my only counseling session with Colonel David. I valued his personal and professional criticisms—easy for me, since they were all positive. In a way, my relationship with him was almost opposite to that which I had with Colonel Fulton. I had worked for David only a third of the time I had worked with my first Riverine boss. Fulton was nearly always the teacher and I was the student, while with Colonel David, I was often the teacher, owing to his lack of prior exposure to the Riverine concept. In a way, I found myself more often in a difficult position with him than I did with Fulton. But, my task was easier with both because of their total honesty, with themselves and with me. At times, I did not show the best judgment in recommendations to each of them, but they never hesitated to ask my view and opinion, and I knew quickly that both could handle hearing what they did not like. I never suffered as a messenger with either of them; regardless of how unwelcome the news might be, even waking them in the middle of the night to share bad news. Both were men of great honor and integrity. But, Bert David's job was harder. He was competent, smart, a professional. He did not like not knowing, but he thrived on learning. He learned fast, and I did not have to tell him twice, something he might not have been able to say about me.

His professional restraint in dealing with Bill Fulton as his boss was admirable. He saw Fulton as a teacher too. He had the confidence and the devotion to his duty and his soldiers to accept good advice from any quarter. However, it was not always easy to do that in working for Bill Fulton, a man of innovation, imagination, aggressiveness and action. He could hardly restrain himself with an idea. Whether in the presence of his division commander as a brigade commander, or before the Chief of Staff of the Army as Director of the Army Staff. I watched him perform admirably in both capacities. It was his personal emphasis on unreservedly throwing your judgment into any discussion that Fulton prepared me to serve Colonel David.

At Camp Bearcat, just before we went south in March of 1967 to Dong Tam, Fulton and I were talking following a planning meeting for an operation we were to run in the Nhon Trach area. He mentioned the presentation by one of the commanders to be in the operation with us. "You know," he said, "you should always speak right up when you don't agree with something."

It was almost a conversational comment, but I saw the clear critique in it, and I knew exactly what he was referring to. The officer who had briefed us on how he would lead our brigade into the Nhon Trach wore a flowing gold scarf, hand grenades on his web gear, and a manner that has to be described as a swagger. He was confident. He was well prepared, and he was articulate. He exuded a manner of courage and boldness. So you will know him, he would soon after be decorated with the Distinguished Service Cross for bravery and action above and beyond the call of duty on the battlefield. Of course, I didn't know this yet, but he impressed me. Most of his presentation also impressed me. He ended, however, with a flourish akin to a commander pumping up soldiers prior to an attack. He said the road we were to travel would be open, and would be open fast, once he ran his lead troop down its length. If true, that could mean our infantry would not have to cut our way through the jungle on either side of the road to remove snipers or, worse still, a VC ambush force.

Fulton asked him, how long he thought it would take him to reach the first objective well down that road. The squadron commander gave his answer. My quick mental calculation was that his armored vehicles were going to negotiate that distance at some 30 kilometers an hour. I had a folder on my lap with several recent aerial photos. They showed three locations along the road that were pitted with large craters from explosions. My aerial photo interpreter had calculated that the holes that traversed nearly the width of the road up to the jungle growth and its marshy soil, were six to eight feet deep and thirty feet in diameter.

I asked a question, but only one, whether the squadron formation would include any field bridging capacity. The lieutenant colonel cavalryman answered, as if a little irritated, that there was no need for such equipment on this operation. My mistake was that I had said no more. I had intended to share with the colonel, or his operations officer who accompanied him, the aerial photos, after the meeting. However, Fulton, who had been standing just beside the podium for a couple of minutes, as a hint I think for the colonel to wrap it up, said, "Let's see what more my S2 has to say about that. Johnnie?" He was looking at me. He probably read on my face that there was something I did not agree with.

I stood and said that I had some information that had probably not come to the cavalry commander's attention. They showed that clearing the roadway, even without enemy resistance, would need much more time because of three deep craters with abbatix in depth in front of them. The colonel looked at his S3. There was a brief silence. Then the S3 said that he believed an officer he called by name had identified some cratering in their planning, but it would not be a significant delay in their advance. The cavalry commander hesitated and then said. "Well, that's something we can look at." He turned to Fulton and said he would get back to him on that point before the operation, and the planning conference ended. Later the colonel did provide an estimate that lengthened the time he would take to lead us into the Nhon Trach. His revised estimate proved to be about right.

I was probably for months after the conversation inclined not to make too much of it, but I was not inclined to take lightly anything Fulton might say, particularly if it seemed critical of my actions or judgment. Fortunately, there were almost no similar critiques of matters large or small. So, I valued that rather easy comment, and had thought I had subsequently taken it to heart, and I suspect that I had done so, at least in dealing with Fulton. But the look I got from Fulton many weeks later at the forward operations center at the mouth of the Rach Ba Rai as he left the discussion with Colonel David and me, was clear. I had failed to speak up aggressively enough with my new commander. I didn't raise it again with either man. I felt that it was Fulton's presence that raised the pressure for David to come up with something to do about the confusing battle above Snoopy's Nose. The result was an unsound tactical notion. Even David, I think, soon saw it would not be practical to push another battalion up that river, blocked by the boats carrying Doty's battalion.

In that counseling session, Bert David mentioned several events that had passed between him and me, all complimentary of my professional judgment.

He spoke of the Snoopy's Nose operation, emphasizing the initial plan, saying that he almost didn't approve the concept because of concern that "we would run into exactly what we did." Then he smiled, and said, "That was why it was a successful operation. We carried the battle right into their front door and then blocked their back door."

"With a little delay," he added.

Then he rose and reached out his hand, and I took it. "The reason I was so quick to approve it, despite my reservation, was your professional judgment. Fulton had told me that you might be a little hesitant to speak your mind at times, but that once you did, I could take it to the bank."

A colorful mix of criticism and compliment, I think, but, on balance, I'll take it.

Chapter Sixteen

Another Reflection

General Fulton asked me to come up to the division headquarters at Camp Bear Cat a day before I needed to go to Saigon for my flight home in December. As a brigadier general, he lived in a bare and rustic, but comfortable, mobile "hut on wheels." We talked of the Mobile Riverine Force and its success in the Delta. We were proud of what had taken place, and we believed the MRF to be one of the innovative applications of ground forces in recent warfare. We had both studied the use of gunboats in the Civil War, Navy gunboats in China before World War II, as well as U. S. Marines in Latin America. We saw the MRF as a proud and major step forward in such activities. We had written some new doctrine for American military fighting. I raised my concern that the Viet Cong were increasing their use of rocket launchers and recoilless rifles against our boats. I thought that we might need to adjust tactics sometime in the coming year. He said perhaps that was true, but there were vast areas in the Delta where the MRF had not yet fought. The new areas might allow another year or so to surprise and defeat the Viet Cong battalions.

He shared some information from briefings at MACV headquarters. I found his words refreshing. I had not been aware of the heavy losses the Viet Cong had suffered in the last year. I also had not known the number of Americans killed in '67 would be around 11,000, double the previous year, which had been the highest of the war. He told me that some were saying we could break the will of the VC in the coming year. I shared with him General Paul Harkins' predictions four years earlier. They had not proven to be accurate. He chuckled and said he thought this time it would likely be different. He said that even if you were to lessen the VC casualties of the last year by a quarter, they could not continue their insurgency with the inadequate number of men they could recruit.

Over the years, I have linked that conversation to a document I had examined, captured by one of our battalions in Kien Hoa Province three months earlier. I could not make full sense of it, and my best guess was that it meant an unlikely convergence of two Main Force Viet Cong Battalions on the town of My Tho. Despite the unlikely implication of the map, we shared the information with the 7th ARVN Division and the My Tho and Province leadership and forwarded it to division. Neither I nor anyone with whom I shared it thought it significant, and, of course, nothing, happened—until after I left Vietnam. In the TET offensive of February , two months after my visit with General Fulton, two converging Viet Cong battalions attacked My Tho. I later learned that General Giap and the North Vietnamese also looked forward to 1968 and concluded their forces in the south could not continue to sustain such casualties. They needed to act to remove any image that suggested they were losing. They chose the Tet Offensive.

Chapter Seventeen
Tactics and Training

Following my duty with the Mobile Riverine Force, the Army hustled me off to the Armed Forces Staff College in Norfolk Virginia. I had arrived home just before Christmas to have Carol tell me the Infantry Branch at the Department of the Army had called her and I was to call a number as soon as I got home. I waited until morning.

They had changed my orders. Carol had already arranged to ship our household goods to Fort Benning, Georgia. I liked going to the Attack Committee of the Tactics Group, Brigade and Battalion Operations Department with the special task of writing and teaching a new class on Riverine operations. The Infantry Branch guy told me two months earlier that the Infantry School was a great place to work, and I wanted to learn and to teach other military tactics as well. I paid little attention to the sales pitch by the officer on the other end of the line: I liked the idea of teaching at Fort Benning. He said they had handpicked me. I impressed them, he said, with my experience as an operations officer at brigade level in both Europe and Vietnam. It would be great for my "career progression," he said.

Now I was hearing the same sales pitch from a different staff officer for a different assignment. It reminded me of how the staff officer six years earlier had the same pitch on getting away from my basic branch for two or three years to play like I was a foreign service officer. I protested. I had never heard of the Armed Forces Staff College (AFSC), the place they had decided I should go as a student. I did not want to miss attending the Command and General Staff College (CGSC), an institution that prepared officers for staff work in large commands and organizations. This officer explained how the AFSC was far more prestigious, and taught more than the CGSC. I thought that dubious, since the CGSC was fifty percent longer. Also it stressed the Army, about which I had more to learn. But, I was stuck.

At the AFSC, I learned that someone had shot and killed Martin Luther King. At the AFSC, I also learned of the assassination of Robert Kennedy. They sent me to AFSC because I had served in the Mobile Riverine Force with the Navy, which was not a joint organization, the specialty of AFSC education and training. At the AFSC, I learned all they said I would need to serve on a joint staff, something I never did. The first time I found myself serving in a position that involved significant joint matters, I was a Lieutenant General and whatever I could recall from the AFSC course was twenty years old.

I did, however, meet some impressive officers at AFSC from all branches of the military, caught flounder in the Chesapeake Bay, and made the AFSC all-star softball team as a short fielder, probably my most notable accomplishment there.

Finally, I went where I wanted to go to start with and had two great years at the Infantry School. But, before I got there, my mind and heart went back to our time in Vietnam. Carol and I learned of the death of our friend Bob Reeves, which I have already shared with you.

It came at a low point in the AFSC program. I listened to talks by General "Buzz" Wheeler, Chairman of the Joint Chiefs of Staff, and General Harold K. Johnson, Chief of Staff of the Army. Their presentations were part of the AFSC program of instruction.

Wheeler's fatigue was the most impressive part of his talk. He had been Chairman for over three years under President Johnson. He was not specific on issues. I thought it must be trying, even frustrating, to work with the Secretary of Defense and the President, both of whom sounded like men with no high regard for senior officers of the services, and a fondness for management in detail. I recalled comments about that in MacNamara's role in the Cuban Missile Crisis. Of course, over the years, I have read much more about that. But with Wheeler's answers to questions, it was not so much the specifics as the mood that caused me to feel discouraged following the session. Probably it was more a reflection of my lack of information then about working at the top levels of the Pentagon, but I thought this officer wanted to tell us more, be more forthright, but could not be. I had to imagine what he thought, or believed, that he was not saying. Finally, I thought he had little confidence that we would be successful in Vietnam.

General Harold K. Johnson gave a moving presentation of a man torn and on the edge of anger. On some issues, I liked his candor, although we knew we were not to repeat the comments of these military leaders. He was apologetic in permitting the rotation policy to become entrenched. That is, we should not have gotten into a policy that brought men back to the states just as they began to understand the enemy, the weather, and the terrain. As I recall, he suggested he should have carried that right to the White House, and had not. Maybe he did not go that far, but I left with that impression. On some other points, he was not so specific, but I left the auditorium with the impression that he had not agreed with much of the policy guiding our efforts in Vietnam. He clearly had wanted to see the call up of the reserves, but that had not happened. He did not directly say we had been wrong to go into Vietnam, but he said we should have gotten the American people on board, and kept them on board with straight talk and sensible expectations. At that point, I had heard nothing about the questionable circumstances of the Tonkin Gulf Incident, and the intent behind bringing in increasingly larger forces because of that incident. He was uncomfortable with the gradual escalation of the war and mentioned that, as a guide, we should only go to war as a final option and with great strength with a commitment to gain our goal quickly.

Both of these men spoke to us after the Tet Offensive. Unlike many of my classmates, I accepted the notion that the battles of TET could well go down as an overall defeat of our effort in Vietnam. Later information made it clear we beat the enemy during the Tet Offensive, but we suffered a defeat in the minds of too many Americans back home. If we were winning, how could the Viet Cong have come in and taken over some of the cities? Many Americans heard no satisfying answer to that question.

The teachings of General Giap had impressed me when I had been exposed to them five years earlier at Fort Bragg. His strategy was there for anyone to read. The phases of warfare, the importance of the will of the enemy, the civilian population main target of the effort. Dr. Bernard Fall had told us that a key part of the war between the forces in Indo China in '53/'54 was fought in the minds of people in the streets of Paris, France.

By the time I learned the growing American opinion against the war in Vietnam, I wondered if the leaders in Washington believed we could gain a favorable outcome by military action. As for me, I felt more uncomfortable with the war after I left AFSC and found myself teaching and training captains at Fort Benning, most of whom were on their way to their first or second tour in Vietnam.

The incident that tipped me in the direction of doubt, privately, was not a single event in Vietnam or a guest speaker at AFSC. It was my high school history teacher—between my return to my family in South Charleston, West Virginia, in December, and my departure for AFSC in January. Carol told me she had run into Mrs. Nellie Melton, who said that if I had time once I was home, she would like to talk to me. And so Carol and I had visited her in the halls of our high school with our two children.

It was good that we had limited time. I think she felt compelled to get some answers, and so she was direct. I was concerned by both the questions and views she had already formed. I felt initially a need to reassure her. As I talked, I realized that I was not so confident. I was trying to reassure myself as I chose the words, and I thought she could see that. I then felt it a matter of integrity and honesty with her, and I spoke words that I had kept in the back of my mind in the day-to-day pressures of fighting the war. I was never confident again, in my own thoughts, about our eventual success. I learned that her questions were not unique. The notion she was forming that it was not worth the costs in lives was widely held. I was a wounded duck when I flew into the vulnerable environment of hard questions about the war that I found, surprisingly, at AFSC. Most often the carriers of the questions were mid-level civilians of our government. Sometimes, protected by confidentiality, they were senior military officers. And there were the magazine articles the faculty provided or told us about. They were supportive of the policies of our commander in chief and top military leaders, but they did not dodge the questions about the war. It was an openness I did not expect, and many Americans would not expect in a major military school. At the Armed Forces Staff College, my greatest positive finding, which I was to experience eight years later at the Army War College, was this readiness of the commandants to allow various views to enter the halls of learning. It is one of the important safeguards in the education and training of military officers.

But, Fort Benning and the Army Infantry School is not AFSC. And cannot be. The task at Fort Benning is more training and less education than AFSC, CGSC, or the War College. At Fort Benning, I soon dived into training those infantry captains who needed what I offered to assist them in leading men into combat in Vietnam. I was not, however, a fortress of support for all aspects of the war in Vietnam.

In those days at Benning, I discovered a new appreciation for the circumstance I thought General Johnson revealed at AFSC. While in many ways a year of duty in Vietnam was a long time, there is no doubt that a large part of that time was a learning experience for both generals and privates. I wonder today if America's sons and daughters had gone to the Vietnam War "for the duration," as our soldiers did in World War II, if the war would not have been much shorter. Whether it would have ended in victory, which I doubt, or not, it would likely have been shorter. Many soldiers stomached the war because they knew they were going home in a few months—if they survived. That, I think, is what General Johnson had in mind. That and the fact that the draft to sustain the war might not have dug so deeply into the marrow of America. I had twice volunteered for duty in Vietnam. Colonel Fulton and others placed high value on my prior experience when I joined his brigade. While that might have been an overstated value, it reflects the notion that experience in war, as in life, counts. Over the years my own take on Vietnam is that there are challenges for nations that are not best met with military force, or, at best, the military role must be secondary to an effort to deal with the causes of the war up front.

Unfortunately for me in mid-1968, while troubled by doubts about the war, I had not yet fully accepted that insight. I stood on the stage and taught scores of captains who were on there way to war. I knew what being torn was.

As time went on, and years passed, I did not return to Vietnam, although I made no effort to avoid duty there. In those days at Fort Benning, I was also busy as researcher and writer of instruction blocks, teaching classes, and enjoying the most stability my family had ever experienced. I enjoyed teaching tactics, and I loved playing tennis with Clancy Matsuda. Clancy had preceded me to the Infantry School and taught in the same, small Attack Committee under first, Lieutenant Colonel Dick Prillaman and later, Lieutenant Colonel Manny Alves. I seldom beat Clancy at tennis, but I hit some rare winners, and he started asking me about my family tree and how my arms had gotten so long. I was not tall, as he pointed out, and suggested I might never catch up with even one of his hammered forehands if my reach didn't cover the entire width of the end line. But the arms were no big advantage to me—the long arms—most of our games Clancy beat me with ease.

The war was with us every day. While we taught conventional tactics better suited for the last war in Germany than in Vietnam, we tried to share what we had learned in Vietnam. I was asked to write and teach five new tactics classes. The first was Riverine Operations. It was a lecture, actually, and served only to orient the students. I taught it as I wrote the second class, which was a block of four hours including lecture and practical exercises. Soon we phased out the early lecture and went entirely to the longer class. I believe it did contain much that could have helped the young officers later in Vietnam.

The third class I wrote and taught only briefly before leaving the Infantry School was Attack of a Fortified Position. It was set in jungle terrain, and I researched and used the so-called Battle of Hamburger Hill, an actual Vietnam fight, as a guide in teaching. That battle, unfortunately, was a source of many things not to do in attacking a fortified position. At times, a member of the class who had been in that battle assisted me in laying out the conditions and flow of the actual fight, from his perspective. The other tactics classes were on combat in cities and operations in northern, or cold climates. In presenting the latter block of instruction, I drew on class members, captains, who had served in Alaska with our airborne brigade there. I had never served in such climates except for winters in Korea. It would be twenty years before I, the

Advance Course expert in such cold weather tactics would serve in Alaska, and then as a division commander.

Colonel Prillaman had commanded the 2nd Battalion, 2nd Infantry Regiment in Vietnam and had black scarves made for all his troops. The unit came to be called, "The Black Scarves." The cloth was the same used to make the "black pajama" clothing so common in that country and worn as a uniform by the Viet Cong. He was a strong and direct officer, given to bragging that he had never served in the Pentagon and did not intend to do so. He had his unique way of introducing me to each of those new tasks of research, writing and teaching. He would come booming into our room of cubicles, stop at my workplace and say, "John, another chance to excel." It was a compliment and an example of Dick Prillaman's great skill in handling people. I bit. He knew I would. I loved the work and the challenge. I stayed quite busy in my two years at Fort Benning.

Oh, yeah, General Jack Vessey grabbed Dick Prillaman a few years later by the collar, and threw him into the fire of the Pentagon as the Director of Operations of the Joint Staff. Carol and I visited Lieutenant General Prillaman and his wife at Fort MacNair when he had that difficult job. While he had a great sense of humor, he did not like being reminded about his boasts of avoiding the Pentagon. Of course, we both knew he would have gone anywhere for Jack Vessey, then the Chairman of the Joint Chiefs.

I served in those cubicles and on the teaching stage at Benning with Clancy and a fine group of officers. It was among my most favorite assignments in the Army, partly because of the chance to dig into Army history, but mostly because of the people. My fellow instructors of tactics were dedicated to the task. They, as I, viewed our work as truly important and we worked very hard.

However, we did have some time to relax. In addition to the brief struggle at tennis with Clancy, there was golf. My failure was that I did not pick up the game—not then. I received invitations to play, from Clancy and others, but I repeated my long-held view that it took too much time. Really, I may have been wary that I would be required to wear the same kind of pants Clancy wore, with the huge, geometric designs in multiple colors, mostly red, white and blue. He did, however, give me a set of old golf clubs. They looked in great condition to me. About fifteen years later, I did take up golf, and now I know how a golfer might have a perfectly good bag of golf clubs, maybe two, out in the garage, no longer used. Once you are hooked, you will do anything and buy anything to get just one stroke off your handicap. Of course, it is little help, whatever you buy, if your primary handicap is that you started trying to play golf to begin with. I came to love the game, although I play it with little proficiency.

But give Clancy credit. He tried to teach me how to relax. He even suggested, through his wife, Connie, and Carol, that I play bridge with them. I never got far with the game. After a full day at work, pushing my brain to learn and remember things, I didn't see how bridge could be relaxing—keeping track of all those cards. Of course, to Carol, who loved the game, that was unfair. Clancy got even, caught me off at West Point researching a new block of instruction and invited Carol to come and play bridge with him and Connie and a male friend of theirs who lacked my fear of relaxing games. I later got even with Clancy—or tried to—tried to hire him as a staff officer in my battalion at Fort Lewis. He was too smart for that. I admired Clancy. He had balance in his life. He could work hard. He could play hard

That was five years after Benning that I had the idea to get him to work for me, in 1973, and I never had a chance. Another battalion commander asked him to work for him, and Clancy jumped at the job. I didn't blame him. I would have been happy to work for the guy too. His name was Sharp, Lieutenant Colonel Richard Sharp. He was already a lieutenant colonel, while I took command of a battalion as a major, a "promotable" major , but a major.

At Benning, I traveled to West Point, which cost me that chance to play bridge at the Matsuda home, to gain information that would let me prepare and teach a new course to Advance Course captains—Military History. The curriculum did not offer a history course although it had been in and out of the program. My sponsor at The Military Academy was a young major who taught mathematics and coached the West Point lacrosse team. He invited me to sit in on one of his classes and attend a lacrosse team practice. He was equally and admirably effective as a teacher and leader in both roles. I was to learn months later of his death in combat in Vietnam.

At the time, the head of the history department at West Point was Colonel Tom Griess, already an institution in himself. He opened all doors for me and talked with me long and enthusiastically about military history in general and the West Point program in particular. His "Threads of History" idea caught my attention and I used it to help our captains identify valuable lessons of military history looking at the thread of a particular interest over many years. The class, which involved many hours of preparation, was well-received based on student critique sheets. I enjoyed teaching it. However, the school dropped the class two years after I left Fort Benning.

That first and only visit to West Point was a great experience. I had seen the black and white movies of the '40s with the marching on The Plain and the marriage of some just graduated cadet at the post chapel. I had sat with my ear close to the radio to hear the Blanchard and Davis exploits on the football field in the last years of World War II. I walked the plain by day and at night and admired the statues of the cadets who had gone on to fame in serving our country. I visited with Major Tony Nadal and his wife in their historic Army quarters. Tony had also been one of the first four officers to command a 7th Special Forces Group Green Beret detachment in Vietnam.

We sat at their dinner table and spoke of family and the days since Fort Bragg. Tony and I talked of the new concept that was being developed of an all volunteer Army. We were both dubious of the concept in its threat to push our Army farther away from the American people. But quickly our subject was Vietnam. Our failure to apply counterinsurgency doctrine foremost, instead of relying primarily on conventional concepts and tactics. Our days in that country commanding our detachments. His return and his big battle in the Ia Drang River Valley, less than two years after I had operated on the northern slopes of that same river. He had been in the middle of the Ia Drang battle during its entire course. He relived parts of it with deliberate preciseness about what he saw and heard, and a seeming reservation about how the media depicted the fight, particularly a major magazine article. Years later, when I read Lieutenant General Hal Moore's excellent book, "*We Were Soldiers Once ... And Young*," I thought of that evening with Tony. It was the only time I saw him after the war. Still later, the book was adapted as a movie starring Mel Gibson. It seemed the scriptwriters, to give Gibson's role as Moore a bit more weight and screen time, enlarged Moore's role in the specifics of the battle. I believe that reduced Tony's role, especially with his initiative and on the scene leadership in the attack to reestablish contact with a group of soldiers who were cut off from Moore'sbattalion. However, I never had occasion to talk to Tony about that. Regardless, both the book and movie reveal him, as they did Hal Moore, fittingly in the heroic roles they played.

That night, at his home, I got no heroics, only a matter-of-fact, summarized version of what had happened as he saw it. The visit with him and his wife in their home was the highlight of my trip to West Point, even surpassing the moving stroll around the grounds above the Hudson River.

Several years ago, I gave the golf clubs that Clancy had given me at Fort Benning to my son Mike for his children. Mike had used them at Fort Benning when he was nine years old and a few times later. All the children have had a few swings with those clubs, but at this point, the youngsters are putting off golf to an older age. The golf clubs and bag now reside in my son's garage, some 38 years later—darn good clubs, but right-handed. Once I began to play, I decided to swing from the left, the "wrong side," according to a colonel I played golf with in California in the mid-eighties.

Of course, Clancy and I went on to Fort Lewis and shared time there. I didn't see him for eight years after For Lewis. But when the Army selected Fulton to be the new commanding general of Recruiting Command, he soon got Clancy there to work for him again. Then, the Army was falling short in recruiting the number of solders needed. They picked a proven leader with drive and innovative practices. When Fulton and Clancy left Recruiting Command, the Army was rapidly getting well.

The Army leadership, impressed with what Fulton had done in raising Army strength and quality, promoted him to lieutenant general and made him the Director of the Army Staff. It is a position charged with moving the huge Army General Staff in the directions needed by the Secretary of the Army and the Chief of Staff.

I was at the Army War College as a student of the bicentennial class of 1976 when Fulton came up as a guest speaker. He wanted to play golf, and, since I had not yet started the game, I asked my fellow classmate, Tom Forburger, to join him in his round of golf. I think Fulton expected me to ride around with them, but it didn't occur to me until Fulton, as he walked to the golf cart to begin play, asked me if I was going to do so. I exaggerated some small task I was to do for the masters degree I was working on, and he let me off the hook, but Tom was unimpressed with my excuse. I think he believed I should at least share the event since I had maneuvered him into the match. I never played golf with Fulton or saw him hit, but at six feet, seven inches in height, I could imagine the long drives that Tom later reported. I didn't ask who won.

The masters degree program I used as an excuse was laughable. I had long wanted to get my advanced degree, and had put off opportunities to do so at a couple of good universities because of other duties. The program the War College ran in conjunction with Shippensberg State College disappointed me. I wrote some positive recommendations in my critique as the course ended. Major General Dewitt Smith, the Commandant, appreciated my critique, talked to me about my ideas, and acted on them to improve the program. I think he already had reservations about the program. When I learned later the changes that were made, I noted they went far beyond my suggestions. The program director did not appreciate my comments. Dick Sharp was in the incoming class and had signed up for the masters degree program. He let me know my name was mud with the new students. Things were being done that would make the course of instruction more time consuming and demanding. Dick wanted to know what I thought the course was all about. Before I could answer, he smiled and reminded me that most officers saw it as getting a ticket punched—nothing more. I knew that, but I saw no reason for the cream of the crop officers who were selected to come to Carlisle to waste their time. Some guys never forgot that straight-laced move on my part. Some might have liked to have played a role in getting the Chief of Staff of the Army to tap me to be The Inspector General some fifteen years later. They likely thought I had demonstrated an "IG" mentality in criticizing that master degree course. Also, if I was selected for the IG job, they knew the Chief of Staff wouldn't tap them.

The tapping happened this way. In 1989 someone put in a call late one night for General Carl Vuono, Army Chief of Staff, to my quarters at Camp Zama, Japan, where I was serving as the Commanding General, United States Army, Japan. General Vuono said something like I didn't wake you did I? I lied and said he didn't. Well, he didn't. The operator did. Then he told me he knew I was having fun in my second straight field command, but he had an important job and I was just the right man to do it. He told me he wanted me to come back and be The Inspector General, TIG. I lied again and said I would be glad to do that. The next morning I told Carol that it was not a memorable beginning to lie twice to your boss as you are being hired as the staff keeper of Army integrity. It didn't bother her at all—the job or my fibs. She knew that after nearly four years away from grandchildren who had been born while we were in Alaska and Japan, we were going to Fort Meyer, Virginia, where two of our grandchildren would be living in our back yard.

Of course, it was an honor to serve as The Inspector General of the Army. Carl Vuono later told me of the strong support for the idea of putting me in the job when he brought it up to his four-star commanders. I think I know why I was asked to do the job, and I am proud he asked me. My strongest recollection of those months as the "TIG" was watching Vuono prepare the Army for DESERT STORM, our operation to drive the Iraqi army out of Kuwait. He was masterful. He anticipated the needs of General Norm Schwarzkopf in areas ranging from bullets to strategy. He daily tasked staff principals to inquire, ask, coordinate, and act. He presided over meetings, sometimes with only three or four staff principals, the same way he did a full Army Staff meeting. He anticipated. He asked. He tasked. He insisted on coordination—with the joint staff, our commands in the field, with one another. He made hard decisions to make sure that Schwarzkopf and his troops got what they needed and when they needed it. He put reality into the much thrown about word, readiness, in the Army. His standard for readiness was high: would the action save American soldiers' lives or put them further in danger. That guided his decisions. It was a memorable leadership performance, behind the scenes, largely unknown, but key to our success in Kuwait.

But back to the guys at the War College in the class of 1977 who would have liked me to drop my critique of the masters degree program in a wastebasket, at least some of the vocal ones would have.

Unfortunately, Dick Sharp would not be one of the remaining Army War College Class of '77 members—not in 1989.

Carol and I met Clancy and Connie at the entrance to the Arlington

Chapel in March of 1981. We were there for the funeral services and interment of Brigadier General Richard H. Sharp, who had died while running, alone, between two Ranger Companies in Georgia. It had been a heart attack.

The four of us stood side by side under a large Maple tree at the graveside as members of the Old Guard helped us pay our last respects. We said little, then or afterwards as we parted and went our separate ways. It was too close, much too close. Surely each of us, Clancy, Connie, Carol, and I, looked at the flag-draped casket and at Dick's widow, Pat, and felt her loss. A loss compounded by the emotion that it could only be as personal if the one who had departed was Clancy or me. No one said that, but I know that we felt it. It neither detracted from our feeling of loss for Dick and Pat nor provided solace. It was a stark reality that we had lost someone almost as if it were we.

Bill Fulton continued to work in retirement at the Association of the United States Army, an imposing presence at each Annual Meeting. When he finally retired from that position, he clearly missed the Army more than anyone I have known. He needed soldiers. He thrived on the vitality and optimism of the young soldiers and the practical strength of the noncommissioned officers. He and I traveled together to a couple of annual conventions of the Mobile Riverine Force Association. As we neared the Louisville or Chattanooga location of the meetings, he became more excited with each mile, and when we arrived, his excitement and elation were obvious to all ranks and were contagious.

At Louisville, Captain Wade Wells was also present. It is special to feel the stirring recollections of times gone by, things more than thirty years before, and to see the once young soldier and sailor or the old Captain and Colonel step back into character. You relive some events and some emotions that seem even more vivid in recollection and stronger in emotion than they were in their origins.

I sat with men who had commanded companies in the Battle of Can Giuoc, 19 June 1967, and learned of new and different perspectives about that battle. Someone spoke of Captain Bob Reeves and there was a pause, no further comment, and then the exchange of memories went on, at times conflicting in versions of what happened or why.

Guy Tutwiler was there. We recalled Snoopy's Nose and laughed at the often-told story of Dick Sharp with a cigar clenched in his teeth and sitting on a box of hand grenades. He was in the CCB with Dusty Rhodes as it spun in the Rach Ba Rai. The addled Dusty shaking the cobwebs from his jarred head and making, Tutwiler agreed, the hard and right decision to pull back.

And Blackie Bolduc and recollections of the Rung Sat Special Zone, Dong Tam, and his starring role as G3 of the Division once he left battalion command. It seemed the contact of the division staff to us brigade operations officers improved overnight when he carried his field "knowhow" into that headquarters at Bearcat.

Whenever we would speak of Dick Sharp, Bill Fulton was clearly wounded. It was as if, having survived the dangers of the battlefield, Dick Sharp should not have left us so soon. But we, Fulton, Clancy, and I, knew better than to linger on that. After all, Dick was running between two companies of Army Rangers when it happened. I see him now, handsome, tanned, creases along the cheeks to inscribe the smile, the cigar, the sparkling teeth…the smile.

We finally lost Big Bill Fulton in the winter of 2006. About seven years before that, I wrote of him in a poem, Big Bill. It accompanies this story.

Carol and I speak now of traveling west to visit with retired Colonel Clancy Matsuda and Connie in the Dakotas. They live on Custer Parkway. At Fort Riley in '66, Carol and I lived on Custer Hill. We met Fulton there—at Custer Hill. That was before we met Clancy and Dick.

She and I plan to wander in our RV around the old stomping grounds of the Sioux, Cheyenne, Arapaho, and the Army infantry out in the Colonel Custer land west of the Matsuda Country. There may be in the future a post Civil War novel about courage and honor and loyalty and friendship. The good guys will be like Fulton, Matsuda, and Sharp. I'll keep a role for myself, say as the involved story teller, an ex-Confederate soldier serving in the United States Army Infantry. Maybe I'll make myself six and a half feet tall, call myself Clint Samuraii, smoke cigars, and, what the heck, maybe I'll sketch myself as handsome as ….

THE MEN IN THE BOATS
By John H. Corns

The mist of the morning cools and softens the air
The last of the soldiers has gone down the steel stair
He crossed the barge that lay along side the big ship
And boarded the craft making sure he did not slip

Now all assault craft and boats are well under way
They are executing the plan briefed yesterday
The boats flow out smoothly and take their place in line
From the air their formation is dark serpentine

Up the brown muddy river they move with the tide
Some sense the jungle beauty on this their first ride
Some seem not to look, unaware of the beauty
They limit their thoughts to just those of their duty

They are veterans, they have been out here before
They have seen the hot fights, they want not to see more
But if a fight does come these men are very good
Their skill by their foe is very well understood

Their force in our history is not often seen
They fight from the water and are called riverine
Grant used them at Vicksburg in the great Civil War
The French used them also on the Red River shore

They combined the power of Army and Navy
Their thoughts of each other at first were quite cagey
But that didn't last long when there was a real fight
Petty officers and sergeants know what is right

Soldiers saw water as moats around a castle
An obstacle that would cost them in a battle
Sailors saw these moats as the track at Daytona
Take some care for mines and then blast right on down 'em

Attacks from the water their foe was not used to
They aimed at highways and watched for landlocked crews
For Riverine it was the way to start a fight
To attack with surprise from water at first light

And this they were doing on their attack today
They thought would their plan work or go some other way
Very early some doubt about this plan arose –
When they learned they'd be running right by Snoopy's Nose

An elaborate plan that probably worked well
But for boat crews and platoons it was hard to tell
The artillery was firing, of this they'd been told
A battalion in choppers found an LZ cold

But what is that pounding on the side of the craft
And where we were once heading is now pointing aft
The antitank rocket that exploded top side
Has sprayed steel on a platoon but they're still alive

There's a monitor turning in the stream ahead
No one at the helm, just a slumped figure instead
The assault craft turns wildly, rams into the bank
The captain's quick decision before the craft sank

The infantry platoon and the whole boat crew too
Scramble ashore where their last artillery blew
Their foe is retreating crawling over a dike
That's getting chewed up by a boat's forty mike mike

There's plenty of action, the new guys have their fill
The artillery pounding, the jets streaking shrill
Guys still in boats to their foe must seem evil
Blazing away in clouds of cordite and diesel

But the noise of battle passes slowly away
There are men to be cared for and some need to pray
Some pursue the enemy by chopper and boat
Medics work wonders but there are lumps in their throats

It seems forever, but then they're back on the ship
They talk of light hurts, swollen finger and bruised hip
But they're thinking of Willy who made them all laugh
And of Stan, Jose and Bob who did not come back

They laugh at Frank's letter that he just got from home
The candy his wife sent had been missent to Nome
The mail man said he'd sent it on though quite tattered
They knew that for Frank the letter was what mattered

They laughed and they joked and there were a lot of pranks
And a few good jokes about guys in higher ranks
But they were glad to know that the brass had announced
It was a main force enemy that they had trounced

That was good, they'd put that fact in their next letter
But what mattered most was they had fought even better
There was this deep sense of sharing great danger
Of meeting a test, risking life for a stranger

Most pictured the stranger as a child, maybe six
Who didn't want much, food, home, and not to be sick
And it was for the young life that they now most feared
It was worth fighting in hopes they would not be scared

Many years have passed since the days of these battles
For each Raider and Rat the memory still rattles
And a few of these warriors have even gone back
For with all they recall there is something they lack

Not as a warrior they feel good for the people
It was always their aim to free them from trouble
And they are warmed by smiles of kids three years or four
But in our old U S A they'd have even more

But the main experience that gives them a chill
Is to fly over the land, lush, green and still
To feel tears sting the eyes looking down at brown moats
Feel the chest swell thinking of the Men in the Boats

A Modest Tribute
For
Captain Robert Linton Reeves
To
The Men of Company A, 4th
Battalion, 47th Infantry Regiment
Who fell in
The Battle of Can Giuoc
19 June 1967

(Captain Robert Linwood Reeves
Colorado Springs, CO, fell eight
Months later, 26 February 1968
during TET in Dinh Tuong
Province)

1LT Philip O. Zum Mallen, Jr.
Homewood, IL

1LT Fred G. Bertolino
Bushnell, IL

SSG George Randolph
Cottonport, LA

SGT Dennis W. Brown
Moline, IL

SGT Daniel J. Sandstedt
Omaha, NE

SP4 Dennis J. Adamski
Appleton, WI
(Engineer)

SP4 Jack E. Cossins
Henderson, NV

SP4 Robert E. Craythorne
Duncan, OK

SP4 Wayne S. Fielden
Sherman, TX

SP4 Thomas L. Gordon
Sylacauga, AL

SP4 Monte R. Harper
Palmade, CA

SP4 John R. Hill
Van Nuys, CA

SP4 James G. Hinch
Wichita Falls, TX,

SP4 John P. Lee
La Crescentia, CA

SP4 Joseph T. Martin
San Luis Obispo, CA

SP4 Lloyd A. Sellers III
Euclid, OH

SP4 Edward H. Stevens
Annapolis, MO

SP4 Jackie D. Weatherly
Sacramento, CA

SP4 Noel T. West
Tacoma, WA

SP4 Robert F. Wright
Bremerton, WA

CPL Richard C. Lundy
Galax, VA

CPL Clyde W. Stephens
Wichita Falls, TX

PFC Allen N. Engel
Calvary, WI

PFC Paul E. Good
Sharpsville, PA

PFC David F. Henry
Hurst, TX

PFC Charles J. Hildenbrand
Chardon, OH

PFC Bobby W. Price
Mount Vernon, KY

PFC David S. Raine
San Bernardino, CA

PFC William P. Shaffer
Batavia, NY

PFC James B. Smith
Phil Campbell, AL

PFC John D. St Peters
Brighton, IL

BIG BILL
[A Friendship Poem]
1992

I entered his office
Up on Custer Hill
Assigned to his brigade
Though not of my will

I saluted smartly
And gave my report
He returned my salute
Seemed a formal sort

In a visit to Riley
Three short weeks before
I met a good friend
Of six years or more

He sat straight in the chair
Said, "Have you been an S2?"
I said, "No sir, I have not."
Thought I'd drop him a clue

I told him I'd seen
The division AG
I was scheduled to be
A battalion S3

"As a matter of fact,"
I said with some glee
"I've always preferred
To be an S3."

My friend from Korea
Was a trainer, class A
Who knew that in Vietnam
I'd been a Green Beret

He did not seem impressed
He did not waste a grin
He said, "You're my S2!"
And stuck out his chin

And now I was back
My assignment changed
Now to 2nd Brigade
My duty was arranged

I reassessed quickly
Thought, "I can if I must."
Besides, the set of his chin
Was of a man I could trust

My friend played a role
He was loyal in essence
To his Brigade Commander
Who valued intelligence

He then said to me,
"Sit down, we'll discuss it."
I sensed that he was
As firm as colonels get

Now I entered the room
A big man I could see
Even while seated
He seemed six foot three

I came quickly to sense,
I now will allow
The discussion would be
Not whether, but how

I wondered what then
He knew about me
I thought that for sure
I'll not be an S3

But I liked what he said
"The S2 is in charge.
We'll go where you say,
Fight forces small or large."

"I will fight my brigade,"
An expression first heard
I would soon come to learn
He was a man of his word

It seemed that my old friend
Of old Korea days
Had told the commander
Of my Green Beret ways

A tour in Vietnam
Some intelligence skill
Seemed to impress this man
Brought me to Custer Hill

When he finished talking
Went to rise on the spot
He was so tall it seemed
That he never would stop

More like six foot seven
Than a mere six foot three
I dared not to repeat
Hope of being S3

Six months of good training
With Clyde pushing each rump
My assistant and I
Taught weapons and Crack-Thump

Then to San Diego
To spar with Wade Wells
A man whose strong views
Matched the Captains of sails

But my boss was equal
Little warmth, little chill
And soon Wade was saying
We can take any Hill

But he meant from a mile
In big water, not creek
He'd fight from long range
Not at range cheek to cheek

He was a tough old salt
But when he got on track
He'd watch boats looking meek
And he'd send them right back

When we wanted to land
Helos on a small ramp
He railed you can't land that
On a small postage stamp

But my boss could goad him
The Old Salt could be turned
If told he was wimpy
He got very concerned

The Colonel and Captain
Made an unlikely team
What they did together
Made the headquarters steam

The Colonel liked challenge
He would think, innovate
The Captain was cautious
Then committed, first rate

Artillery on Barges
Guard Houses up on skids
Big Barges alongside
No steep nets for our kids

"You must tell your story."
He one time said to me
So briefings to Westy
Got us early to sea

We fought on the rivers,
Hit from water and air
We changed the direction
VC never knew where

For more than a year
The force won by surprise
Then antitank weapons
Spun in before our eyes

We added more caution
Using scouts in the air
And "Scouts Out" on the ground
We heard our boss declare

By this time our Colonel
Had moved to greater things
But even as a General
He'd return on a fling

Riverine was in battle
Meant that out of the sky
He'd return to the barge
Suggest how or stand by

His heart was with soldiers
Those who fought in the mud
Those who dug in and prayed
When the mortars went thud

It was like Italy
And his unit again
Had to clear the valley
For regiment to win

He hated the casualties
The hurt and the fear
I recall our first killed
Brought his grief and a tear

I tried to console him
Me, his junior by years
His patience amazed me
I, naive of his fears

His fears from the battles
When he was my age
When he lost men to bombs,
88 guns in rage

For he had seen battle
Much different than mine
He had seen units lost
And in so little time

I had seen terrorists,
Irregulars, guerrillas
Where our losses were few
Though gallant young fellas

Before it was over
I would more clearly see
This experienced man
Feared and felt more than me

But that was just one thing
He taught me o'er the years
How to look in the eye
Your feelings and your fears

And then to meet duties
Not with acts cavalier
But with decisions always
That held men's lives most dear

There was once I failed him
Late one night at Dong Tam
When his boss on the phone
Told of problem and plan

First Brigade in battle
Had lost their fine S3
I realized the plan
Centered now right on me

Straight away my boss asked
"Are you ready to go?"
My concern was not small
My response was not slow

"Yes sir, I am ready."
I replied with no thrill
With strong sense of duty
I felt I had the skill

My boss put his big hand
On the end of the phone
The look then on his face
Hinted I'd spoken wrong

"I have had it in mind,"
He looked straight at me
"For you to follow Clyde,
And to be my S3."

What I'd done then stung me
I thought I should have asked
Or have been less ready
And waited to be tasked

For to fight with this man
To serve close by his side
I came slowly to grasp
Was now mine to decide

He'd not decide for me
Need was in two places
I wanted to remain
With familiar faces

Yes, Clyde soon would move on
I would miss his great skill
But there still would be Tom,
Jim, Nate, Dan, and Big Bill

Big Bill was the main guy
We said not that to him
But that was his fond name
For Clyde, Tom, Nate, and Jim

So I stayed and I fought
I fought the brigade
I served close by his side
Best decision I made

I was so very proud
To serve as his S3
But it was as S2
That he really taught me

He taught me in tactics
The S2 sets the thrust
He taught me in people
The prime need is to trust

He taught me that many
Excel with hand-picked men
But the true leader wins
With those the lot gives him

There are many lessons
How to train, how to fight
He taught by example
Or wise comments in flight

One that is still special
A thought he shared with me
In a Huey flying
O'er the South China Sea

He said, "John, remember
As you look down the years,
You're young, have the Army
Wife, kiddies, little fears

But there will be the day
The Army says Well Done
The kiddies are on their own
To your home you will come

If you're lucky; work hard
If you live and you care
There will be your wife
To share every year."

Of all that he taught me,
This I cherish the most
In the years that have passed
I have held the words close

My kiddies are now grown
My Army days wind down
But, I cherish my wife
She too knows his words sound

How do I just thank him?
What is there now to do?
Except just to tell him
"I'll always be your S2

Printed in the United States
by Baker & Taylor Publisher Services